Summers at Pemberley

A Pride and Prejudice Retelling

Jennifer Kay

For Maria

Contents

Title Page

Dedication

Part One   1

Chapter One   2

Chapter Two   14

Chapter Three   27

Chapter Four   40

Chapter Five   46

Chapter Six   59

Chapter Seven   73

Chapter Eight   86

Chapter Nine   99

Chapter Ten   116

Part Two   127

Chapter Eleven   128

Chapter Twelve   141

Chapter Thirteen   159

Chapter Fourteen   173

Chapter Fifteen   192

Chapter Sixteen   206

Chapter Seventeen   221

Chapter Eighteen   237

Chapter Nineteen   253

Chapter Twenty   268

Chapter Twenty-One   282

Chapter Twenty-Two   295

About The Author   313

Books By This Author   315

Part One

Derbyshire, England
1798

Chapter One

Derbyshire, 1798

I t was a morning meant for exploring. At least that is what Elizabeth Bennet thought as she made her way down the path heading out of Lambton towards what she'd heard locals refer to, with a wave of their hand in the general direction, as "the park." She understood vaguely that seven-year-old girls did not go exploring on their own in strange counties, but that paled in comparison to the pull of the path beneath her feet, curving away deliciously out of sight and surely leading to treasures like babbling brooks and baby birds. Besides, it wasn't like anyone had actually forbidden her from exploring—the only reason she knew it was wrong was because her sister Jane would never do such a thing.

But Jane, placid and sensible and very grown up at nine years old, wasn't here. Only Elizabeth had accompanied her father and her Uncle Gardiner to Derbyshire, where Mr. Gardiner was to marry a young lady that Elizabeth had only met for several minutes but thus far liked very well. As Mr. Gardiner was understandably preoccupied by his soon-to-be-bride and Mr. Bennet was equally engrossed in the offerings of the local bookstore, Elizabeth made the decision that no one would miss her soon, and gleefully headed into the woods free of any sense of guilt.

It was truly delightful, and Elizabeth forgot all about the adults as she darted from tree to tree, pretending to be a fairy. A stream did appear, and she crossed it by jumping from rock to rock, debating if she ought to go wading on the return journey, when it was warmer. It looked like a good stream for wading, even better than the one that crossed her father's estate in Hertfordshire.

Elizabeth had been wandering long enough to wish she'd tucked an apple or roll into her pocket when she heard splashes, followed by the unmistakable sound of voices. For the first time on her rambles, she hesitated, unsure if she wanted to be seen or not. In Hertfordshire, everyone knew her by sight, and while her mother liked to complain about the other inhabitants in the neighborhood, Elizabeth liked most of them. She wasn't sure yet how she felt about people in Derbyshire, other than Miss Madeline Foster.

"Oy!" a voice said directly behind her, and Elizabeth jumped, spinning to face the newcomer. It was a boy, likely twice her age and certainly twice her height, with dark hair and a hint of a sneer. "What are you doing here, little girl? Did you run away from your nursemaid and get lost?"

"I'm not lost!" Elizabeth exclaimed, indignant. True, some of the turns were a little fuzzy, but she was positive she could find her way back to Lambton. A great deal of the path ran parallel to the stream, after all. Any idiot could follow a stream, and she wasn't an idiot. Papa had told her so.

The boy, who she did not like, raised his eyebrows. "Oh, really? Then how did you wind up in Pemberley's woods in a fancy little dress?" He took a step closer.

Elizabeth jumped back, crossing her arms. "I walked, you goose."

The boy opened his mouth to retort, then darted his eyes to something over Elizabeth's shoulder. She swung around to see yet another dark-haired boy, even taller than the first, with a scowl on his face instead of a sneer. Maybe Miss Foster was the only pleasant person in Lambton.

"George, what are you—oh. Who are you?" He stopped, scowl changing to a perplexed, slightly wary expression as he looked at Elizabeth.

"She hasn't told me that yet, but she walked here, and she's *not* lost," the first boy said, sotto voice.

"I'm *not!*" Elizabeth exclaimed. "If you don't want me here, I'll prove it and take myself back to Lambton!"

The second boy's eyebrows shot up. "You walked from Lambton? How old are you, five?"

Now she was well and truly vexed. Letting out a huff, Elizabeth grabbed the edges of her skirt —it really was too fancy for exploring, but her mother had insisted on the extra lace—and gave the second boy a rather shoddy curtsey. "My name is Lizzy Bennet, and I am *seven*."

"Look at that. Even babies recognize the future lord of the manor."

"Shut up, George," the second boy said, sparing his companion a look before facing Elizabeth. He bowed back to her. "Pleased to meet you, Miss Lizzy. My name is Fitzwilliam Darcy. I apologize if I offended you. It is just that Lambton is rather far from here, and you may have noticed that your legs are a great deal shorter than mine. I am impressed you made such a long expedition, although I am concerned that you are alone. Are you staying with someone in the village?"

Elizabeth studied him for a moment, considering if he was mocking her by bowing and talking like she was an adult rather than a baby. Deciding he was genuine, she took a step closer, which forced her to look up to meet his eyes. He really was quite tall.

"I am staying with my papa at the inn. He's at the bookstore, or at least he was when I left, and Uncle Gardiner is off courting. As long as I'm back in time for dinner, they won't mind. Uncle Gardiner might not even notice at all. He's getting married soon. That's why we're here."

The expression on the second boy's face had slowly edged towards a smile. "Your uncle must be marrying Miss Foster," he said.

"Yes! Do you know her? She's very pretty. I hope that someday I'm that pretty, even if Mama says I'll never hold a candle to Jane. But Miss Foster has brown hair like I do, so maybe I'll be lucky and look like her."

The boy blinked, clearly not having expected that response. "Yes, I know Miss Foster," he said after a pause. "She is pretty, and I'm sure you'll be just as pretty as she is once you grow up. But I'm also sure your uncle will miss you, and your father as well. Would you let me escort you back to Lambton, Miss Lizzy?"

"I don't need help Fit—Fiz—" Elizabeth stopped, biting her lip. It was polite to call someone by their name, but she couldn't remember all of his.

The boy laughed, the last of his stern expression melting away at last. "Don't worry, my sister can't pronounce my name either. You can call me Will like she does."

The first boy, who Elizabeth had been happy to forget about, hooted. "Where did stuck up Mr. Darcy disappear to?" he asked.

Will's face snapped back into a scowl. "This isn't Cambridge, George, and I hardly think she's going to take advantage of me. Go away if you're going to be a pain."

George brushed by Elizabeth, shrugging. "Fine. I'll go tell Mr. Darcy to expect all the gossip when you ride Jupiter into the middle of Lambton with a little girl and cause a fuss because you just had to be gallant. You'll make quite the picture. Perhaps one of your admirers can capture it on a canvas."

A host of emotions flickered over Will's face before settling into resignation. He closed his eyes for a long moment and sighed, then focused on Elizabeth again. "Miss Lizzy, it is my duty as a gentleman to make sure you get home safely. However, George is correct. If I take you directly back to Lambton, we will be noticed and you might end up getting in trouble. Would you be willing to come back to my home with us and let my father determine a better solution?"

It was Elizabeth's turn to frown. "I can get back on my own. And you don't have to call me Miss Lizzy, if I get to call you Will." Her father's tenants and servants called her Miss Lizzy. Will didn't act like either.

He gave her a tight smile. "I am sure you could get yourself back on your own. But I would worry, so please indulge me. Do you like horses?"

Clearly expecting an emphatic yes, Will looked surprised when Elizabeth hung her head. She *didn't* like horses. Papa had purchased a pony to teach the girls to ride. It tolerated Mary, and adored Jane like every other creature in the world, but it hated Elizabeth and she loathed it in return. "I would rather walk."

"Are you afraid? You can ride with me, and it will be perfectly safe. Sometimes I take my sister for rides, and she's much younger than you. We can go as slow as you like."

"Why can't I walk?"

"Because it's two and a half miles to either Lambton or Pemberley."

Elizabeth stood perfectly still for a moment, considering. "What's Pemberley?" she asked at last.

"My home. It's an estate. You're technically on Pemberley land right now."

She considered again. She could certainly see more from a horse, and her legs *were* getting tired. They might even have food for nuncheon at the house. Elizabeth looked up at Will. "Promise you'll really go slow?"

*

George Darcy was in the middle of reading yet another tiring letter from his late wife's sister when voices in the hall caught his attention. One of them belonged to his son, and if Fitzwilliam was coming this way, he was headed for the study. Grateful for the excuse to put Catherine's letter off for a while, he set it aside and leaned back in his chair. It was his favorite. Anne had commissioned it for him several years into their marriage, and the comfortable brown leather was made all the better by its association with her. It would last long enough to be Fitzwilliam's chair someday.

Smiling to himself, George wondered what his son needed now. It was good to have him home from school, he and young George Wickham both. Fitzwilliam was talking to someone, so— but no, that wasn't Wickham's voice. It wasn't Georgiana's, either. But what other child would be with Fitzwilliam here?

A moment later, Fitzwilliam entered the study and George received his answer. A stranger stood next to his son. The little girl clearly belonged to someone of property, in a light blue dress boasting altogether too much lace, with dark brown curls and the biggest eyes George had ever seen. She barely cleared Fitzwilliam's hip, but she danced along next to him, taking three steps to each of his strides, unphased by the house or the study. Another indication of her upbringing.

"Hush, Lizzy," Fitzwilliam said, and her chatter dropped off. Interesting. George raised an eyebrow and waited. His son was a good lad, perhaps too serious for fifteen, but that could be helpful in this situation.

"Pardon the interruption, Father," Fitzwilliam began. "George and I were down by the creek resting the horses when we came across Miss Elizabeth, here. She's staying in Lambton with her father. I thought about taking her back directly, but didn't know if that might cause any trouble." The girl opened her mouth, and

Fitzwilliam looked down at her. "Yes, I know you could have walked yourself back. You are being a proper young lady and letting me assist you, and I appreciate your patience. Which reminds me, Father, this is Elizabeth Bennet. Lizzy, this is my father, Mr. Darcy."

The girl took a step forward and dropped a crooked but altogether adorable curtsey. "Hello, Mr. Darcy, sir." There was the tiniest hint of a lisp to the last word.

George smothered a smile to remain suitably stern as he greeted her in return. "Hello, Miss Elizabeth. Where are you from?"

"Hertfordshire."

"And what brings you to Derbyshire?"

"Her uncle is marrying Miss Foster," Fitzwilliam said.

George covered his smile once again. Fitzwilliam had always been one for bringing home strays when he was small: birds with hurt wings, a stray dog, a kitten his mother had loved dearly. It seemed he had not shed this trait just because he was now a young man attending Cambridge instead of a boy. Although—

All desire to smile fled. Fitzwilliam had not brought home a stray since Anne died the year prior. In fact, he had not worn the easy expression currently on his face since that time, either. Fitzwilliam smiled at Georgiana, was polite to all of the servants, and paid careful attention to anything George cared to teach him, but he never looked relaxed like this. And because of a strange little girl!

It was not a surprise that Fitzwilliam would do the right thing and make sure Miss Elizabeth was taken home. He was responsible and conscientious and would make a fine master when the time came. It was surprising to realize just how perpetually serious his son had become. The house had been quiet since Anne's death, but surely Fitzwilliam still found ways to laugh on occasion? Staring at his son now, George realized he didn't know the last time he had even seen Fitzwilliam grin.

Clearly catching the strange look, the smile dropped from Fitzwilliam's face. "Father?" he asked.

George waved the concern away. "Forgive me, it is no matter," he said. "You did well to bring Miss Elizabeth here. With such a long walk, she must be hungry. Have you had refreshments?"

"Not yet," Fitzwilliam replied.

"Why don't you go to the green parlor?" George asked, standing. "I will join you momentarily."

He followed the children into the hallway and met the eyes of his housekeeper, who stood waiting for his direction. Mrs. Reynolds had been at Pemberley for over a decade now, and George knew she likely had several plans ready to go, depending on what his next words were. "Refreshments to the green parlor, suitable for the child, Mrs. Reynolds. And please ask Sally if she knows anything about Miss Foster's betrothed and his party."

A look from the housekeeper and a maid disappeared, likely to see to the tray. "Of course, sir," Mrs. Reynolds said. "As to Sally, I took the liberty of asking her when Master Darcy came in. Mr. Gardiner is the betrothed's name, and he is traveling with his sister's husband and a girl-child. The word is that, while Mr. Gardiner is not a gentleman, his brother-by-law is one."

George nodded once. "Thank you. Anything else?"

Mrs. Reynolds gave a tiny smile. "She was awed by the entrance hall, but not so awed that she stopped talking Master Darcy's ear off. And Mrs. Foster herself told me that she thinks Madeline has made a good match. You know how hard she is to impress, particularly when it comes to her daughters."

He nodded again. "Very well. I will join them now. Please alert us if anyone comes in search of a child." Feeling confident that their visitor was not a trap, George headed towards the less formal parlor they had used frequently when Fitzwilliam and his cousins were all small. Miss Elizabeth did not seem at all worried, but George was a parent. He was certain that her excursion would not go unnoticed, and in this part of the county, someone would inevitably end up at Pemberley in search. They met so few new people in their secluded area of the country, although he hadn't cared about the lack of company since losing his Anne. Right now, however, George was quite intrigued to meet the individual who had produced the precocious, fool-hardy girl who so delighted his somber son.

Chapter Two

To say Fitzwilliam Darcy was delighted with Elizabeth would have been a gross misrepresentation. She intrigued him. She was utterly different than his own sister, despite being closer to Georgiana in age than to him. Then again, Georgiana was only two years old, so perhaps that was an unfair comparison. Elizabeth—Lizzy—was like a sunbeam. Blink and she had darted off somewhere else, energy coursing through her every movement. She confused him. At her age, Darcy had still been shy around all strangers. He never would have chattered away at someone twice his age or more. He didn't even know where she came up with all the things that she had to say. At a certain point, when the flow of chatter didn't wane, she annoyed him.

But most of all, she worried him. Darcy remembered very well what George Wickham had been like as a child. He had the same mix of confidence and vivacity that Elizabeth embodied, and it was a combination that Darcy's father found charming. The problem was, once away from his godfather and namesake, George Wickham was anything but charming. Darcy couldn't help but worry that Elizabeth would be the same.

So he indulged her, answering her questions about various items in the room. Darcy was a gentleman, all signs indicated that Elizabeth was a gentleman's daughter, and manners dictated that he act as a proper host. If on occasion he found himself smiling in spite of his best intentions, that was beside the point. But all the while, Darcy kept a close eye on the girl, waiting for the moment when she would turn petulant or tuck some item away into the pocket of her dress.

He was still waiting when his father joined them, followed almost immediately by a tray of sandwiches, cakes, and tea. Elizabeth's face lit up when she noticed the food, and for a moment Darcy thought she would dart across the room and grab something immediately. Instead, she visibly restrained herself and managed to wait until she was seated with a plate before tucking into the food.

"You must have been famished, Miss Elizabeth," George Darcy remarked as she finished her second sandwich—less remarkable than it sounded, since they were cut into small triangles—and reached for the cake on her plate.

The girl froze, looking abashed. "Yes," she said in a smaller voice than usual, as if waiting to be scolded. Then, in more of her normal tone, "Your food is very good."

His father smiled. "Thank you. Let it never be said that anyone ever went hungry at Pemberley. Would you like another sandwich?"

Darcy cringed internally, watching. What was it about other children that brought out his father's playful, indulgent side, when he was so stern with his own two? Even Georgiana, tiny and delightful, rarely evoked this level of gentleness and generosity from her father.

To Darcy's surprise, Elizabeth did not immediately accept the additional food. Instead, her eyes darted to him. "No, thank you. But Will is all done, maybe he needs another one. He's a lot bigger than me," she added earnestly. And then, clearly considering the matter to be settled, she picked up her cake and took a big bite, ending up with a bit of powdered sugar on the tip of her nose.

Time drug by. The elder Darcy continued to ply Elizabeth with questions and convinced her to take a second piece of cake. It was not until he caught his father glancing at the clock that Darcy realized they were stalling on purpose. For at least the third time that day, his heart sank. There was only one reason for Father to wait for someone to fetch Elizabeth rather than discreetly returning her to Lambton, and that was because he'd decided to prolong their acquaintance. *Why* his father would want to associate with someone who let their daughter —their very young, unprotected, impressionable daughter—wander off into the woods was beyond Darcy.

It had been somewhere between thirty minutes and an hour when there was a commotion in the hall outside and Mrs. Reynolds appeared in the doorway. "A Mr. Bennet to see you, sir," she told the elder Darcy, then stepped aside.

From the corner of his eye, Darcy noticed Elizabeth sit up straight. She did not appear fearful, only expectant and perhaps a little confused. Her father was neglectful, then, but not abusive. She was not afraid of him. That expressive face could not hide fear, if it indeed existed.

Mr. Bennet, on the other hand, clearly *was* worried. He was a moderate man in all ways, Darcy thought as he took him in—moderately tall, medium brown hair, moderately handsome, moderately well-off. Mr. Bennet would disappear into the background of many situations, and while there were some gentlemen who would resent that, Darcy's initial impression was that Mr. Bennet embraced it.

"Lizzy!" The pinched, worried look morphed immediately into relief, followed shortly by exasperation. But he did not scold. Instead, he dropped to his knees and Elizabeth hurtled off the couch where she was perched and into his arms, nuzzling her small face into her father's neck. After a long moment, the gentleman pulled back. "Lizzy, how on earth did you get here? Where have you been?"

"I went for a walk," she said, as if that explained everything. "You were looking at books and Uncle went to see Miss Foster. I wanted to explore. They have a stream that is even better than at Longbourn, and I was going to wade, but then I found Will and he said I had to come here with him even though I could have found my way back on my own, I wasn't lost a bit, but they have good sandwiches here and I was hungry, so that was pleasant, and—"

"Lizzy," Mr. Bennet said sternly, and the flow of words stopped. "Lizzy, you know this isn't Hertfordshire. You aren't on your own estate here; you can't just wander off. I let you come because I thought you were old enough to behave."

"But no one said I couldn't explore!" she exclaimed. "And I was going to come back. I would have been there by dinner."

Mr. Bennet closed his eyes briefly. "Lizzy, we have been looking for you for the last three hours. I would have been frantic by dinner time."

Clearly confused, Elizabeth stared at him with wide eyes. "But you never worry at Longbourn."

"Yes, because I know the tenants will help

you if needed, and you have Shephard with you in case of trouble. It is different here. What if someone unkind had found you? They might have taken you away, not brought you to a fine home and fed you."

Elizabeth's face furrowed. "Like the first boy. He was mean," she said, but only Darcy was paying attention.

Mr. Bennet had looked up at Mr. Darcy, still kneeling in front of his daughter. "Good afternoon, sir. I apologize for my lack of manners, and for my daughter's intrusion. I am Mr. Thomas Bennet, of Longbourn in Hertfordshire, and I am in your debt for your care of Elizabeth."

George Darcy smiled, rising from his chair. Mr. Bennet stood as well. "Pleased to meet you, sir. George Darcy, and this is my son, Fitzwilliam. He is the one who found Miss Elizabeth and brought her here. We have been happy to host her."

Mr. Bennet turned to Darcy and bowed his head. "I thank you very much, sir. It is not every young man who would put aside his day's enjoyment to ensure the wellbeing of a child wholly unrelated to himself. And with that in mind, we will excuse ourselves, by your leave. I am sure Lizzy has already taken up more than enough of your time."

"About that," George Darcy said. Darcy froze, halfway to standing to bid his farewells. "Miss Elizabeth mentioned that you were staying at this inn until your brother's marriage to Miss Foster. While it is a fine establishment, I wanted to offer you accommodations here as an alternate. If your daughter is inclined to wander, far better to do it on the grounds near the house, and no matter how good the bookseller stocks his shelves in Lambton, I can assure you my library is better."

"Mr. Darcy, I could not dream of intruding upon you in such a way," Mr. Bennet said, eyes wide. He was either truly shocked or a far better actor than Darcy expected. "We are strangers, and I would not like to see Lizzy wreak havoc on your home." He gave a wry smile. "We have five young girls at home, and the house is geared towards the children."

"Five! Gracious!" George looked at Elizabeth. "You did not tell me you had so many sisters."

Elizabeth shrugged. Apparently her nurse had yet to break her of that habit. "You did not ask."

George smiled at the girl, then looked back to her father. "I have a daughter of my own. Georgiana is two years old, and the nursery is well set up. This parlor has been maintained with children in mind, as have other areas of the house. It would be easier than you imagine to accommodate Miss Elizabeth, particularly since I believe she would prefer to spend her days outside, am I right?" He directed the last to her.

Elizabeth looked at her father, clearly picking up on some of the tension in the room. "I do like being out of doors," she said haltingly, keeping her eyes on Mr. Bennet.

"Be that as it may—" Mr. Bennet began, then stopped as George Darcy held up a hand.

"You would be doing me a favor. I do not like going to town, but the company here is often unvarying. Furthermore, my late wife's sister is insisting we visit her this summer, and I am disinclined to acquiesce. It would be simpler to tell her that we have houseguests, particularly ones with children, so she does not worry about Georgiana alone in a house of men."

Mr. Bennet's eyes twinkled. He was amused. "Mr. Darcy, I am sympathetic to your plight, but I am not a good houseguest. I do not shoot, care little for billiards or other such games, and ride only when I cannot avoid it. My wife is forever bemoaning that my nose is buried in a book, and when I do emerge it is only to argue policy with the neighbors."

George smiled brightly. "That is perfect! Come, you must see the library. If you are not impressed then I shall accept your decision with grace, but I have faith that I shall yet prevail. I have never met a bibliophile who could resist Pemberley's library."

From his expression, it seemed that Mr. Bennet had anticipated, perhaps even counted on, a very different response. He agreed to see the library, however—there was little else he could do without being inordinately rude. As the two men left the room, Mr. Bennet clearly unsure of what he had stumbled into, Darcy leaned back in his chair and resisted the urge to groan. His father was being persuasive, and that meant only one thing: Mr. Bennet and his daughter wouldn't be departing any time soon.

*

Thomas Bennet followed George Darcy into Pemberley's library with no intention of accepting the other gentleman's offer to stay. He was a man who liked what was comfortable and predictable: his own book room, his preferred brand of scotch, the same people to be encountered at events in the same rooms, even the same complaints from his wife. He did not like being asked to stretch himself, and he did not like being manipulated—and George Darcy was manipulating him. George Darcy, however, was not the kind of man to whom one refused anything unless they had a very good reason. Bennet only had to glance at the furnishings and artwork in the hallway around him to know that while they were both gentlemen, he and his temporary host were worlds apart. Bennet did not like feeling lesser, either.

Then Mr. Darcy opened one of a pair of large doors and stepped into a room that could have come straight from Bennet's daydreams. Rows and rows of bookshelves stretched away from him, stopping well short of windows that let light in for reading, but never allowed it to touch the stored volumes. Here and there, tables and lamps stood ready for a closer inspection of maps or diagrams or whatever other wonders might be unearthed in this glorious place. A swift, cataloging glance told Bennet that this room would hold first editions he had never hoped to lay eyes on, let alone handle and peruse at his leisure.

All of a sudden, being manipulated into staying seemed like a much better idea.

"Now," Mr. Darcy said, breaking into Bennet's awed thoughts, "I realize that I may have spoken out of turn, in my enthusiasm. If you are missing your wife and other children, or need to get home to oversee your steward—or perhaps you don't have a steward at all—I completely understand. I will not force you to stay against your will."

Bennet did not miss his wife, not really. Lizzy, his favorite, was with him—and wouldn't she love this place as well! The other girls would barely notice his absence. Jane would miss Lizzy, and vice versa, but their separation might be for the better. They relied on each other a bit too much, each girl tending to a different extreme so they were only balanced when they appeared as a pair. As for his steward, Bennet cared little for the man, or for the work he brought with him. Both of them would be relieved to let the steward handle matters at Longbourn for a while longer.

"I hate to think that we would be imposing on you, arriving as we did in such an unorthodox manner," Bennet began slowly.

Mr. Darcy laughed. "But is that not part of the charm? When our grandchildren tell the story in years to come of how our families became friends, they shall embellish what really happened beyond all reality and Fitzwilliam will have saved Miss Elizabeth from horrible danger, or perhaps it will be that she arrived just in time to stop him from making a tragic mistake, or some other delightful fiction. All good friendships ought to have stories like that, don't you think?"

For the first time, Bennet decided he may actually enjoy Mr. Darcy's company, rather than simply wishing for access to his books. Any man so ready to embrace the absurdities of life was one he would like to know better.

"Oh, certainly it was Lizzy who saved your son," he said, chancing a smile and watching intently to see how his new acquaintance would react to an opinion that might not match his own. "The juxtaposition works much better that way; the headstrong nymph and the privileged but troubled young man who thinks he's saving her but is actually the one saved in return."

The reaction was not at all what he expected. Mr. Darcy's face turned solemn. "You jest, but you're not as far off as you might think. Fitzwilliam has struggled since his mother's death. Despite their age difference, I think having Miss Elizabeth around will be good for him."

Bennet snorted. "And here I was thinking having to spend time around someone older would be good for Lizzy. She is quite convinced of her own wit and opinions. I have likely done her no favors in that regard and there is no one to check her amongst her sisters."

"Does that mean you are willing to continue with my harebrained scheme?" Mr. Darcy asked, cocking an eyebrow.

What was there to say? It seemed that there were a great many benefits to be gained from staying at Pemberley, and next to no ill consequences. "What is harebrained about it? Two country gentlemen with a love of books decide to spend time in like-minded company, while their children run wild in a safe location and challenge each other in ways that need to happen. I will admit, I was not convinced from the start, but it has grown on me. Only, it occurs to me that my brother-by-law must still be frantic for Lizzy, and I ought to return to bring him up to speed ere long."

Mr. Darcy smiled. "Bring him back with you. I am well acquainted with Mr. and Mrs. Foster, as Mr. Foster has served as the clergyman here for the past fifteen years. There is little that would make Mrs. Foster happier than being able to boast that her daughter's new husband stayed at

Pemberley prior to the wedding."

Bennet eyed his new acquaintance, a multitude of clever replies darting through his mind. He held his tongue, not yet confident that Mr. Darcy would appreciate someone else making a witty response. But as he secured Lizzy's continued welcome and made his way back to his horse outside, he allowed himself a small smile. Maybe, just maybe, this hare-brained scheme was going to be exactly what all of them needed.

Chapter Three

Pemberley! What in the world do you mean, you are staying at Pemberley?"

Edward Gardiner turned to face his betrothed, who had stopped in shock, and raised his hands. "Just that. I am staying at Pemberley. I technically know how it came to be, but it is a fantastical story. I'm not sure if Mr. Darcy is playing with us, or has a hidden agenda, or will tire of our company soon and send us back to the inn. All I know for sure is that my brother Bennet came back to the inn yesterday after Lizzy scared us all to death by disappearing and said she'd been found by young Mr. Darcy, and would I like to join them? They were invited to stay for a few weeks."

Madeline Foster gawked at him. "I forget you aren't from here. That's just the thing. None of what you suggested will occur. Mr. Darcy—the elder, although I hear generally good things of the son as well—isn't given to either brooding or caprice like so many high-born gentlemen. He doesn't give universal handouts, but if someone deserving is in need, he finds a way to make sure they receive help. The servants are loyal to a fault. It's extremely rare to hear even a whisper of complaint against the family, and when a position opens at Pemberley house or grounds, there are a line of applicants. The Darcys don't just take care of their servants, they take care of their families as well, you see."

Mr. Gardiner felt his eyebrows creeping higher throughout Madeline's speech. "So you mean to tell me that I've been randomly selected by an eccentric but highly honorable gentleman to stay in his country estate and enjoy all the luxuries it has to offer until we wed next week, and there are no secret pitfalls waiting to trap me?"

Madeline made a face at him. "Are you sure you'll be wanting to marry me, with Pemberley as your other option?"

"When it comes to you, my dear, there isn't even a choice. Pemberley is a pleasant house—" he grinned at her affronted expression "—but you are essential to my happiness."

There was a long pause, then, "I think you'd better tell me the story, fantastical or not."

He complied readily, interested to hear her opinion; his bride to be was a shrewd woman who saw connections and details he missed. She would be the perfect partner as he worked to grow his yet-fledgling business in London.

Madeline paused for a long while when he

finished the tale, and Gardiner could tell she was thinking about it from different angles. At last, she said, "I can't be certain, as Mr. Darcy is far from an intimate acquaintance, but I have an idea. All of the Darcys are rather serious, but Mr. Darcy has always enjoyed being entertained. I think he likes being around playful people, even if he is not one himself. Lady Anne may have been playful in private; she gave me the impression of putting on a public persona when she came to Lambton or the parsonage. Earls' daughters are not encouraged to mingle freely with the locals.

"My guess is that Mr. Darcy was amused by Elizabeth, who *is* quite enchanting, and decided to let her father collect her so he could take his measure. Young Mr. Darcy has been at school since his mother died, but the elder has been shut up with little company. He may have decided Mr. Bennet's company was just what he needed to break the monotony."

Mr. Gardiner thought it over. "That is more insight than I was able to muster," he said. Then, smiling, he added the final part of the story he hadn't been sure he'd even bring up, when he had no reference for Mr. Darcy's behavior. "So would you like to join us for dinner? Mr. Darcy asked me to invite you and your parents."

Madeline's shriek of excitement was quickly stifled and covered by a hand, but the answer was clear all the same.

*

My dear Mr. Bennet—

I am not sure what to make of your sudden change in plans. It is most unlike you, and set my nerves all aflutter. I could scarcely wrap my mind around the idea all of yesterday, but you will be proud to know that I rallied today, and once I had discussed it with Mrs. Long and my sister Philips, decided that it was just the thing. I should much prefer a journey to the seaside—Brighton or Bath would be delightful—but as you pointed out, spending time with a country gentleman with a large library is exactly the sort of vacation you would choose, and to be able to indulge for little to no expense! It was most kind of you to suggest I buy myself a treat to better balance out your enjoyment. I've had my eye on a silk shawl that will be the envy of the neighborhood ladies, and it is just the right color for my complexion.

And so my brother is married at last, and to a gentleman's daughter at that! He did not tell me; do you know if she came with a significant dowry? It would help his business, and I suppose he must wish to eventually purchase an estate of his own. How fine that would be! My mother always said Edward had the makings of a true gentleman. It is sad he was not able to remain with you and experience what life on an estate can be, but newlyweds do want their privacy, after all. By the bye, Mrs. Philips and I are in your debt for your uncharacteristic description of our new sister Gardiner. Did you have Lizzy tell you what to write? That girl and her flights of fancy may be the death of me, but she does have a way with words. I like your idea of inviting them for Christmas; I will have to make my own judgment then. Although I must say, noting that my new sister is pretty but nothing to what Jane will be one day is only cruel—our eldest will be the envy of many, and so telling me that says far less than what you might think.

I will end here, for Lydia needs her Mama. I simply wished to tell you to enjoy your trip, and let me know when you are planning to return so we may be ready for you.

Yours,

Mrs. Bennet

*

By the time she awoke two weeks later, nestled into a multitude of pillows on her bed in the nursery, Elizabeth had a good read on the happenings at Pemberley. She knew that Georgiana was likely to be awake already, but would not make a sound until the nurse came in to dress her for the day. Her father and Mr. Darcy would be buried in the newspaper, both drinking coffee instead of tea for some unfathomable reason. Will would be awake as well, but his whereabouts seemed to change—some days he joined the adults, others he would be out for a ride on his stallion, Jupiter. The younger George, who Elizabeth still thought of as the mean boy, would likely be asleep.

Accustomed as she was to a house full of late risers, the first few days had been strange and rather unpleasant to Elizabeth. But this was not like Longbourn, where her mother droned on about neighborhood intrigues, or wailed because Lyddie had not been born a boy, or told Lizzy how she would never measure up to Jane. *No one* wailed at Pemberley. And secretly, despite missing Jane daily and not knowing exactly how she fit in, Elizabeth wished that they never had to leave.

There was one creature who was not predictable yet, and so Elizabeth slipped from her bed, pulled on one of her favorite play dresses, and set off to track down her quarry.

She was flat on her stomach in the gallery, once again beginning to think she needed to remember food for her adventures, when a voice behind her enquired, "What in the world are you doing? Ladies don't lay on the floor!"

Elizabeth rolled over onto her back and glared at Will. "You spooked her!" she admonished, flopping her arms out wide to either side. "Besides, I'm not a lady, not yet. And no one was around until you came barging in, so who cares if I'm on the ground?"

"I'm not barging in, it's my house."

"I was here first."

He huffed. "I'm not having this argument with a little girl."

"That sounds like giving up to me."

"Leave my mother's cat alone, okay? She doesn't like anyone, not anymore."

Elizabeth hesitated for just a moment, weighing her annoyance against the unexpected pain in his voice. In the end, her desire to be heard, to be correct, won out. "She'll like me. All the cats at Longbourn like me."

"It's not a game, Elizabeth. Princess Sheba only liked my mother. Leave her alone. She doesn't want—"

Will broke off. Confused, Elizabeth froze, only to feel something tickle her forehead. Going on instinct, she tilted her head up incrementally and looked into the upside-down face of the white cat she'd followed around the house whenever she wasn't allowed to go outside. "Hello, Princess Sheba," Elizabeth breathed.

The cat meowed. Elizabeth meowed back, matching the pitch. From the corner of her eye, she noticed Will stiffen in surprise, but she had other priorities. Ever so slowly, she reached a hand up and did her best to pet the cat's head in the correct direction while completely upside down. It was a shoddy attempt, and she was unsurprised when the cat jerked away, darting back under the console table from whence it had emerged.

Elizabeth pushed herself into a sitting

position and looked up at Will. "I'm not going to force her," she said contemptuously. He clearly didn't understand cats, but that wasn't unusual. "She wants to be friends; she just doesn't know how."

Will stared at her for a long moment, unspeaking. Emotions flashed over his face, and Elizabeth waited for him to shout, or grumble, or tell her she was a silly child. To her surprise, he did none of those. Instead, his face closed down altogether and he turned sharply away on the ball of one foot. She was left staring after him, wondering briefly if he was the next creature she ought to befriend.

Then she shrugged and rolled back over, attention once again on the cat who now had a name. Princess Sheba would be much easier to coax out now that she had come once. Will would just have to deal with it.

*

He made himself walk calmly out of the gallery. It wouldn't do to yell at a child, even if he had wanted to so very badly. She didn't know what that cat had meant to Lady Anne Darcy. She didn't know that he had found the kitten and brought it, soaking wet and freezing, back to his house. Mrs. Reynolds had wanted to turn it out, and his father had called it a lost cause, but his mother had swooped in and claimed the kitten as her own. She was pregnant with Georgiana at the time, although Will hadn't known that until later. All he knew as the cat made her smile when she felt ill so frequently, and in return it had loved her fiercely. While Lady Anne lived, others were allowed to stroke its shiny white fur while it sat on her lap. After her death, it ran from him whenever he attempted to pet it.

Elizabeth didn't know. She couldn't know. No one talked about Lady Anne, at least not outright. Even her cat seemed to be forgetting her.

Darcy turned and drove his fist into a hard piece of paneling. She didn't know. Perhaps his mother would have preferred this. She would have hated for Princess Sheba to be lonely, after all. Perhaps he should have tried harder, been more patient in his coaxing to get the cat to come. Elizabeth had said she wouldn't hurt the cat. It wasn't like Wickham, who had once tried to put honey down the length of the poor creature's back, where it couldn't reach it with its tongue.

Elizabeth didn't know that when Darcy saw the cat he saw his mother's hands, fragile and trembling as they passed over the fur that was only a shade paler than her skin. She didn't know that Princess Sheba had been the first one to notice that something was truly wrong at the end, had yowled and raced from the room before the doctor could give his final prognosis. She didn't know.

She didn't know any of it, and Darcy wasn't sure that he could forgive her for that.

But he was glad that Princess Sheba would finally have another friend.

*

The routine continued with minimal variance for the next week, and so Elizabeth was caught unawares when George Wickham sauntered into the nursery one day when she was sitting on the floor playing with Georgiana.

"Well, hello, my darling Miss Darcy," he said to the younger girl with an exaggerated bow.

She giggled and held her arms up. "Dorge!"

Wickham scooped her up and did a dance with the toddler around the nursery before at last turning back to where Elizabeth still sat on the floor. "I suppose you're happy you got lost in the woods now, aren't you?"

Elizabeth glared at him. "I have no idea what you mean. And I wasn't—"

"Yes, yes, you weren't lost, I know. I've half a mind to test your claims, what say you? Could you find your way back to Lambton if I dropped you off by the creek?"

The creek crossed the road just north of town, so Elizabeth was confident that she *could*, actually, but it wasn't worth telling Wickham that. "You don't have to be mean to me, you know. I'm not here to bother anyone. If you don't like me, just ignore me like Will does."

Wickham's eyebrows went up and one lip curled slightly before he seemed to catch himself and looked back at Georgiana. "I just worry about my dear Darcy friends, is all," he said to her, tousling her blonde curls. "I wouldn't like it if anyone tried to hurt them."

It was turning into a conversation she didn't want to have from the floor, so Elizabeth climbed to her feet. "I'm not going to hurt anyone!"

"Getting ready to run off and tattle, are we?"

"I'm not a crybaby or a tattletale. Which you'd know if you'd bothered to spend any time around me since we've been at Pemberley. I didn't miss you, though, so I'm glad you stayed away."

"Is that so? I suppose—"

"Ind!" Georgiana exclaimed, smacking a chubby hand against Wickham's shoulder. "Be ind!"

Elizabeth had learned almost immediately that the younger girl hated conflict. She found Georgiana rather boring, but she was a sweet girl, very unlike Elizabeth's own little sisters. Upsetting her was the last thing Elizabeth had intended to do. "Of course, Georgie," she said placatingly. "Being kind is the right thing to do, isn't it?"

"It certainly is," Will said from the doorway. Elizabeth spun to face him.

"Willum!" Georgiana shouted, reaching out and wriggling in Wickham's arms.

He ignored her. "Are you upsetting my

sister?" he asked, looking between Elizabeth and Wickham.

So much for backup. Enough was enough. "I was *trying* to keep the peace so she didn't get upset," Elizabeth snapped. "Clearly no one wants me to be here. I'm going; you can all be grumpy together."

She pushed past Will, who looked surprised. "Elizabeth—"

Elizabeth kept walking, then that became too hard so she grabbed her skirts and broke into a run. It wasn't like she expected Will—or George Wickham—to like her. They were both fifteen, almost adults; she was seven. They were *boys*.

She just wished that Will didn't seem so eager to *dislike* her. He was pleasant, for a boy. He'd defended her from Wickham and brought her to Pemberley to make sure she was safe, which had been kind of him even if Elizabeth still knew she could have managed on her own. He clearly cared for Georgiana, talked about interesting things with their fathers, and had never pulled her hair or shoved her the way her annoying neighbors, the Lucas boys, did on occasion.

But despite his good manners, Will had also been cold towards her from the beginning. She felt him watching her whenever they were in the same room and knew he was waiting to catch her doing something wrong. He never smiled at her the way he did at Georgiana, rolled his eyes at her questions, and of course there had been the incident with Princess Sheba. He made her feel unsure and small, and Elizabeth didn't like either of those, which made her angry in turn. She hadn't done anything wrong! It wasn't fair.

Two hallways from the nursery, Elizabeth slowed to a walk once again, catching her breath. Well, she'd show them. She didn't want to spend time with the fussy Darcy's or mean George Wickham anyhow. There was a new litter of kittens in the horse barn, and Elizabeth didn't care if she had to get covered in hay, she was going to find them and make friends.

It was far too pleasant a day to waste any more time thinking about Fitzwilliam Darcy.

Chapter Four

I t was nearing the end of the Bennet's scheduled visit when Darcy was invited to spend the evening with his father and Mr. Bennet. George Wickham had been invited as well, disappearing only at the last moment. Mr. Darcy laughed off his absence as the enthusiasm of youth; his son was not nearly as sanguine. George was not the same this summer, but the only other person who wasn't charmed by him was Lizzy, and how useful was a seven-year-old in convincing adults? Not at all, as far as Darcy was concerned.

Regardless, it was pleasant to be able to sit with the grown-up men rather than being lumped in with the little girls. He'd even been given his own glass of port, something he did not care for at all but knew better than to complain about. All gentlemen drank the stuff, after all. And Darcys were always, first and foremost, gentlemen.

They'd covered a variety of subjects, some that

Darcy understood and others that completely befuddled him, when the topic of the Bennet's visit arose.

"I'm of a mind to make this an annual occurrence, provided you don't mind making the journey," Mr. Darcy said, pouring both of the older men more port. "You'll have to bring your wife with you next year."

Mr. Bennet made a face, then took a hearty swallow. "As for returning, I am certainly amenable. I have enjoyed myself more than I expected, and I know Lizzy has as well. But my wife accompanying me, well, I do not know if that would be a good idea." At Mr. Darcy's surprised look, he sighed and ran a hand through his hair before explaining. "Mrs. Bennet is a good wife and mother to our girls, but the truth of the matter is that she was not raised as a gentleman's daughter, and her behavior reflects it. In Meryton, where everyone knows her and we are the preeminent family, it matters little. But to bring her to a place like Pemberley and expect her to comport herself with restraint—I cannot see it. If you had a wife she could emulate, it might be different. As it is, she is remarkably resistant to any suggestions I might make as to what behavior befits a lady, and would ignore anything I might say. She is not interested in books or the outdoors, either. It would make for an unpleasant visit in a multitude of ways."

Darcy looked at his father, keeping his face

impassive. Mrs. Bennet sounded awful, nothing like her husband or Elizabeth.

Clearly, his father's thoughts trended in a similar vein. "I will respect your decision, Bennet, as it is your family," he said after a pause. "Forgive me, I am simply surprised. Miss Elizabeth does remarkably well for a spirited girl of her age; I had assumed that was Mrs. Bennet's influence at work."

"Thank you for the compliment to my daughter. No, Lizzy and Jane spent a great deal of time with their grandmother—my mother—while she was still alive. My wife did not care to listen to the previous Mrs. Bennet either, but she was able to instill a sense of comportment in my eldest two. It is entirely to their credit that they have retained the good habits."

Mr. Bennet likely didn't catch Mr. Darcy's flared nostrils in the low light, but Darcy did. His father was angry, very angry. To dismiss the behavior of his children, young ladies who would one day need to take their place in society, as a matter of chance! It was unimaginable, especially given that he was relying on the good sense of two girls who were not even ten years old.

There was no hint of the anger when Mr. Darcy spoke, and the younger Darcy listened intently. He'd been working on masking his emotions and managed decently well until he opened his mouth. His father was a master, speaking or silent.

"It is a challenge, is it not, to raise young ladies. As gentlemen, we can only know a portion of what they face, and there is so much expected of them! I worry for Georgiana already, growing up without a mother and so isolated here. It has been suggested I send her to one of her aunts when she is a bit older, particularly since both have daughters, but I cannot stomach the idea. A great deal will depend on finding the right nurse, and governess, and eventually companion."

Mr. Bennet said nothing; Darcy wondered what he was thinking. Mr. Darcy sighed, drained the rest of his port, and set the glass aside. "Enough of that for this evening. I am glad I have a little more time with Georgiana before I must truly worry about her education. Do say you'll bring Miss Elizabeth back with you; I believe she would be a good example for Georgiana in several ways."

Mr. Bennet's tight expression eased into a small smile. "Gladly. She would never forgive me if I denied her the pleasure. I think Lizzy has quite fallen in love with your grounds and would be happy to never leave. Another visit would be a tremendous treat."

"Wonderful. Like I said, perhaps we can make it an annual event. But for now, I am for bed."

All three rose; Mr. Bennet said his good nights and exited. Darcy looked at his father, who had motioned discreetly for him to stay. They both stood silently for several moments. At last, Mr. Darcy said quietly, "Let that be a lesson for you. Mr. Bennet made a very poor match when he married. Do you understand why?"

Darcy nodded. "She is not a gentleman's daughter. He did not say exactly that, but it is obvious enough."

To his surprise, his father shook his head. "No. Well, that may contribute to the matter, but it is not the main concern. Mr. Bennet is a gentleman from an established but not highly elevated family and he cares little for town. He could have married a tradesman's daughter and made a huge success of it, had he chosen a lady who would be a helpmeet to him and a proper guide to their children. I do not know the circumstances of their marriage, and I will not ask. He may have needed her money, it may have been a love match, or perhaps there was a compromise involved. But I suspect Bennet saw a beautiful face and thought more of that than he did about what is required from the mistress of an estate." Mr. Darcy paused. "I hope you find love with your future wife, son. But never forget that marriage is a partnership. Both sides must understand the requirements and be willing and able to keep up their end of the deal."

Both Darcys retired to their respective beds, but sleep evaded Darcy for hours. He'd never given much thought to choosing a wife before.

It was always something that he knew would occur in the future, and thinking about it wasn't necessary. Now, though, he wondered. What kind of lady would he like for a wife? She would have to love Pemberley, of course, and get along with his father and Georgiana. Beyond that, however, he couldn't say. It would be preferrable if she were beautiful and liked to read the same books that he did. He didn't want a boring wife. And yet—

Darcy rolled over, pushing the thoughts from his head. He was only fifteen. There would be plenty of time to select a wife later. Much, much later.

Chapter Five

Longbourn, 1799

"Well, Lizzy, are you of a mind to accompany me back to Pemberley, or would you prefer to stay here with your sisters this summer?"

It was after dinner and Elizabeth had felt very grown up indeed when her father invited her into his study. They were ensconced in the pair of leather chairs by the fireplace, both scratched and stained to the point where Mrs. Bennet refused to keep them in her sitting room, but perfectly worn in and comfortable, with high arms just right for supporting a book.

The arms also hid her father's face, so Elizabeth pushed herself forward and searched his face to make sure he wasn't joking. He did that sometimes, and while she generally appreciated his humor, this wouldn't be funny.

The question was, did she want to go? Pemberley meant unlimited books and grumpy disapproving Will, new puppies in the barn and putting up with George Wickham, new areas to explore on the estate and rainy days cooped up in the nursery with Georgiana instead of Jane. But Longbourn would be noisy and unvarying and, with her father gone, Lizzy was sure to be in trouble with her mother more often than not. In Derbyshire, Lizzy was expected to behave herself like a small adult, which was so very hard when she wanted to run and shout. But she was treated like a small adult, and that was worth the effort to behave.

"I'd like to come, Papa. But can't Jane come, too?"

Mr. Bennet smiled, as if he'd expected this response. "I've already talked to her, and to your mother. Jane will be staying here. Your mother wants her help with the younger girls, and remember, Jane has not met the Darcys. She didn't want to go stay with strangers."

"But we would be there! And they were strangers when we met them last year!"

"Lizzy, my girl, are you just like Lydia?"

"No!"

"Jane is not just like you, either. You enjoy meeting new people and going new places. She likes being at home, where she knows who everyone is and how they will react. At some point, she will need to learn to be more in the world and deal with new situations, but it will not be right now. Tell me, what are you most looking forward to at Pemberley?"

"The library, and the grounds, and seeing Princess Sheba, and—"

Mr. Bennet held up a hand and Elizabeth stopped. "Does your sister like reading?"

"Well, no, not like I do. But—"

"Does she like going for long walks outdoors?"

"No."

"You girls are very close, and that makes me happy. But you will both do better with time on your own. I have talked to your Uncle Gardiner. Jane will be spending a month in London over next winter, now that he and Mrs. Gardiner are established enough to house her. Apparently Mrs. Gardiner suggested it, and I am happy to comply. That will be Jane's adventure, and it is one better suited to her nature. You, my bibliophile wood nymph, will come to Pemberley with me. Do you understand why?"

Elizabeth bit her lip and tried to think logically instead of shouting that she wanted Jane to come. Her papa never gave in if she shouted, only said that her logic couldn't be very good if she needed volume to back it up. Only, there was no alternate logic to employ. Her father was correct.

She nodded reluctantly. "Might I spend time with my aunt and uncle Gardiner someday, too?" Elizabeth asked. "I liked Mrs. Gardiner."

Mr. Bennet smiled. "I am sure they would be delighted to host you. Now off you go. We leave in four days, and I have several letters I cannot put off writing any longer."

Darcy set his shoulders and locked his hands behind his back as he stood on the front steps. He'd always hated the idea of waiting for guests, even if they didn't have to wait very long thanks to the notice from Pemberly's staff that the carriage had been spotted. Today, when he'd already received a dressing down from his father, and the sky was spitting intermittent drizzle, it felt very much like torture. The Bennets weren't *his* guests, and it wasn't like they were important.

However, since he'd just gotten a lecture about being considerate towards George Wickham, who was less fortunate than himself and therefore deserving of more leeway—the worst logic Darcy had ever heard, especially given Wickham's constant flouting of the rules of polite society—he knew better than to protest. At least his father hadn't required Georgiana to wait in the rain.

The carriage arrived in due time, even if it felt like forever, and a footman stepped forward to fold down the step. Mr. Bennet emerged, then turned back to his daughter, picking her up directly from the carriage and swinging her to the ground. Darcy waited for the girl to sprint towards them, the way his classmate's sisters did whenever they encountered rain.

Elizabeth Bennet did no such thing. Instead,

she tipped her head back and let the light rain fall directly onto her face. She *smiled.* Only when her father turned from giving instructions to the footmen and put a hand on her shoulder did Elizabeth start towards the house, still smiling.

"Welcome back to Pemberley, Mr. Bennet, Miss Bennet," George Darcy said. He gave Elizabeth a tiny grin and addressed her directly. "I had thought to serve tea, but perhaps you would like to stay out here and soak up rain like a flower?"

Elizabeth gave a curtsey and shook her head, making her curls bounce. "Hello, Mr. Darcy, and Will. The rain is very pleasant after being in the carriage forever and ever, but I like tea. And your cakes," she added, glancing sideways.

George Darcy laughed. "Of course, I haven't forgotten your love of cakes. Come in, come in. We're very glad that you are here."

Mr. Bennet gave his own greetings as the party filed into the house. Footmen carried in trunks and Mrs. Reynolds directed them to the nursery and Mr. Bennet's guest room. Mr. Darcy and Mr. Bennet walked ahead of the group, discussing the state of the roads. Darcy trailed behind them, silent amidst the hubbub, a sinking feeling in the pit of his stomach once again. How long would it be until he was receiving lectures about allowing Miss Bennet's poor behavior? Years? Weeks? Hours?

"You attend Cambridge, don't you?"

Surprised, Darcy looked down. Elizabeth stood

next to him, looking up with big eyes under slightly frizzy hair.

"I do."

"How long does it take to get there?"

"Generally two or three days, depending." He'd made it in a day and a half, once. That hadn't been an enjoyable ride.

"Depending on what?"

"If the roads are in good condition, if I ride or take the carriage, how soon it gets dark at night, and how long I'm willing to push on."

Elizabeth was silent for several moments, clearly thinking through all that he'd said. "Two days sounds much better than four."

Darcy had never minded traveling much, but then, he wasn't sure how well the Bennet's carriage was sprung, or if they had decent squabs. "Do you not like travel?"

She shrugged. No one had broken her of that habit yet, apparently. "I like it well enough. But Papa gets tired and prefers to stop early. He says riding in a carriage gives him a headache."

They'd reached the green parlor. Will ended up between his father and Miss Elizabeth, once everyone was seated with tea and cakes. He debated saying nothing, but that could very well mean another lecture, just as much as saying the wrong thing. What he would give to be a charming, preferred child like Elizabeth and Wickham.

Pushing the thought away, Darcy looked at

their young guest and said, "It usually takes us four days to get to Kent, when we visit my aunt there. We generally break in London, but even so it is a long journey. I greatly prefer riding for part of the way to make it more interesting."

Elizabeth wrinkled her nose. "Even if I could ride, ladies have to be in a carriage."

"You don't ride?" Darcy asked, shocked. Riding fit so well with Elizabeth's impetuous outdoor-loving temperament he'd never considered that she wouldn't know how. Vaguely, he recalled her reticence to return to Pemberly via horseback when they first met.

"Lizzy and our mare had a disagreement when she was younger," Mr. Bennet said, clearly having overheard the exclamation. "They've avoided each other studiously ever since."

"I don't like horses and they don't like me," Elizabeth said stoutly, as if that settled the matter.

Turning from Mr. Bennet to look at the girl beside him, Darcy caught a glimpse of his father's face, where a small smile showed only in the wrinkles of his eyes. George Darcy had a plan, and he meant to carry his point.

"Why of course, you cannot be expected to learn on a horse that is not suited to you," the elder Mr. Darcy said agreeably. "I recall the first pony I tried to mount. It was the most temperamental beast I've ever had the pleasure to encounter, and as you might imagine, I ended up in the dust more often than not. My second mount proved to be far better. There are several horses in our stables that I believe would do well for you, Miss Elizabeth. With my own experiences in mind, I will personally help you find the very best one." He glanced at Darcy. "Fitzwilliam has been teaching Georgiana the basics of riding. I am sure, given your age and confident nature, that you will pick it up admirably. By the end of the summer, Fitzwilliam could take you to explore some of the further areas of the estate, the ones that are too remote to reach on foot."

"You'll turn my daughter into even more of a hoyden," Mr. Bennet said in his usual good-natured sardonic way.

Darcy stiffened. He'd happily tell off anyone who dared to speak of Georgiana in such a way.

His father only smiled. "Nonsense. All gentlewomen ride, particularly those on estates like Pemberley. There is a chance we will be joined by my brother-by-law and his family for a short time, and if so, you will see that his wife and daughter both ride."

Surprised that Elizabeth had not broken into the conversation, Darcy turned back to see a strange look on her face. It was so foreign he could barely believe it, but it was there nonetheless. Elizabeth Bennet was afraid of horses, or at least afraid of riding them.

He did not know how to persuade the way his

father did, but Darcy opened his mouth all the same and heard himself say, "There are several areas of the estate I believe you would love, Miss Elizabeth. If you practice every day, it would be easy to show you at least a few of them before you leave."

Her small face was uncharacteristically solemn as she looked from one gentleman to another. "Horses do not like me," Elizabeth said again.

"Nonsense," George Darcy said, smiling at her. "There is a horse for everyone, Miss Elizabeth. The trick is simply finding the correct one. More cake?"

*

George Darcy watched from the corner of his eye as his son led Miss Elizabeth down the aisle of the main barn. Elizabeth had spent plenty of time in the barn last year, playing with the kittens that had been born there. He'd never thought to wonder about her feelings towards the barn's main occupants.

Slightly behind him, Bennet grumbled indistinctly. Forcing Elizabeth to face her fears was not his style, and it would not have surprised George if the other gentleman was also worried about cost. No doubt it suited him to allow Elizabeth's avoidance of riding, for it meant one less lady's mount to purchase, feed, and house.

George had other ideas. There was a spark of potential within Elizabeth Bennet, and it was well within George's means to draw it out and see what she could become. He thought it quite possible that she would manage well enough on her own—she was stubborn and strong-spirited, but had a good heart, and Bennet had mentioned the plan to send her to her aunt and uncle in the future. Madeline Foster—Gardiner, now—was a well-behaved, genteel young lady despite her lower position in life. She would be a good influence on the girl. But Elizabeth was here now, and George did not believe in doing things halfway. Gentlewomen rode, and if her father did not intend to teach her, George would see it done.

Besides, it would be a good lesson for his son. He'd pulled back from young George Wickham lately. The elder George was disappointed, but not terribly surprised. They were very different young men, and in that age when one rebels against the patterns and strictures of their youth. It was likely they would grow back together in time, but for now, Fitzwilliam needed to practice his manners with those outside of his family circle. Elizabeth needed a patient teacher who was good on a horse and knew the estate. Really, it worked out so well it seemed predestined.

*

Elizabeth walked down the steps as slowly

as she could manage, but the bottom still arrived. By the time she was halfway across the courtyard, dragging her feet, it was clear that Will was thoroughly annoyed. Well, she was too, and no one seemed to care that she didn't want riding lessons in the first place.

"You know, we'll spend the same amount of time with the horses no matter how long it takes you to get there," Will commented, eyes on the puffy clouds in the sky.

Elizabeth didn't reply.

"Why is it that you're so sure this will go poorly? Riding is exactly the kind of activity I would expect you to love."

She shot him a sideways look. "I told you, horses don't like me."

He was looking at her now, directly, with that focus he usually reserved for books. "Horses don't like you, or the one you tried to ride at home didn't?" When she didn't answer, he continued, "Do you have a problem around carriage horses? Do stranger's mounts go out of their way to bother you?"

Well, put like that— "I suppose it is the horse we have at home. She's a perfect horse for Jane, but as soon as I come near or mount, she gets all skittish and refuses to stand still. She goes backwards or sideways and puts her head down so I can't even correct her." Elizabeth realized she'd stopped, remembering. She started walking again "Everyone, even horses, love Jane.

But I'm not her."

Will stared at her for several long moments, clearly thinking through something. He thought a lot—too much, Elizabeth thought sometimes. "Do you like everyone equally?" he asked at last. Seeing her expression, he continued, "Me and George Wickham, for example. Do you think about us the same?"

"No!" She didn't like George Wickham at all.

"I'm guessing you don't care much for Wickham, am I right?" At her nod, Will continued, "Well, there are people who think he is wonderful, and find me boring and staid. If people prefer different companions, why can't horses?"

It was Elizabeth's turn to think it through. They'd reached the stables before she came to any sort of conclusion.

Stopping both of them short of the door, Will dropped a hand onto Elizabeth's shoulder. "You don't have to be afraid of Sir Lancelot. He didn't react poorly to you yesterday, but if it is a bad fit, we'll try a different horse. I guarantee there is at least one horse in the stable that will like you."

"What if there isn't?"

Will sighed, his hand moving off her shoulder. "If you really are an aberration and all the horses truly hate you, then I'll tell my father and we can stop this. But I will be watching you, Elizabeth. If you try to provoke Sir Lancelot or any of the other mounts into misbehaving because you're trying to prove a point, it won't end well for you."

"I wouldn't do that! And my name is Lizzy."

They'd reached the stall, where one of the grooms had saddled and bridled the giant dapple grey gelding she was supposed to ride. Elizabeth looked at the side saddle, pommel higher than she could reach, and tried not to gulp.

"Your name is Elizabeth. Stay in the saddle for five minutes without falling off or crying, and I'll see about calling you Lizzy."

She glanced up at Will. His face was impassive, not at all demeaning, but something inside of Elizabeth rebelled. She'd show him.

"Very well," she said in her best grown-up tone of voice, hoping she sounded resigned instead of afraid. "Let's go ride a giant horse."

Chapter Six

To Darcy's complete surprise, he came to enjoy Elizabeth's riding lessons. Sir Lancelot, despite being huge—or maybe because of it—was very hard to spook and stood calmly beneath his new rider. Elizabeth had still managed to fall off half a dozen times in the last three weeks, but she never once cried. Yesterday they had finally left the stable yard for a short excursion around the house, and Darcy was sure that Elizabeth would be up for a longer ride with just a bit more practice.

They wouldn't be doing any riding today, however. The uncharacteristically beautiful weather had turned overnight, and now rain streamed down the window panes. Darcy had stopped by the nursery after breaking his fast to see Georgiana, only to be roped into a game of hide and seek with both of the girls. The first few rounds had gone well, but then Georgiana had grown tired of the game and Elizabeth convinced him to search for only her one last time. And now, as he made his way further and further away from the nursery without any sign of her, Darcy was beginning to get worried.

"Lizzy?" he called out in a low voice. "Lizzy, the game is over. You win. Come out." He backtracked, repeating the message several more times. Darcy knew very well by now that she loved to win and was not above gloating about it—hardly surprising for a child of eight years old. If she wasn't responding, it was because she couldn't hear him. And that was what worried him. Pemberley was a well-maintained house, and new enough that Darcy wasn't concerned about Elizabeth finding an old section and falling through a floor. It did sprawl, however, and the labyrinth of dark service corridors could be extremely hard to navigate if you didn't know where you were going. Throw in a sticky latch on a rarely-used door, and it was only too easy to imagine Elizabeth wandering into an area where they could not hear her and winding up stuck there.

"Lizzy!" Darcy called again, louder this time.

A crash came from down the hall, and Darcy sprinted in that direction. He'd been right; she had made her way further away from the nursery and into a corridor of second-rate guest rooms. Grabbing a corner to maintain his momentum, Darcy swung around a turn and nearly ran straight into Elizabeth.

He stumbled to a stop, taking in the scene. She

sat awkwardly on the floor beside an overturned cabinet, doors askew and shards of ceramic littering the entire area. It took only a second to reconstruct what had happened: Elizabeth had hidden in the cabinet, which was allowable in their set rules since she hadn't entered a guest room. She'd likely heard him and, upon attempting to open the door, found it stuck or hard to operate from the inside. In her struggle, perhaps growing more frantic, she'd pushed hard enough to turn the whole thing over, shattering the vase or bowl or whatever had once sat on top.

"Why didn't you shout for me?" Darcy asked.

Elizabeth hung her head. "Only babies get stuck. And I'm not supposed to shout indoors."

Right. The second answer was clearly what had stopped her.

Opening his mouth to respond, Darcy was cut off by quickly approaching footsteps. The next moment, his father rounded the corner. He must have been on his way to visit Georgiana, which he did several times a week. "What on earth happened here?"

He'd be hearing about this for months. Resisting the urge to hand his head and instead squaring his shoulders, Darcy faced his father. "Apologies, sir. It was an accident. We were playing hide and seek. Georgiana is with her nurse, so you needn't worry about her. I'll see that everything is cleaned up." There. He'd gotten out the pertinent information.

George Darcy's face had darkened throughout the speech. "Really, Fitzwilliam, you ought to know better. Are you a young man or a child? Miss Elizabeth could have been hurt, and the servants have plenty of work to do without cleaning up after scrapes. You will clean it up, not ask someone else to do so. I appreciate you entertaining your sister and our guest, but I expected better of you."

"It's not his fault."

Surprised, both Darcys turned. Elizabeth had pushed herself up to standing during the speech and stood gingerly amongst the broken shards—and despite her disheveled appearance, her chin was up in the same way she faced the horse after she fell off.

"Will set the rules and the boundaries of where we could hide. I decided to climb into the cabinet, and when I got stuck, I pushed my way out instead of calling for help. I broke the vase. I will clean it up."

She linked her hands together in front of her, showing a bloody scrape across the back of one hand. Catching Will's widened eyes, Elizabeth promptly shoved her hands in her pockets instead.

Mr. Darcy stared down at her. Elizabeth stared back.

"I trust my son to watch over you and his sister when he removes you from the care of the nurse," Mr. Darcy said in a much lighter voice than he had used before. "I can understand your actions, seeing how you are half Fitzwilliam's age. I expect him to know better. You could have been hurt or lost for quite some time."

Elizabeth's chin jutted out further. "It was my fault. I will clean up the mess that I made." Apparently seeing a hint of the father Darcy knew too well, her eyes slid sideways. "If you think it necessary, Will can help me."

Darcy looked at his father, waiting for the commands that would determine what he did next. The older gentleman surveyed Elizabeth for several more moments before turning and nodding once at his son. "I will check in with Mrs. Reynolds this afternoon. Make sure that everything is taken care of."

"Yes, sir," Darcy heard himself say automatically.

Without another word, the elder Darcy turned and left. Unsurprisingly, one of the upstairs maids had appeared during the conversation and stood waiting with broom and dustpan. As soon as Mr. Darcy was out of sight, she moved forward to begin sweeping.

Darcy stopped her with a shake of his head. "No, Hannah, we will do it. Lizzy, give me your good hand."

She frowned, confused, but held it out readily. Darcy leaned over the mess on the floor and grasped it tightly, then lifted her to stand beside him. "We don't need you bleeding anywhere else," he told her. "Now let me see your scrape."

Luckily, it was only a minor surface wound, already clotted by the time he laid eyes on it. She let Hannah wrap a bandage around it, but said nothing about the pain as they swept the area and righted the cabinet, which thankfully hadn't broken. Elizabeth ran off once they were done, either to the portrait gallery or her favorite nook in the library. Clearly, she was already moving on, happy to put the incident from her mind. Darcy, however, walked back to his room deep in thought.

Nothing had required her to speak up. Her own father wasn't there to reprimand her, and his father hadn't even glanced in her direction. Had it been Georgiana, she would have frozen like a rabbit, hoping not to be seen. Had it been Wickham, he would have been only too happy to let Darcy take the blame, not to mention do the cleanup work. Only Darcy's cousin Richard would have stood up for him in such a way —but then, George Darcy expected such trouble when Richard came to stay, and would have reprimanded both boys from the beginning. And not only had she taken the blame, she'd hidden her injury instead of milking it for more attention, more sympathy. Even when he was friends with Wickham, the other boy never would have acted like Elizabeth had today.

Darcy continued to twist the situation around

in his mind for the rest of the day, picking it apart and looking at it from every angle he could conceive. He couldn't find a single reason why she would act like that, if it wasn't genuine. At last, just before bed, Darcy made up his mind. He didn't consider Elizabeth Bennet to be true friend material, not when she was—as his father had pointed out—half his age, and a girl besides. But no longer did he expect her to turn into someone like Wickham. He could stop watching her every move and worrying that she would purposely hurt Georgiana.

Well, Darcy reflected as he laid back in bed, folding his hands behind his head, he probably ought to still watch her. Lizzy did have a tendency to get herself into scrapes, and it would be better for everyone involved if he was there to get her out of them before they became common knowledge. He smiled at the thought, and the unease in the pit of his stomach dissolved fully for the first time since the Bennets had arrived. At least he would have something to do for the next three weeks.

*

"Willum, look!"

Startled by Georgiana's uncharacteristic shriek, Elizabeth tensed in the saddle, then turned to follow the younger girl's finger. They were on the bank of Pemberley's lake, coming back from a ride. Georgiana sat in front of Will, held tightly on his lap. Elizabeth had found herself vacillating between envy at Georgie's complete lack of fear at being on the horse, and pride that she was in control of her own mount. It helped that she no longer believed that Sir Lancelot hated her.

Now, convinced that she wasn't about to fall, Elizabeth was free to turn her attention to the carriage and accompanying rider that had caught Georgiana's eye.

"Are you up for a canter, Lizzy?" Will asked. To her shock, he was grinning, a carefree look that seemed strange on his usually serious face. He was excited, very excited, about their visitors.

A spark of jealousy shot through Elizabeth. She'd been at Pemberley for five weeks now, and had spent a significant portion of it with Will, since he gave her near-daily riding lessons. She didn't want to lose his attention to the strangers in the carriage, even if she was only here for one more week.

But she wasn't willing to show him how she really felt, or turn down a challenge. "Of course!" she replied, leaning forward and grabbing the end of Sir Lancelot's mane before giving the gelding his head. Will had told her at least a dozen times it was poor form, but she hadn't yet decided to care. Today, preemptively annoyed at him for ignoring her, Elizabeth would have done it just to bother Will.

But he only grinned at her and pushed his

own horse into a canter alongside Sir Lancelot, Georgiana tucked securely into one of his arms while the other managed the reins. The rider adjacent to the carriage noticed them as they approached the yard and broke into a full-on gallop, thundering down the rest of the drive before pulling his mount to a sliding stop what seemed like inches from Will and Georgiana.

"Richard!" Will shouted, half greeting and half admonishment. "You could have hurt Georgie!"

The newcomer reached out and plucked Georgiana from Will's arms; she giggled, clearly unconcerned. "Never," he declared as all three horses turned back towards the stables. "I've been working with Ares for months; I can stop him wherever I want, and he's too well-aware of his own surroundings to bash into something even if I do make a mistake. Georgiana, can you believe your brother would accuse me of something so plebeian?"

Will only snorted in reply.

They trotted into the stable yard, where even more grooms than usual waited to receive the animals once they were free of their burdens. Richard dropped the reins on his horse's neck, kicked free of both stirrups, and swung his right leg forward over his mount's lowered neck, sliding down and landing on the ground without even shifting his hold on Georgiana.

"Show off." Will dismounted in the usual way, handed his horse off with a nod and a thank-you, then stepped up to Elizabeth and Sir Lancelot. She unhooked her leg from the side saddle and slid into his arms. At first, dismounting had been nearly as terrifying as sitting on the horse, but she'd become accustomed to the maneuver, and Will had never even come close to dropping her.

Today, he gave her one of his rare full smiles before setting her on the ground. "Good job today," he added quietly.

Elizabeth felt herself beaming.

"And who do we have here?" The tan young man was watching her closely, the way Will used to do. Some of her smile faded away.

"Richard, meet Miss Elizabeth Bennet. Mr. Bennet is a friend of Father's. Lizzy, this is the other Fitzwilliam, and the bane of my existence. My cousin, the Honorable Richard Fitzwilliam."

"The bane of your existence? Surely that title must belong to someone else," Richard said, his face far more serious than his words.

The smile dropped off of Will's face, and he gave a single shake of his head. "Richard, surely you know that no one can compare to you."

Simultaneously, the front doors opened to let Mr. Darcy out, and the carriage came to a halt at the bottom of the steps.

"Come," Will said, taking Georgiana from his cousin and making his way towards the rest of the group.

Elizabeth looked back to make sure Sir Lancelot was taken care of and smiled at the groom who led the gelding away. Typically, her lessons ended with learning how to untack and brush her horse, but clearly there were different plans today. Then she fell in behind Will and Richard, trotting to keep up with their long-legged strides.

The carriage door opened to disgorge a man roughly the same age as Mr. Darcy, who then turned back and offered his hand to a girl a couple years older than Elizabeth.

"Milton didn't join you?" Darcy asked.

It was Richard's turn to snort. "Since when is Milton the type for visiting family, unless said family has plenty of young ladies to amuse him?"

Elizabeth couldn't see the look that Will threw at Richard, but she caught the way his entire body stiffened, and the sharp movement of his head.

"Don't give me that look, I'm not the one with the problem. Mother didn't come either—you know she always goes to Brighton in the summer."

Whatever Will intended to say in response was cut off as they stopped next to the group. Greetings were given between the family members while Elizabeth hung back, still half hidden between the young men. At last, the older gentleman looked directly at her. "Well, you don't look like a Darcy or a Fitzwilliam. Who might you be?"

Mr. Darcy smiled, while Elizabeth tried to

decide if she should be offended or not. Before she could make up her mind, she was waved forward and managed a curtsey. "James, this is Miss Elizabeth Bennet. She and her father are staying with us for part of the summer, you'll meet him soon. Miss Elizabeth, my brother the Earl of Matlock."

Elizabeth managed to keep from frowning in confusion, but only just. A moment later, her brain caught up and she realized that the earl must be actual brother to Will's late mother; Mr. Darcy meant he was a brother by marriage. "Pleased to meet you, sir," she managed.

"And you as well, Miss Elizabeth," the earl replied, then turned back to Mr. Darcy.

"I imagine you'd like a drink after your journey," Mr. Darcy said. "Fitzwilliam, Richard, why don't you join us?"

"Delightful idea," the earl said. "My son has some news to share."

Will's eyes shot to Richard, face tense. The other boy only gave a bland smile. All four gentlemen climbed the stairs and disappeared inside, Will handing Georgiana off to a nurse who stood waiting inside the door.

Alone at the base of the steps, the two girls looked at each other. The newcomer had curly reddish gold hair and pale blue eyes. Elizabeth guessed she was the same age as Jane.

"My brother bought a commission," the stranger said. "He's going to be a lieutenant,

70

because he's a second son." Her face turned dark. "I wish my other brother was the one going away."

Elizabeth considered her for a moment, then offered up her own unchangeable truth. "My mother is still upset because I was supposed to be a boy. Our estate is entailed and the heir can turn us out into the hedgerows as soon as my father dies. There are five of us girls, but no boys."

"Five! I wish I had sisters."

"You wouldn't think that if you had to live with my youngest two."

There was another pause.

"I'm Sophia."

"Elizabeth. You can call me Lizzy."

Sophia frowned at her. "Do you like playing games?"

"What kind? I got stuck in a cupboard playing hide and seek last week, and Mr. Darcy is probably still mad at me for breaking a fancy vase getting out."

For the first time, Sophia smiled, and her entire face transformed. "Oh, perfect. This is going to be so much more fun than usual. Want to go beg cakes from the kitchen while the boys are stuck acting like gentlemen? Cook loves me."

Elizabeth hadn't known it was possible to beg for cakes, but she'd long ago made friends with the cook and kitchen maids at Longbourn. Surely it couldn't be that much different at Pemberley.

"Yes," she said with a grin.

"I think I like you, Lizzy. Come on," Sophia said, moving away from the main door with purpose. "Let's go in the back way."

Elizabeth followed her, feeling her earlier worry ease. Maybe these cousins wouldn't be so bad after all.

Chapter Seven

Derbyshire, 1801

H ey, Lizzy! Elizabeth! Wait for me!"
Turning slightly, but not stopping,
Elizabeth debated telling George
Wickham that he had never been given leave
to be so informal with her name, but she bit
her tongue. That would lead to him calling her
a child, or some nasty commentary about her
preference for Will. Normally she wouldn't mind
the chance to argue her point, but not today.

"Your legs are twice as long as mine," she
called back instead. "If I wait for you, I'll just have
to run once you get here."

To her surprise, he grinned and lengthened
his stride.

"What do you want, George?" It was her fourth
summer at Pemberley, and he was seventeen
now, almost as old as Will. He'd never shown her
any sort of attention before, let alone sought her
out.

"I heard what happened."

She sped up, continuing towards the gardens.

"No, Lizzy, wait!"

Elizabeth stopped, turning to face him directly. "What?" she asked flatly.

He shrugged, giving her the half-smile she'd seen before when he talked to others. "It's just, I know what it's like being here, but not being a Darcy. The family isn't the problem, it's everyone else. They don't trust you, or want to take your place, or think that because you don't have the Darcy name, you're fair game for whatever games they are playing." His smile turned wry. "It's part of the reason I didn't like you at first. There are plenty of children from Lambton who have tried to pull pranks and didn't care if I got hurt."

"How did you hear what happened?" It had only been the three of them in the room, as far as Elizabeth knew—the two ladies, gossiping while their husbands spoke with the gentlemen, and Elizabeth herself. She didn't *think* she had been meant to overhear, but who could say?

I heard from Madeline Gardiner that the elder sister is a right beauty, and so well behaved. It's a pity for the family that she hasn't come to visit; young Mr. Darcy may decide to snatch her up as the next mistress, and they would be set for life.

It wasn't the statement that bothered Elizabeth, not really. She knew that she could never compare to Jane in either looks or comportment; that had been an established fact for the entirety of her life. She had just grown accustomed to not needing to care while they were here. To be reminded suddenly of that fact by strangers, aided by the aunt she looked up to like no other grown lady, hurt more than Elizabeth would allow herself to admit. She had liked feeling good enough as herself, here at Pemberley. She liked not living in Jane's shadow every day.

"I know the maid who was coming in to serve tea," George said, pulling her from the unwanted reverie. "She's a friend of mine. No one else knows."

There was something in his smile Elizabeth didn't like, but she ignored it. She wanted nothing more than to disappear into the gardens until she could pretend that coming in second best every time didn't bother her.

"They are blind, Elizabeth," George said, walking around to stand in front of her. "I don't need to meet your sister to know that you are beautiful. You are far prettier than Mrs. Chester or Mrs. Norris have ever dreamed of being, and they are bitter old ladies who gossip about others to avoid the drudgery of their own sad lives." He reached out and tugged on one of her curls. "You're one of the prettiest girls in Derbyshire, if not the prettiest."

"Don't let Sophia hear you say that," Elizabeth replied dully. She didn't like George. She didn't want him to see her like this. But it was so hard to ignore him when he said what she wanted to hear.

"Let her hear it," George replied, his trademark half grin making an appearance. "I'm not afraid of Lady Sophia Fitzwilliam. And you are at least as pretty as her. There's something almost horse-like in her face, have you noticed?"

"Stop it!" Elizabeth exclaimed, and then to her great annoyance she laughed instead of crying or shouting, because she *could* picture her dear friend as a horse, just for a moment. "Go away, George Wickham."

He sketched a bow. "Your wish is my command, beautiful Elizabeth."

She hid a smile as she walked away. She still didn't like him. Certainly didn't trust him. But her heart felt ever so much easier, for letting him flatter her.

*

"I feel, Bennet, like I ought to repeat my initial invitation. It does not have to only be you and Elizabeth that join us each year, you know."

"I see how it is. You grow bored of our company and wish for additional entertainment." Bennet leaned back in his chair and smiled sardonically at George Darcy over his glass of port. The drinks were not what he looked forward to most each year, but they certainly didn't hurt his enjoyment of Pemberley's hospitality.

"I merely wish for you to enjoy your time with us. One needn't stumble upon Pemberley via the southern stream to be welcome here."

"Ah, but you have given me the perfect opening to my rebuttal. For I *do* enjoy my time here, and it is due in large part to the fact that only Lizzy accompanies me. Your children are silent for the most part, Darcy. Mine are not, and Longbourn is not nearly so large as Pemberley. There are many times throughout the winter I cast my mind fondly out to the peace of your library, and think with not a little longing of the summer to come."

George smiled, having reached the point from whence he could reasonably broach his desired subject. "So you mean to continue the sojourn? No, no, do not look like that. You are welcome, Bennet, for as long as you wish to come. I only mean that you do not care for carriage rides, and we are several days from your estate. I had wondered if you would care for a shorter journey in the future. Fitzwilliam is eighteen, and while I can foist him off on Matlock for another year or two, I foresee a time when I may once again be obliged to open Darcy House for the season. You could join us there far easier than you do here."

He opened his mouth to continue, but Bennet was shaking his head, the expression on his face one that would not be swayed. "I thank you, but no. It is comfortable here, Darcy, in more ways than one. But that is in part due to Pemberley's remoteness. Here I feel judged on my mind; my opinions and my wit are my currency. London would never be the same. My brother by law is no earl with great sway in the house of lords; he is a tradesman with great promise but only little to show for his work thus far. I send Lizzy and Jane to him each winter. Perhaps in time you may have cause to encounter them, but London holds no interest for me. I highly doubt it ever will."

Then how do you mean to secure your daughters' futures? George Darcy wondered, but he said nothing. Time had taught him that Bennet was perfectly capable of shutting down any persuasion he did not wish, and all that would come from pushing the matter was estrangement. The matter would come up again later, when Elizabeth was older. Perhaps Bennet would be more open to suggestions then.

*

Little girls and house guests were the last thing on Darcy's mind as he strode into the library. The afternoon had resulted in an argument with his father, again. It was about Wickham, again, and Mr. Darcy senior had refused to listen to a single point from his son despite how valid Darcy knew them to be—*again*. It was infuriating.

A flash of white appeared in his vision, but Darcy ignored it.

He never fought with his father, not the

way some of his classmates described. Both Darcys were far too civilized for that, the elder convinced he was correct and would carry his point in time, and the younger not yet willing to break a lifetime's habit of respect to say what he actually thought straight-out.

A sudden crack, followed by a crash and thud, yanked Darcy's attention from his frustration, and he whirled towards the sound. When nothing appeared before him, he set off at a jog, glancing between bookshelves, until he at last arrived at an aisle with a chair laying on its side, one leg broken off.

A sharp intake of breath drew his gaze upwards to where— "Good God, Elizabeth!"

She hung off the side of the bookcase at an awkward angle, one hand on top and a foot jammed into the shelf below.

"Will." It came out as a squeak, and Darcy heard the fear in her voice.

"Elizabeth, what in the world are you doing?"

"Can I explain *after* I'm on a flat surface? Up or down, I really don't care."

Darcy sighed, taking a step back to get a better view of the situation. Elizabeth was at least eight feet in the air, but unlike her, he wasn't sure he could simply clamber up the bookshelves like a ladder and expect them to bear his weight. "Can you hold on for a moment longer?" he asked.

"I'm not going to fall on purpose."

Shaking his head, Darcy hurried back up the

rows until he found one of the rolling ladders. Thankfully it wasn't too heavy for him to carry back, and in less than a minute he was standing adjacent to Elizabeth, one hand on the ladder and the other reaching out to steady her.

"There's a rung just below your foot, can you step onto it?"

She nearly lost her grip on the top of the shelf, but on a second try it turned out that yes, she could reach the step with a foot. A hand followed, then the other, and at last Elizabeth stood in front of him on the ladder with all four limbs properly secured and in the correct positions.

"Thank you, Will!" And with that exclamation, Elizabeth promptly scrambled back *up* the ladder onto the top of the bookshelf, turning around on the top to grin back down at him.

"You know, if you didn't insist on doing ill-conceived, childish things, you wouldn't get yourself into nearly as much trouble, Elizabeth! What were you even doing?"

Her face crumpled, and Elizabeth scooted away from him, back towards the area where the wall and bookshelf met. Darcy took another step up the ladder and looked after her. The wall curved as the bookshelves met it, and instead of simply ending them on the curve, the shelves had been angled so both turned before meeting the wall in a ninety-degree angle. The gap between them had been infilled, creating a wide triangular area just the right size for a half-grown girl to curl up with a book. Her actions suddenly made more sense, although her reasoning for hauling a full chair up the side of the shelf was still beyond Darcy.

"I just wanted a place of my own, where I could read when I don't want to have company. Whenever I try to read in the nursery, someone is always coming in and bothering me."

Darcy sighed, backed down the ladder, rolled it closer to her, and climbed back up again. He leaned over the top, resting his forearms on the top of the shelf. "Pemberley is so large that we have to make sure new guests don't get lost," he said, doing his best to keep any sort of accusation out of his tone, "and yet you're telling me the only place you could find to be alone was on top of a bookshelf in the back of the library?"

Elizabeth scooted even further backwards until she sat with her back against the library wall, then drew her knees up against her chest. It was dark in the corner, and Darcy made a mental note to warn her about the dangers of lanterns and candles on top of the wood and stacks of paper books, once she didn't look quite so desolate. Thank goodness it hadn't been something like that to fall, rather than a chair.

"It doesn't make any sense when you say it like that. I just wanted a place of my own, and when Princess Sheba jumped on top of one of the shelves, I thought it looked delightful. She comes up here quite a lot, I think."

Perhaps that had been the flash of white Darcy had dismissed when he entered. How much had he missed, wrapped up in his worries and annoyances with his father and Wickham?

"Is anything the matter, Will?"

Darcy looked up, surprised. "What do you mean?"

Elizabeth lifted one shoulder in a half-hearted shrug. "You seem, I don't know. More than exasperated with me. Sad, maybe."

For a moment, he could only stare at her. It was clear Elizabeth was upset herself—she was not the type of person to hide away from the world. And yet she had noticed and asked about him instead of focusing only on herself.

"Come on," Darcy said, making up his mind. "I'll show you a better place to hide. It has the benefit of allowing both of us to sit down."

She perked up immediately, intrigued, and even allowed him to help her onto the ladder without much grumbling. Safely back on the ground, Darcy set the chair upright at the end of the row and led Elizabeth across the room. Just before he reached his destination, a white cat dropped from a nearby shelf to join them; Elizabeth stooped to pick her up.

"None of my cousins know about this," Darcy told Elizabeth, then reached into a shelf on the wall and pulled the whole thing forward to reveal a narrow staircase behind it. He led her into the short-lived gloom, then emerged onto a balcony that sat slightly back from the high windows around the perimeter, just large enough for a side table and two chairs. "You can see it from below, but you have to know what you're looking for. Otherwise it just looks like paneling keeping the light from touching the books on the shelves."

Elizabeth settled in one of the chairs, and he could tell from her grin that she was as delighted as he'd hoped. "It's so clever," she said, looking around herself with wide eyes.

Darcy took the other chair, leaning back into it with relief. He hadn't decided where he was going when he entered the library, but this place had been on his mind. Strangely, he didn't mind sharing it with Elizabeth.

"You'll have to be in on keeping the secret, now. It wouldn't do for Richard to discover where I disappear to when I need to escape him."

She gave a single giggle. "I won't tell a soul. Except Princess Sheba, although I'm sure she already knew this was here." A pause. "Will, why is she called Princess Sheba and not Queen Sheba?"

"She was very small when I brought her home, but decidedly regal even then. My mother named her. I think she enjoyed the sound of the name."

Elizabeth sighed. "Mama won't let me have a cat. Or a dog, or a horse of my own. Well, Papa is really the one who made the last rule, but Mama would cry about how unfair it is if I had one. None of my younger sisters even care for horses, but it wouldn't matter to her." She fixed her gaze out the window, one hand absently petting the cat on her lap, and Darcy realized that her desire to hide away was about more than something that had happened that day.

"Your mother sounds like a very different person than you," he remarked at last. "It must be hard for you to talk to her, sometimes."

"Sometimes?" Elizabeth shot back. "I'm not beautiful or good like Jane, or small and cute like Lydia, so she either ignores me or complains. Papa just laughs and lets me join him in his book room, and says she doesn't mean anything by it."

It was the sort of thing Darcy would have expected from Mr. Bennet, and it made him appreciate his own father's guidance more, if only a little. He opened his mouth, intending to say something about having patience, but what came out instead was, "I miss my mother." Shocked, he hesitated a moment before deciding to continue. "She understood the things that bothered me, but always had a way of making them seem trivial. My father is a wonderful master and I look up to him, but he can't talk me into liking social gatherings the way Mother could."

The pair of them sat in silence for several minutes. Darcy appreciated that Elizabeth didn't try to force a comment, or tell him any of the platitudes he'd heard ad nauseum since his mother's death.

When she did speak, it was with the bare hint of a smile. "I would loan you my mother, you know. Once she got done cataloging the attics and determining the cost of the chimney pieces and counting all the windows, she would set about organizing a whole host of parties. You'd welcome the social gatherings just to have a reason to avoid listening to how delightful the next event is going to be."

"Elizabeth," he said, slightly reproachful. "You don't mean that!"

She gave him a full grin. "No. But it made you smile. I like making people smile and laugh."

She'd pulled herself out of her own poor mood, Darcy noticed. That was a trick in and of itself, to take two bad moods and turn them both around. But he was beginning to realize that was Elizabeth Bennet's great skill, and he wasn't fool enough to cast off such a gift—or such a friend. Even if she was only a little girl.

Chapter Eight

Pemberley, 1803

L izzy!"

Elizabeth beamed as Sophia stepped down from the Fitzwilliam carriage, then dropped a curtsey that would more commonly be seen at court than a country estate between friends. "Lady Sophia."

The older girl wrinkled her nose as she hurried up Pemberley's stairs. "Are we being fancy? Since when are we fancy?"

Elizabeth tipped her head towards Georgiana, who stood next to her new governess with as much gravitas as a seven-year-old could manage. "We've been practicing the proper forms of greeting," she said.

Immediately, the easygoing smile dropped off Sophia's face, smoothing into pleasant but untouchable genteel agreeability. She dropped into a curtsey of her own, posture perfect, and not a single wobble. "Miss Darcy, how delightful to see you again," Sophia said. Even her voice was different, silken instead of impish. *Since when are we fancy, indeed.* Delighted, her cousin curtseyed back, then looked up at her governess to see if she had done well.

"I see we are quite *de trop*," Lord Matlock remarked, turning from his own greeting with Messrs. Darcy and Bennet to observe the girls. Elizabeth took the chance to drop a curtsey in his direction; he replied with a nod of his head and a smile.

"Gentlemen are always *de trop*, unless they are in uniform or needed for dancing," Mr. Bennet remarked. "Or so my wife has led me to believe."

"Don't forget paying for new wardrobes and introducing new acquaintances," Mr. Darcy returned.

Lord Matlock shook his head. "You two are bad influences on each other," he said. "Bennet, good to see you again. I'll have you know that Sophia turned down a trip to Bath with my lady in order to see your daughter."

Next to Elizabeth, Sophia shed the ladylike persona and wrinkled her nose again. "Mother would make me take the waters, and they are *disgusting*," she whispered. "Besides, I'm not out yet, so I'd have to sit at home while she goes out with her sister every night. I'd much rather get into trouble with you."

The gentleman's conversation had continued, and Elizabeth turned her attention back to that in time to hear Mr. Darcy ask, "Was Richard not able to join you, then?"

Lord Matlock gave a single shake of his head. "No, and we have Napoleon to thank for that. I agree with the decision to declare war, seeing how France refuses to stay within her boundaries, but my son will have far less time to spend with his family until we put them back in their place. But where is Fitzwilliam? I thought we would have had one of the boys here, at least."

It was Mr. Darcy's turn to shake his head. "He was invited to join a house party with a classmate from Cambridge at the last minute. He will be home in two weeks, maybe three, but he is so rarely interested in socialization I thought it best to encourage the event."

The party moved to the parlor, Georgiana and her nurse breaking off. Tea was served, Sophia doing the honors of pouring, and only after the girls were settled to one side of the room did Elizabeth ask the question that had been on her mind since the declaration of war that May. "Will Richard have to go to France to fight?"

Something ugly flashed across Sophia's face before she smoothed her expression into a flat mask not very different from the one Will so often employed. "I don't know. There was a huge argument about it, between Mama and Papa and Richard. Mama insisted he give up his commission, Richard swore that he wouldn't, and then Mama tore into Papa for not providing Richard with a smaller estate where he could make enough income to not need a trade. Papa said he wouldn't have a spoiled son, Richard said he wouldn't accept charity and called Mama unpatriotic, then Papa lost his temper with Richard for not respecting his mother. It went on for what seemed like hours. Finally Richard stormed out. He sent me a letter, but he hasn't been home since then." She paused, then said very determinedly, "Is Fitzwilliam really at a house party?"

Elizabeth allowed her friend to change the subject. "Apparently. Do you think he stands in a corner and glowers silently, or does he actually act like a young man when he is away from Pemberley?"

"You mean silly and boastful?"

"That is how all my neighbors act. Particularly around Jane, now that she is fifteen and more beautiful than ever."

Sophia thought about it for a moment. "I am not sure Fitzwilliam knows how to be silly. Or boastful, for that matter. My money is on him standing back awkwardly. *Particularly* if there are young ladies at the party. Goodness, Lizzy, no one would have told you! You ought to have seen him this winter, my parents hosted a ball at Matlock House in London, and of course I snuck down so I could watch all the dancers. Richard had a wonderful time, and Henry even smiled which he certainly doesn't do for *me*, but Fitzwilliam got the most hunted expression every time a young lady approached. And then Mama glared him into dancing; he acquitted himself quite well with the steps themselves, but I don't think he said more than a sentence during each dance! Can you imagine?"

Elizabeth could, actually. She'd spent several rainy days in the library with Will, and he hadn't spoken a word without prodding for hours. She grinned at Sophia. "Clearly, the ladies he danced with don't know that the trick is to chatter away until he gets annoyed. Then he forgets about being silent and serious."

Sophia smothered a laugh with her hand. "The ladies of the *ton* would never dare. They are to always be polite and proper and prim and polished and a whole bunch of other positively preposterous platitudes."

Elizabeth didn't manage to restrain her own laughter.

"You laugh now," Sophia hissed. "Wait until it's your turn to be poked and prodded and trussed up like a prize sow, and you can't say a single thing you actually think. A young lady with her own thoughts and opinions is not what gentlemen want, you know. At least my mother told me I can *think* whatever I want, I just have to learn how to convince the gentleman in question it was all his idea to begin with."

It was Elizabeth's turn to wrinkle her nose. "Mama is making Jane come out next year, but all that she talks about is flirting and dancing and lace. And how beautiful Jane is, but that is not really a change from her usual remarks. Apparently her beauty will save us all from ruin."

Sophia snorted. "As if you would be destitute, even if you had to leave Longbourn. Father and Uncle Darcy would fight over who could offer assistance the quickest, if it came down to that. Your sister may be beautiful, but *you* are the one who could have the better part of Derbyshire at your fingertips if you were in need of aid."

Elizabeth opened her mouth to reply, but in the end was only able to look down, blinking quickly. She loved Jane dearly and did not begrudge her sister a bit of the attention she received, but it *was* pleasant to be so clearly preferred on occasion.

"Enough of that," Sophia said firmly. "I do not mean to think about coming out or comportment or gentlemen for the rest of the visit. Please tell me you are willing to go for a long ride tomorrow. I brought my old riding habit with me, for I wore it less than a dozen times before I outgrew it, and if it does not suit you very well, I shall eat my riding gloves. It is quite fetching."

"I am of a mind to sabotage it, just to see you attempt the gloves," Elizabeth replied, at last dislodging the lump in her throat. But she would not, and both of them knew it. To Sophia, a new riding habit was no more than her due. To Elizabeth, even a second-hand one was a treat.

She was lucky that the older girl was so diligent in caring for her clothing, and so happy to part with them when they were outgrown.

"You wouldn't dare," Sophia told her. "What say you, shall we ride out after breakfast and see how far we can go?"

They would have to take a groom if they meant to go beyond the main grounds, but to have all of Pemberley spread out before them, treats from the kitchen stuffed in their pockets, a new habit, and the older girl's humor and attention all to herself for the day? "Absolutely."

*

Fitzwilliam Darcy turned into Pemberley's drive and felt a weight lift from his shoulders. Yes, he would have to answer his father's questions, and likely face some disappointment that he had left the house party several days early, but just now he didn't care. He was home, where no one spoke in riddles and the young ladies in residence would never dream of sneaking into his room.

Actually, they would, he corrected himself. Given sufficient motivation, Sophia and Elizabeth would both happily come up with a plan and execute their mischief without a whit of remorse—but they would sneak in to leave a toad in his bed or steal every single left glove in his possession, not to attempt a compromise.

Not like Miss Drayton had done.

Darcy had known for some years, theoretically, that he would be considered eligible and young ladies would do their best to lock him into matrimony. Wickham brought it up often enough he couldn't forget even if he wished to do so. Still, Darcy had managed to convince himself that such concerns and consequences were for the future, not now. Not before he had even reached his majority. He was lucky his valet had been prepared to step in, or else he may be returning home an engaged man, to a lady he could never hope to esteem.

His mount let out a whinny as they crested the hill, pulling Darcy's thoughts back to the present. His stomach dropped for a moment as he took in two young ladies not a hundred yards away, both elegant in habits and matching hats. His panicked mind recognized the horses first, and only then did he recall where he was. Miss Drayton was several counties away, and there was only one pair of young ladies welcome to ride wherever they liked on Pemberley's grounds.

His recollection came just in time, for one of the ladies gave a whoop and leaned forward on her mount, urging it towards him. Darcy rolled his eyes, but moved Boreas to the side of the path so they stood on grass rather than rock. This was all Richard's fault, having introduced his sister to a few of the cavalry tricks he'd learned since enlisting. Sophia had of course told Elizabeth at once, and all four of them had spent a fortnight last summer practicing, somehow ending up with nothing worse than bruises and scrapes to show for their mistakes. Of course, that was before Richard intended to see real combat. His cousin likely wasn't playing with circus tricks now.

But Elizabeth was still a child, and this had been her favorite trick last year, the one that worked best with her because she was smallest and lightest of the four. Darcy caught sight of her smile as she approached, checking her horse's speed just a bit, and couldn't help his own grin in response. Then she was pulling directly alongside him, horse facing the opposite direction, so close it was a simple matter to snake his arm around her waist and lift her from her saddle to sit before him on his own.

Sir Lancelot came to a halt with a long-suffering huff, turning without direction and coming to stand a little behind Darcy's horse. The gelding had come to love Elizabeth, and they had learned he would follow her—or at least the treats in her pocket—unless something prevented him from doing so.

But neither rider paid him any attention just then. Darcy looked down into Elizabeth's face, turned up so she could see him past the brim of her hat, cheeks flushed and eyes shining. "Hello, Will," she said. "We didn't expect you for several days yet!"

She was so clearly happy to see him, vibrant and full of life in that particular Lizzy way. There were no questions, no expectations, no disappointment like he might face from his father. The relief of it surged through Darcy, and for the first time since he'd realized what Miss Drayton was about, his icy, controlled façade cracked and for a moment he wondered if he would cry. Which was utterly preposterous, since gentlemen did not cry, and certainly not Darcy gentlemen. They were above that.

Her smile faltered, and Darcy wondered what she'd seen on his face as she asked in concern, "Will?"

He forced a smile. "It was time for me to leave. Besides, I couldn't in good conscience stay away any longer. What sort of mischief have you gotten into, without me here to keep you in check?"

Lizzy held his gaze for several long seconds, searching. Then Sophia halted beside them, and in greeting his cousin, Darcy managed to put his composure fully back into place. Both of the girls would be full of righteous fury, should he tell them what had occurred, and for a moment he debated doing just that. But he didn't want to relive the horrible realization, or go through the might-have-beens again. And so Darcy allowed himself to push it all away. He didn't mention the house party he had run from, or the supposed friend who would have been happy had his sister succeeded. He simply sat there and traded jokes with the only two young ladies of his acquaintance he trusted, the smell of Pemberley in his nose and the tickle of Lizzy's hat occasionally grazing his cheek.

That was another indulgence, for the curve of Elizabeth's waist beneath his arm told him she was growing up as well, for all that she didn't seem to realize it yet herself. A gentleman in good regulation of himself and his emotions would have set her back on her own horse and let her know politely she was no longer of an age for circus tricks that ended with her on someone's lap. She was innocent, and he owed her guidance as a friend, as a gentleman, and perhaps as the closest thing to a brother that she had.

Darcy knew exactly what ought to be done, and yet he couldn't bring himself to do it. And so he sat, letting Lizzy's laughter wash over him like a balm. He would put her down soon enough, and they would never perform this trick again. But for just a few more moments, Darcy drank in the feel of her relaxed against him, different in every way from Miss Drayton's contrived embrace, and let himself pretend that his childhood wasn't irrevocably behind him.

*

Fitz –

I wish I could say I am surprised about what

happened with Miss X (it is so like you to protect a lady's name against gossip when she cared naught for your feelings) but like you, I must admit I knew this was coming. I cannot even pretend surprise at how soon it started, for I was there when Milton began to receive attention from ladies who fancied themselves the next countess. It is times like this when I believe I prefer my lot as the second son. Better, I think, to know exactly who my enemy is and engage him openly than to spend the rest of my life fearing a surprise attack in my own bedchamber. Of course, you will be safe once you marry, but who wishes to do that at twenty?

From what I hear, my sister is all too ready to commiserate with you. Mother has her come-out set for next Season, since she will be eighteen in the fall. I believe one of them is excited, but it is not Sophia. If she has not seen fit to tell you this, do not mention it to her. However, since I am not able to attend events freely, may I beg a favor of you? My sister seems brash and confident to us, but I have seen flashes of anxiety as she contemplates what it means to take her place in adult society as the well-dowered daughter of an earl. Watch out for her, will you? At least you know there is one lady who will not be looking to compromise you this next winter.

This is to be a maudlin letter, but I have more bad news to impart. I was imposed upon the other day by none other than our dear friend Wickham, who must have been ridiculously far into his cups to believe I would willingly provide any sort of assistance. Is your father still refusing to see him for the reprobate he is? Sending him to London on errands is the last sort of task that Wickham needs. In short, I was required to pull rank as both an officer and the son of an earl to extract the pair of us from a rather hulking brute to whom Wickham owes money, seeing how the fool had introduced me as a friend. He ought to be on his way back to Pemberley now, so at least you needn't fear that his work here will not be completed, but if you have any sort of influence with my uncle, keep him from London for a time. I'm not sure if the man was collecting payment in regards to cards or a brothel, but you don't want the sort of trouble that will come from one of those sorts following Wickham home.

I must end here. Do tell the girls hello for me, and that I wish I could join you as I have in the past. Perhaps when you are back at Cambridge we can meet face to face and you can tell me everything you did not see fit to set down on paper. Until then, I remain,

Your favorite cousin,
R. Fitzwilliam

Chapter Nine

Pemberley, 1806

Mr. Bennet smiled indulgently as the young Mr. Darcy swept by with Elizabeth in his arms. He'd proven so patient with her over the years—less so than with his own sister, but then Elizabeth had never needed as much reassurance as Georgiana. And now he'd stepped in for dancing lessons with the barest hint of a smothered sigh. Bennet was grateful; by all rights it should be him teaching Lizzy the steps. But Darcy was young and far more noble, and Bennet was only too happy to relinquish his role.

Fanny was set on Elizabeth coming out following her sixteenth birthday later this year, young though she was. Jane had been out at sixteen, and so her sister would join her. No doubt Jane would appreciate the company, and Lizzy would do well with the crowds. Knowing George Darcy and Sophia Fitzwilliam, Bennet wouldn't be surprised at all if a ball cropped up next summer, but for now Lizzy danced in a sunny parlor instead of a candlelit ballroom, laughing at Darcy as she made a misstep and he corrected her with his near infallible patience and the barest hint of a smile.

They were good for each other, those two. Bennet looked forward to their visits over the next few years, when Elizabeth was allowed to escape into a world that let her be free in a way she couldn't be at Longbourn. At fifteen, she was expected to comport herself as an adult during their visits to Pemberley, but here she also had room to try out ideas and personas instead of constantly fighting for space of her own against the five other ladies who lived at Longbourn. Mr. Bennet found his wife and daughters exhausting as a spectator; he could not imagine the energy it would take to dive headlong into the fray each and every day.

The song finished, and someone clapped behind Mr. Bennet, surprising him.

"Brava, Lizzy, and Georgie as well," George Wickham said, bowing to each of the ladies in turn. Lizzy smiled back—not much of an achievement, as she'd already been laughing at something Darcy had said—and from behind the pianoforte where she sat with Sophia, Georgiana blushed.

"I don't suppose you'd indulge us with another song? I would be remiss if I didn't offer my tutelage as well. Not all gentlemen scowl silently throughout a dance, Lizzy. You ought to practice conversing with your partner."

There was a beat of silence, then Sophia hopped up. "Here, Fitzwilliam, I'll dance with you. Forget talking, the real challenge is navigating around the other couples. We ought to give Lizzy a sense of how that feels."

Mr. Bennet smiled and made his way out of the room, convinced that no one noticed that he was gone. He would leave the young folks to their amusements. Everyone would be happier that way—especially himself.

*

Elizabeth pulled Sir Lancelot to a stop and sat, gazing out at the vista before her. They were to leave Pemberley in three days' time, and this year more than ever she didn't want to go. Sophia and Lord Matlock had left a fortnight prior, and their departure had rendered Pemberley's serenity ever quieter. Instead of being bored, Elizabeth soaked it up, relishing in the free time to read in the library, stroll through the garden with Georgiana, and go on daily rides. To think she had once hated horses! Now horseback was the most freeing experience Elizabeth could imagine.

"Are you waiting on someone?"

Startled out of her reverie, Elizabeth jumped at the sound of Wickham's voice. "No. Why do you ask?"

"You're stopped. I thought perhaps you were waiting for Fitz to catch up with you."

Elizabeth rolled her eyes. "Just enjoying the view. We don't have peaks in Hertfordshire. And you know he hates when you call him that."

"So protective!"

She didn't reply. Elizabeth didn't dislike George Wickham the way she once had—he'd been far kinder to her the last few years, this year in particular—but she never grown comfortable with the dynamic between him and Will, especially since it felt sometimes like Wickham was trying to put her in the middle of it.

He nudged his horse forward and Elizabeth followed without thought, letting him lead the way until they were by the creek not far from where they had originally met. She never had tried to find her way back to Lambton, Elizabeth thought absently. Wickham grinned at her and jumped down; she slid to the ground before he could make a production of helping her. His overt displays of chivalry made her uncomfortable, a fact she generally tried to keep to herself.

"I've been hoping for a chance to talk to you alone," Wickham said, closing the distance between them.

"Oh?"

"Oh indeed. You've grown up so much, Lizzy. I realized that the other day while we were dancing. It's strange to think you weren't here your entire life, I'm so accustomed to your visits. I rather like having another person at Pemberley who is like me. We're a pair."

She was beginning to regret getting down from her horse, but there was nothing to do for it now. "How so?"

"We're not family. We'll never be on the same level as the family, but we're here all the same, living in their world. I think they keep us around so the place isn't just insufferably dull all the time."

"That's rude, George," Elizabeth said, turning to look for a stump or fallen tree that would allow her to remount without help. "Not to mention it isn't true at all."

A hand descended on her arm, grasping her shoulder as he peered down at her with intense eyes. "Are you still blinded by the act? I thought you were more astute than that, Lizzy. I don't want to see you hurt. They'll never truly care about you. Oh, we're friends, sure, but the connection will never matter as much to them as it does to us. If I loved Georgiana or Sophia, it wouldn't matter, even if they loved me back. We would never be allowed to wed. You can't dream of Fitz or Richard. You know that, right?"

She looked up into a smile that held no sort of joy, only sadness and resignation. "I care about you, Lizzy. I understand you. Maybe you're more removed from it than I have been at Eton and Cambridge. I hope you never feel slighted in the same ways that I have, when people learn my last name and where my family is from. I know your uncles are in trade, after all. But then, you aren't out yet, are you? That might be when the trouble truly starts. I'm sure Sophia will be happy to invite you along to balls, never realizing the sneers and comments you'll suffer as soon as she is out of earshot. None of them will ever understand that feeling."

"What do you want, George?" Something was wrong, seriously wrong. She couldn't put a finger on it, but alarm bells were sounding in her head and all Elizabeth could think was that she didn't have a way to re-mount her horse and get away.

"I want to be happy, Elizabeth, and I want you to be happy as well. I know you don't want to deal with coming out in society." He gave her a sudden, wild grin. "I like you a great deal, you know. What do you say we find a way to be happy together? It's not that far to the border. And as much as Mr. Darcy loves the pair of us, he would never let us go destitute if we married. It would be much easier on you if you simply came out as my wife. What do you think?"

Elizabeth tried to laugh it off, tried to back out of his hold. "I think a lady prefers to be courted a bit more than that, George."

"I can court you later, if you would like." He pulled her forward to stand right in front of him, reaching out and touching her cheek with his free hand. "But it would be a shame to waste the carriage I have waiting on the road across the creek."

"Why me?" she asked, easing backwards. There had to be a way out of this situation, where George had gone mad. Idiot, idiot girl, for following him here! "We've never been close. I've certainly never considered marrying you, or marrying *anyone*. You don't even like me!"

He followed her across the clearing, his grin turning smarmy. "I like a great deal of you, Lizzy. Besides, it makes sense. Mr. Darcy hasn't been nearly as liberal with his support as I expected, no doubt because of Will's jealousy. But if we marry, he has the perfect excuse to provide for us. You look very fine in Sophia's cast-offs, but wouldn't you like to choose your own colors? Just think of what we could have together. Perhaps we haven't always been close, but that can certainly change. With your fire, we'll have a great deal of fun together."

Quicker than she could process, he yanked her towards him, one hand gripping the dress behind her back and the other knotting in her hair so she nearly yelped at the pain. His mouth descended on hers, hungry in a way she had no experience with.

"No!" Elizabeth yelped, revulsion overruling the pain of moving her head. She shoved back against his chest, for all the good it did her. "I don't want to marry you, George. I don't want to marry anyone at fifteen."

He gave her a grin that turned her blood to ice. "And if I give you no choice, my dear?" His hand dropped to her bodice and yanked, the fabric tearing away with a loud rip.

Elizabeth gasped, reaching up to grab the frayed edges. "Stop it!"

"Scream all you like, Lizzy dearest. There's no one around to hear you."

She did scream, praying that there was someone—anyone—who had wandered near, just like she had done on that fateful day so many years ago. She screamed, drew breath, and screamed again, only to cut off as Wickham's palm connected with her cheek.

He shoved her, sent her flying backwards, and Elizabeth tripped over her skirts. She couldn't get up fast enough, couldn't scramble backwards out of his reach as he advanced on her, still smiling that eerie smile. Then he was on the ground before her, one knee on her skirts pinning her in place as he bent over her. He was playing with her, Elizabeth realized as she struggled. He enjoyed watching her try to escape. He had liked making her scream.

"George, no, don't, no!" She didn't know what had come over him, didn't want to think about what he intended to do. A blink, and she felt as though she was watching the scene from above, separate from what was happening. It couldn't be happening to her, it simply couldn't.

Wickham only smiled wider and reached for

the torn bodice she was frantically trying to hold in place.

His hand never reached it. Instead, he was hauled up and back, and Elizabeth watched as Will spun Wickham around and drove a fist into his face. There was a moment where Elizabeth thought Wickham would hit him back, but instead he yanked himself free and took off along the creek, disappearing into the woods.

Will dropped to his knees beside her and reached out, then froze. "Lizzy, are you hurt?"

She stared at him for a long moment, brain attempting to catch up, swimming through the sea of adrenaline that had flooded her.

"Lizzy, did he hurt you? Did he touch you?"

She pushed herself up into a sitting position and huddled into a ball, pulling her knees into her chest.

Will moved closer, eyes trained on her face. He looked like that when he was trying to train a new horse, she thought from very far away. Was she a horse in need of calming? Another blink. These were her eyes, she saw through them, not from above. The horrible kiss didn't matter, she understood enough to know that. That wasn't what he was asking.

He'd come closer, inch by inch, hand hovering just to her side but careful not to touch. Did she want him to touch her? What had he asked? Thinking was so hard, words were so hard, but she drug them up from the recesses of her mind.

"He tried," she managed, not recognizing her own voice. And then she collapsed sideways into Will, closing her eyes and trying very hard to think of nothing at all.

*

"Sir? Master Darcy is asking for you, urgently."

George Darcy looked up from his account book and frowned at the footman, but pushed himself up without comment. Fitzwilliam never asked for him to come, let alone with urgency. "Where is my son?"

"On the south lawn. He's headed towards the house."

Icy fear made its way down George's back. An incident, then. Fitzwilliam wasn't hurt, but someone likely was. "What has happened?" he asked as he strode down the hallway towards the doors.

The man's hesitation spoke volumes. "It involves one of your guests, sir. I don't know the full story, and it isn't for me to speculate."

Well, it was hard to argue with that. George gave a decisive nod of his head and lengthened his stride.

He came out the door, where there was already a flurry of activity in preparation for whatever calamity had fallen, and spotted them immediately. Fitzwilliam was on foot, appearing to support Elizabeth as she walked beside him. He was distracted momentarily by the horses that trailed them, the reins of his son's mount looped around the knee hook of Sir Lancelot's saddle. Clever, that. But Elizabeth wasn't walking normally, and George turned his attention back to the problem at hand, hurrying out to meet them.

She flinched back at his approach, curving already hunched shoulders further in and turning her face into Fitzwilliam's chest. His opposite arm came around her, saying something too low for George to catch. Then his son looked up and met his eyes.

"Get Mr. Bennet." The words were calm, direct, but there was a sea of fury in Fitzwilliam's gaze. He was livid.

George glanced to the side, to the footman still trailing him, and gave a nod that sent the man hurrying back into the house.

"What happened?"

Fitzwilliam's face twitched, betraying the emotion he was shoving down. To keep from making a scene, or because of Elizabeth? His son swallowed, pushing it back, and shook his head. "Not here."

So they made their way inside, meeting Bennet not far from the door. To George's surprise, Fitzwilliam led the way to the study. Only after all four were inside, with the door firmly closed, did he speak, each word clipped with anger.

"Wickham attacked Elizabeth. I was out riding

and heard her scream, but it still took me a moment to reach them. He was—he attempted —"

Bennet's face turned white, and he started towards his daughter, but she shrank back from him in the same manner as before, huddling into Fitzwilliam.

"Lizzy, you have to show them," his son said, the horribly flat tone dropping away to something coaxing and gentle.

She shook her head vehemently.

"They won't judge you, Lizzy. But they need to know what happened. You have to let your father see you."

A long look passed between the pair, and at last Elizabeth stepped away from Fitzwilliam, one of his hands still held in a death grip from the look of her white knuckles. Her other hand came up to hold the torn bodice of her dress, inadvertently revealing a developing bruise on her arm.

Bennet gasped, but stayed where he was. "Lizzy..."

George did not have time for his friend's roundabout ways. "George Wickham did this?"

She met his eyes slowly, and he took the time to look her over more fully. Hair askew, dirt and grass stains on her knees, a scratch on her face, that horrible bruise—were those finger marks? —and the torn dress. It did not paint a pretty picture, but George could not reconcile it with his namesake. Wickham did not attack. He was the type to seduce, and while George worried a bit about the rumors of his time with young women in the parish, he did not think they were all that bad.

Elizabeth nodded.

"You are certain?"

She held his eyes, something in her expression shifting from fear to anger. "I am sure."

"As am I," Fitzwilliam said. Was that a split lip that his son sported? He hadn't noticed it before. "I saw enough of the attack to know what Wickham intended."

"Where is he now?"

"I have no idea. He took off, likely towards Lambton, but I didn't watch him. My focus was Elizabeth."

George stood and crossed the room, yanking the door open. "Find me George Wickham. Check the village if he's not on the grounds."

He returned to the office and an argument ensued, vicious for all that little was said aloud. In the end, Elizabeth was surrendered into Mrs. Reynolds' care, with specific instructions for the girl to be returned once she'd been looked over and donned a new gown. Fitzwilliam sat fuming after her departure, and through every other emotion a thread of wry humor emerged: his son was far more visibly ready to defend Miss Elizabeth than her father, who sat numbly now that the first shock had worn off.

George Wickham wouldn't have tried to force her. He was a good lad, high-spirited, but not malicious. This had to be a misunderstanding, fueled by the silly animosity between his son and Wickham, and further inflamed by the high emotions of youth. Mrs. Reynolds, with her gentle insistence, would get more of the story —more of the truth—from Elizabeth while she ensured the girl was well. And then they would all resolve this.

But when the two women returned, the housekeeper's face was set in a grim mask and there was nothing in her expression that spoke of a childish misunderstanding. Perhaps more telling, she walked Elizabeth directly to the chair beside Fitzwilliam's and helped her sit, murmuring something too low for George to catch. His son did, however, and replied in the same low tone. Then she departed without another word, and for the first time George felt a sliver of doubt. Mrs. Reynolds had ruled over dozens of servants for years, sorting through hurt feelings and fights and lies, and George was not aware of a single instance where her intuition had been wrong. Whatever had happened, Mrs. Reynolds was convinced that Elizabeth was the injured party, and his son was in the right.

The door opened again and George Wickham stepped into the room, flanked by the butler. George Darcy took in a multitude of things at once: the black eye developing on Wickham's face, the way his easy smile faltered at the sight of Elizabeth. Fitzwilliam locked his hands together, displaying bruised knuckles, and even Bennet sat up straighter. But it was Elizabeth's frozen look of fear that stood out the most. What little color had been left in her face drained away, and she sat perfectly still save for a tremor that shook her curls, the way a rabbit would watch a fox intent on eating it for breakfast.

Wickham had re-affixed his smile. "Mr. Darcy, you asked to see me?" And then, taking a step further into the room, "Elizabeth, I am glad to see you recovered from your accident. Are you well?" He moved another step in her direction and Elizabeth yanked her legs up so fast George blinked in shock, curling herself into a ball in the chair. Her huge eyes were fixed on Wickham's face until Fitzwilliam, who had shot up from his chair in the same instant, put himself between the two.

"If you ever speak to her again, I'll tell Richard exactly what happened this afternoon, and I won't try to reason him out of giving you what you deserve."

George Darcy blanched; he'd never heard the low tone that came from his son. Beyond that, Fitzwilliam *never* threatened. It was a joke between himself and Matlock, that Darcy's son thought every problem could be solved with words, while Matlock's always gravitated towards fists or the sword. For Fitzwilliam to condone violence was no small matter.

Slowly, Bennet stood and walked across the room to stand beside Fitzwilliam. "I understand that you hurt my daughter," he said, in a deceptively calm voice.

Wickham fidgeted, rocking back on his heels as if to put distance between himself and those accusing him. "It was all in fun, Miss Elizabeth knows that, surely."

Bennet smiled, and it was an ugly, terrifying thing. "My daughter has not shown fear like this even once in her life. I would have thought it beyond her. She thinks you are worthy of terror. I saw the ripped gown; I saw her bruises. Did you do that, Mr. Wickham?"

Wickham's hesitation lasted a hair too long— he was beyond the point where an innocent man would have protested. "Mr. Bennet asked you a question, George," George Darcy said, pulling the young man's attention to him. The pair of them locked eyes. "Did you hurt Miss Elizabeth? Whether you meant to cause harm or not, did you do this?"

The truth was in his eyes, and it hit George Darcy like a punch. His godson had done this, and beyond that, he had probably intended harm. For years, he'd dismissed Fitzwilliam's complaints and concerns about George Wickham, waving off the tales as misunderstandings or even jealousy. It had all led to this: a young man unrepentant beyond being caught out, and an innocent young lady injured. At last, George Darcy looked—really looked—at the boy he had helped raise, and did not attempt to alter what he saw. He had made a horrible mistake, and now Elizabeth Bennet, the dear daughter of one of his closest friends, was paying the price. George couldn't reverse that, but he could stop it from going any further.

"Get out of my house," he said, just as quiet as Bennet, just as quiet as his son. A threat didn't need to be shouted in order to be felt. Fitzwilliam had taken that lesson to heart, it seemed.

George Wickham turned and ran.

Chapter Ten

Longbourn, 1806

The newspaper sat folded beside Elizabeth, its edges fluttering in the bitter wind. She'd read the notice contained within at least a dozen times before bringing it out into the garden, and now it occupied the place beside her like a specter.

Mr. Darcy was dead.

The paper had said it so plainly. There was no mention of his presence, his humor, his annoying but somehow endearing way of assuming he could arrange everything and everyone around him to suit him best. It mentioned Will, but not the huge feeling of loss and overwhelming responsibility he must be facing now. Georgiana would have retreated into music the way she always did when faced with strong emotions; Elizabeth wondered vaguely if anyone was attempting to coax her into talking, into eating. Will would be buried under details —would he have the time to give Georgiana as much attention as she needed?

She should be there. Except Wickham had been right about one thing on that awful day 6 months ago: she was not part of the Darcy family. She had no reason to appear on their doorstep without an invitation, and certainly not now. They were in mourning, and custom required that she be turned away even if she did appear. They'd always managed just fine without her for forty-six weeks of the year, anyhow.

But it still felt like she should be there.

Footsteps scuffed through the dead leaves littering the path and Elizabeth looked up, ready with an excuse for why she wanted to be alone. Her mother and sisters knew next to nothing of the Darcys—Mr. Bennet found it amusing to not even mention their surname. Longbourn and Pemberley may as well have existed in two separate universes. The inhabitants of Longbourn could not possibly understand her grief.

To her shock, the intruder was Mr. Bennet. Her father sat down on the opposite side of Elizabeth from the newspaper, and she noticed that he was holding a letter.

"They must have delayed the announcement in the paper," Mr. Bennet remarked, "for I just received a letter from Matlock. It is lucky that Hill brought the missive straight to me, or I may never have heard the end of hiding *that* connection from your mother."

Elizabeth turned to him with raised eyebrows, curious but in a strangely muted way. The *why* didn't matter nearly so much as it usually would.

"The letter is in regards to Mr. Darcy's will," Mr. Bennet said, and Elizabeth frowned in confusion until she recalled that *will* was a document as well as her friend. Come to think of it, she'd never heard anyone other than herself call the younger Mr. Darcy—the *only* Mr. Darcy, now—Will. Not even Georgiana, once she learned to speak fully.

"What does it say?" she managed to ask.

"You were named. What I am going to tell you can be shared with Jane if you wish, but no one else, and I would recommend you consider fully before you tell your sister." Mr. Bennet paused, shaking his head. "Even in death, Mr. Darcy had the last say, for he has always prodded me about how I meant to ensure your future. You have a dowry of two thousand pounds, my dear. Matlock has suggested that we invest it, perhaps with your uncle Gardiner. I mean to follow his advice."

Elizabeth sat in shock, attempting to wrap her head around the news. "But—why?" she managed at last. "Wouldn't he wish for that money to be used for Georgiana?"

Mr. Bennet's smile was sad. "There are twelve years between the Darcy siblings. It would not surprise me if they expected another child much sooner, and funded Miss Darcy's dowry accordingly. You will not take anything away from her. Regardless, Elizabeth, this is something he wished for you to have. Treat it as the gift it was meant to be, and do not spend too much time worrying about the reasons why."

*

Mr. Bennet walked away from his daughter, wondering if he ought to have ordered her to join him indoors. It was cold in the garden, and she wore only a spencer over her dress. Bennet had long wondered why ladies were not allowed greatcoats like gentlemen; they were certainly more practical garments. A proper father would have ordered her in, the voice in his head that sounded slightly like Mr. Darcy said. But then, Elizabeth had always done better when she was allowed ample time out of doors, and this was her first true experience with loss. Forcing her inside and away from her respite seemed cruel to his way of thinking. She was *his* daughter, after all.

Looking back at the small figure huddled on her bench, Bennet wondered what would have happened had they not made the acquaintance of the Darcys. Would Elizabeth be happier now? Oh, she would be sillier and more judgmental, still afraid of horses and not at all afraid of young men. His other daughters seemed content with their lot in life. Would Lizzy have longed for more? Or would she not miss what she'd never known?

Well, it was too late to wonder now.

Two thousand pounds was no small sum, particularly when one compared it to the fifty pounds his other daughters would receive upon their marriage, plus a thousand each at the death of their mother. Coupled with Elizabeth's vivacity, her pleasing manners, and her acquaintance with the Darcy and Fitzwilliam families, she could make a very satisfactory match. It would elevate the other girls, to see her married well.

Bennet reached the back door and shook the thoughts off in the same motion he removed his coat. That was his wife's sort of thinking, and better leave it to her.

Damn Darcy, who had always made Bennet ashamed of his own actions—or rather, inactions. Damn him for leaving Elizabeth a gift her own father could never hope to match. Damn him for leaving. Damn him for leaving, and taking away the best friend that Bennet had ever had.

*

Matlock –

I have been staring at this paper for the last five minutes, waiting for my usual semblance of eloquence to strike, and have come up with nothing. I hardly know what to say. Darcy told me only once that he felt his age a bit more keenly this past year, but I thought nothing of it. Haven't we all been made to realize our age or mortality at different times of life? I certainly have. Perhaps you lords and great gentlemen live according to different rules, but then, I suppose death has been proven to come for us all.

In regards to your letter, I am equally speechless. I knew Darcy was fond of my Lizzy, but I never expected that she would be remembered in such a way. I mean to take your advice and invest the sum through my brother Gardiner—I shall include a note for you to pass on to him, should that prove the simplest course of action. I do not believe you have met him, for his single stay at Pemberley was at a time you were not in residence. His wife hails from the Lambton area; it is to her that I owe our introduction, although she removed from the area some years prior. I know you to be a fair man, so I shall say only that I would take Gardiner's company over a large majority of the gentlemen I knew at school. Whether it is you or your man of business who deals with him, I give permission via this letter for him to act fully in my stead; he is shrewder than I in terms of business and will not do anything to jeopardize Elizabeth's future.

I shall end here. I fear I am even worse of a correspondent than usual, and my wife quite despairs of me in that matter. Forgive my bumbling words and know they are all meant with great appreciation and sorrow—I have not said, but I send my condolences to you and all your family. I

can only imagine how keenly you feel George's loss.
Most sincerely,
Thomas Bennet

*

Fitzwilliam Darcy lowered himself into the chair before the fire in his father's study and stared dully at the flames. It was his study, now, but he could not bear to think of it as such. Glancing up at the door to ensure it was indeed still closed and locked, Darcy let out a long sigh and dropped his head into his hands. Alone. He was finally alone, and that meant he was finally allowed to show his grief, instead of remaining strong for everyone around him.

It had been a brutal two weeks. His father's health had been in decline for several months, not that Darcy had noticed it when it began. Only in his last week of life had he seemed truly ill, pale-faced and short of breath. But even then, it had not felt serious. One often felt poorly over the winter months, and Darcy was sure his father would be back to his old self by the time summer rolled around.

Just now, it seemed that summer would never come again.

The death itself had occurred suddenly, with George holding onto life just long enough to say his farewells to both of his children. Thank goodness Darcy had been home and able to receive that final goodbye. The days that followed—Darcy wasn't sure what had happened during those days. They came in flashes. Informing the staff. Mrs. Reynold's face. Georgiana's sobs, followed by a seemingly impenetrable silence. Writing to his uncle Matlock and aunt Catherine—any immediate next of kin on the Darcy side had long since died. Someone had arranged a service and perhaps it had been him, for he remembered standing there next to his uncle and listening to the service, though he could not recall what had been said.

Lady Catherine had come and gone, full of advice he had no interest in taking and demands he never meant to fulfill. Darcy endured her as politely as he could manage, because that is what his father would have wanted. Only when she gave the order for the staff to pack Georgiana's things, intending to take the girl home with her, did he lose his patience. The shouting match that followed stood out in his memory as one of the few clear moments after George Darcy's death.

When Lady Catherine departed at last, only her own trunks accompanying her out the door and onto her carriage while she spat her final insults, Darcy attempted to feel shame for his actions. Instead, all he could muster was a voice that sounded very much like Lizzy whispering, "Good riddance!" Was it rude of him to wish that his aunt had stayed away, when she clearly shared none of their grief? Was it wrong to hate the social conventions that require him to answer so many polite condolences that meant nothing, when all he wanted was the company of people who actually cared?

Well, he was alone now, finally free to sit in silence and let the enormity of the situation sink in. That was likely the best he was going to get.

What he would give to have Lizzy here now. Darcy leaned back in the chair and closed his eyes. He could very nearly picture her, standing beside him with that all-too-grown-up look she got on occasion. Darcy had no idea how, but somehow, she would say something to make everything seem just a little bit more manageable, a little less bleak. And if all else failed, she would sit with him in silence and offer her company in his grief.

She would also know what to say to Georgiana, would know the necessary mix of gentleness and guidance to coax his heartbroken sister back into the land of the living. If Georgiana had been skittish and silent before Lady Catherine's plan to remove her from Pemberley, she was now completely withdrawn, flinching at anyone who came near and refusing to eat or speak. Darcy had removed his aunt, but he had no idea how to reach his sister. Perhaps Sophia would be able to help, but he still couldn't help but think that Lizzy would be able to help Georgiana best.

Blast George Wickham. Lizzy wouldn't have been here now, regardless, but it felt so much more permanent this way. The wonderful summers they had shared at Pemberley had shattered into ruin, and before there was any hope of mending the break, the entire world came crashing down. Georgiana was withdrawn and heartbroken and he—well, Darcy honestly didn't know if he was coping much better than his sister. He was at least managing to eat on occasion.

At least his father had seen Wickham for what he was in the end. Darcy would never wish that pain on Elizabeth, but it had broken through to George Darcy when nothing else had. It was in large part why he had said farewell to his father with no regrets in their relationship, for they had discussed many things over that last six-month with a deeper understanding than ever before.

Of course, now Darcy knew exactly how much he had lost. But if his father had to be gone, he was happy to have esteemed the man so highly during his last months on this earth. That was because of Elizabeth as well.

And somehow, thinking of her—what she would say, how much she too would grieve—Darcy finally felt the tears well up and spill down his cheeks. In that moment, he couldn't have said what he was mourning. Perhaps it was only for his father, tears released at last once he had a chance to sit alone. Perhaps it was the loss of his childhood, of an irreversible shift in the fabric of his life. Or perhaps he mourned only for Elizabeth, because in that moment her loss was the one he could tolerate, knowing as he did that she lived on even if their paths would never cross again.

Darcy didn't know. But he sat in his father's study and let himself cry until the edge of the pain finally dulled. Unwilling to leave the only place he had found relief for weeks, he settled himself further into chair and let sleep carry him away from this horribly lonely new world.

Part Two

Hertfordshire, England
1811

Chapter Eleven

Meryton, 1811

I s that them? I think it is them! Charlotte, lend me your eyes, you're taller than I am!"

Charlotte Lucas, Elizabeth's dear friend and neighbor, laughed and rose onto her own slippered toes for a moment. "You could have positioned yourself closer to the door, Lizzy, if you were so worried about being the first to see the new arrivals."

Elizabeth grinned at her friend. "I am not *that* concerned. It's just exciting. It isn't every day that we have new people in the neighborhood, not to mention 'young men of fortune.' Or young *man*, at least."

Charlotte laughed again. "Has your mother picked which daughter he is to marry yet?"

"Oh, Jane for certain, unless he prefers livelier ladies and then Lydia will do very well."

"Lydia! She is not yet sixteen!"

Elizabeth was laughing in return when the crowd parted slightly and her gaze fell on the newcomers, just as one happened to turn towards her. Before she fully comprehended what had occurred, a rush of joy shot through her and Elizabeth felt her face light up. In an instant, the past five years fell away and she nearly called out in delight. *Will.*

And then, from the corner of her eye, her mother appeared. Jane and Mary were already clustered behind her, and Mrs. Bennet's eyes were sweeping the dance floor. Clearly, she was looking for the rest of her girls, and would be dead set on forcibly introducing the lot to the newcomers. After so long of keeping Will separate from her family in Hertfordshire, and then the years that had passed since their last meeting, Elizabeth could not fathom standing there and enduring the humiliation that would certainly come from such a reintroduction. The joy turned to a pit of dread in her stomach. She would not do it.

"Hide me," she hissed to Charlotte, dropping down and ducking to the side so she was concealed from her mother by the crowd.

"Lizzy? What on earth—"

"Charlotte, it's Will—pardon me, Mr. Darcy —with the group. Remember? My friend from Derbyshire? If I go to Mama now, she'll take friendliness for something more and torture both of us for however long he's here. He's *rich*. Netherfield is nothing to his estate. She'll find out and she'll ruin any hope I have of renewing our friendship. Oh, goodness, don't let Lyddie see me."

"But Lizzy, what if he would *like* something more? If he is rich, well, a young man in possession of a fortune must be in want of a wife."

Shaking her head at Charlotte and not risking a backwards glance, Elizabeth darted away. Her father, thankfully, had not come to the assembly this evening. She could warn him in private that his friend's son was in the community, could convince him to see it as a game to continue keeping the depth of their connection from Mrs. Bennet. At least until she could figure out what else to do. Because Elizabeth simply would not let her memories of Will be ruined by the realities of Meryton life.

*

"I say, that woman is the most deluded, aggrandizing lady I have ever had the pleasure of meeting," Miss Bingley proclaimed.

Darcy, well aware they were still just within earshot of the matron in question, said nothing. So Lizzy had not exaggerated when she spoke of her mother's frantic desire to see her daughters wed. She also had not overstated the eldest Miss Bennet's beauty. Laying eyes on Jane, Darcy could understand far better why Lizzy occasionally bemoaned her own looks throughout her childhood and adolescence. Bingley, of course, was enraptured. Jane Bennet was just his type, and her shy smiles were far more enticing to his friend than the bold confidence exhibited by so many ladies of the *ton*—currently displayed by the one who refused to let go of Darcy's arm. What he would do to be free of Miss Bingley! Especially since there was another lady in the room he desperately wished to find, and not with Caroline Bingley in tow.

Elizabeth's delighted smile had been a balm to Darcy's heart, soothing the guilt he still felt over their last meeting and giving him that sense of joyful freedom from expectations that only she had ever been able to bring out. It had vanished as her smile dropped, and he had barely been able to stop from chasing her deeper into the room to find out what caused the sudden fear on her face.

Perhaps she associated him with Wickham, hadn't recovered from Wickham's attack and his own inability to keep her safe. Perhaps she had simply moved on, their time together not the bright spot of memory that it was for him. Did she never long for summer mornings at Pemberley, coaxing him and Georgiana into laughter, either on her own or with Richard and Sophia for assistance? Did she prefer life in Hertfordshire with her mother and sisters?

Bingley asked Jane Bennet to dance; Miss Bingley looked at him expectantly. In his head, Lizzy laughed at him. *Will, it's only dancing. You act like you're being asked to submit to torture.*

A strange man approached, one of the locals to whom they had been briefly introduced. Glancing first at Darcy, he asked Miss Bingley to dance. She gave Darcy a hard stare; he remained silent and she begrudgingly accepted as Darcy had known she would. She didn't want to eliminate the possibility of dancing with him later.

And now, finally, he was free. Making sure his impassive expression was firmly fixed in place, Darcy made his way through the crowd, scanning for chestnut curls. For once, he appreciated that his height let him tower over almost everyone else. No, no, close but not her—there! He adjusted course slightly, heading in her direction. Only as he closed the last few yards did Darcy realize that approaching Elizabeth in a very public area when she'd literally run from him was exactly the sort of oafish behavior she'd call him out for. But it was too late now; she was there and he could not make himself turn away.

"Lizzy." He turned, leaning on the wall next to the column she had ducked behind—really, was she that opposed to speaking with him!

"Hello, Will." Her voice was calm, measured.

"Are you well? I—"

"Don't look at me," she said, cutting him off. "Put on that frightful Darcy mask and act like you're lurking here to avoid the crowd, it shouldn't be hard."

He huffed, but did as she asked before

repeating himself. "Are you well, Lizzy? I never would have pictured you hiding on the edge of a dance floor. Would you care to dance?"

"No! I—Will, I can't dance with you. I can't stay here and speak with you."

His heart dropped. "I had wondered if my presence might be uncomfortable for you, given how we last parted. I apologize, I will not impose upon you in the future."

"What? Will, no, that's not it at all. It's only —my mother—oh, *drat*," Elizabeth hissed, as a group of young ladies came laughing in their direction. "Don't find me again tonight," she said quickly, her eyes meeting his for one long moment, and then she was gone, leaving him less inclined to dance than he'd ever felt before.

*

"Oh, Lizzy, he is everything a young man ought to be!" Jane exclaimed. "You must think me silly for saying so after only two dances, but I have never met his equal. So handsome, and kind, with such pleasing manners—"

"And rich enough to lease Netherfield, which speaks well of his ability to keep you," Elizabeth added, grinning at her sister.

"*Lizzy!*"

"What? It is the truth, Jane. It neither raises nor lowers him in my general estimation, but you have to admit, it is an important aspect of letting yourself decide whether or not to fall in love with him. And it seems you have made a good start this evening."

"Oh, Lizzy. I cannot think of love, not now. He is so new to the area, and we know nothing of him or his party. I would like to get to know him better, but do not think me so silly to fall in love in a single night."

Elizabeth walked to the window as calmly as she could manage. "I was not there when you were introduced. Tell me, what is his connection to Mr. Darcy?"

"Let me see. Mr. Bingley introduced him as a friend, and then while we were dancing, he said he was lucky that Mr. Darcy had agreed to accompany him. It seems that Mr. Darcy has been master of his own estate for some years now, and is considered by all a very admirable master and landlord. When Mr. Bingley professed his interest in purchasing an estate, Mr. Darcy volunteered to assist him. From everything that was said, I judge them to be fairly close."

Had she ever heard of a Bingley? Elizabeth could not remember. Mr. Bingley seemed young, in comparison to Will, who had already graduated from Cambridge when her visits to Pemberley came to an end. Had they become friends there and she simply didn't remember the name? Or had they met in a different manner, at an event in town or introduced by mutual friends? She would have to ask, once she determined what she was to do about his presence in Hertfordshire.

Elizabeth turned from the window and studied her sister, whose face glowed with hope in the flickering candlelight. Jane would dislike the deception, but not telling her was impossible.

"If Mr. Darcy likes him, and finds him worth his time, that is high praise for Mr. Bingley."

Jane's brow furrowed. "Do you know of him, then?"

"Mr. Darcy holds the rather remarkable distinction of being the only person other than you who has proven capable of talking me into good behavior," Elizabeth told her sister. Despite herself, she couldn't keep from smiling. "Jane, do you remember my trips with Papa each summer, and my friends in Derbyshire?" She waited for her sister's nod before continuing. "Mr. Darcy is Will."

Jane's eyes widened, and one of her hands came up to her mouth. "Lizzy! But why did you not greet him this evening? Surely he would not reject the acquaintance; he was so polite when we were introduced!"

She'd have to thank him for that, later.

"Jane, you heard the same whispers I did. I know what his estate is like, and ten thousand a year is not an exaggeration. Tell me, what would Mama do if I greeted him like an old friend and allowed him to sweep me off to the dance floor?"

Unlike Charlotte, Jane understood

immediately. Her face fell, a frown tugging at the corners of her mouth. "Oh, dear. I suppose that would be a problem."

"Yes, it would. I have not spoken to Will—Mr. Darcy, I must think of him as Mr. Darcy now—in half a decade. We may renew our friendship, or we may be too different, but I refuse to meet him again under Mama's opportunistic gaze. It would be cruel."

There was a long pause before Jane spoke again. "Does he know that you are here?"

"Yes. We spoke very briefly tonight. I think I offended him, and for that I am dreadfully sorry, but it couldn't be helped at the time."

Jane considered her. "You are different, Lizzy."

Elizabeth laughed. "I was always better behaved in Derbyshire than I have been here. Perhaps it was Will's influence all along."

Jane smiled, still looking rather worried. "Will you tell Papa? I assume he must know Mr. Darcy as well."

"He does. And yes, I shall tell him tomorrow. I mean to enlist his assistance in managing Mama."

There was silence in the room as Jane thought through everything, and then she smiled. "Well, you know Mr. Darcy's character and find it sufficient to call him friend, and I am predisposed to think well of anyone that Mr. Bingley so clearly likes. If we assume Mr. Darcy must esteem his friend in return, then we are off to a delightful start. Oh, Lizzy, I do look forward to spending more time with our new neighbors!"

Elizabeth did as well. And if she suspected that Jane cared as little about Mr. Darcy's presence as she herself did for Mr. Bingley, well, no one need admit to either fact aloud.

*

"I cannot imagine a more backwards place that you could have brought us, Charles! These people have no taste, no sophistication. I grant you that Miss Bennet is pretty enough, but the rest of her family! I was told by several people that the eldest two are the jewels of the country, and yet Miss Elizabeth couldn't be bothered to greet us and was barely seen all night. If that is what constitutes prime behavior in this county, the younger sisters no longer shock me at all!"

Charles opened his mouth to argue, but to Caroline's utter surprise, Mr. Darcy spoke first. "You have no way of knowing what else is occurring in Miss Elizabeth's life at the moment, Miss Bingley. Perhaps she had a perfectly good reason for remaining on the fringes tonight. Mrs. Bennet was brash, yes, but I have seen worse displays from both mothers and daughters of the *ton*. As for Miss Bennet, her calm demeanor is a refreshing change."

Caroline had been ready to expound on several more faults she had noticed of the Bennet ladies, but at Mr. Darcy's statement, her world shifted slightly on its axis. He had never—*never*—spoken up in defense of a lady. Perhaps he would in regards to his sister or cousin, but Caroline wasn't enough of a simpleton to demean either of them. And to choose the Bennet ladies to defend! Theirs was exactly the sort of behavior Caroline had expected him to abhor; she introduced the topic primarily for the delight of hearing Mr. Darcy agree with her statements.

"We are in the country now, Caroline," Charles said. "Socializing with the locals is part of being a landed family. I know you wish to marry a gentleman as well. Consider this good practice for your future, whether you make your home with me or not."

"But surely, the families around, say, Pemberley, do not act in such a way!"

Mr. Darcy gave a huff that may have been laughter, but surely wasn't. "I saw nothing tonight that would have surprised me in Lambton. Not everyone in attendance is at our level, but that is rather the point of an assembly. There is a full assemblage of the local populace."

Caroline opened her mouth but could not think of a single thing to say. By rights, she ought to be triumphant—Mr. Darcy was to stay with them for the next two months or more, where she could show off her superb skills as a hostess, and he had not danced with a single local lady tonight. And yet....

There was something about him that had

changed since they walked into the door of the assembly house, and Caroline could not put her finger on what it was. She didn't like it. She didn't like it at all.

*

"Well, my dear, how was the assembly? Did you dance every dance?"

Elizabeth shook her head fondly at her father as she settled into the chair across from him. "I ran away from a gentleman and refused to dance at all for the rest of the evening," she said.

Mr. Bennet sat up at once, fond indulgence dropping off his face. "The newcomers—it was not—"

"No, nothing like that," Elizabeth cut in quickly. "In fact, it was rather the opposite. Mr. Bingley is here with his sisters, his elder sister's husband, and a friend who is to teach him about running an estate."

One eyebrow went up. "And who is this friend, who knows so much at a presumably young age?"

"You've already guessed, I know you have. It's Will—Mr. Darcy."

The side of Mr. Bennet's mouth quirked up, confirmation enough for Elizabeth to know that she had been right. "And why, pray tell, did you run away from Mr. Darcy?"

Elizabeth leaned back in her chair, meeting her father's eyes and raising an eyebrow of her own. "Why have you never told my mother that you

139

address the Earl of Matlock informally and still correspond with him on a semi-regular basis?"

There was a pause, and then Mr. Bennet sighed. "Well, Lizzy, I suppose the ruse is up. I will not ignore Mr. Darcy's son, nor should I expect you to do so. Although—tell me, did he seem opposed to renewing your acquaintance?"

She couldn't help her smile. "Hardly. He managed it well, but he chased me across the dance floor to ask if I was well, after I fled. I know I ought to have greeted him properly, but, Papa, I couldn't stomach the scene that Mama would have undoubtedly made. I would have sunk through the floor in mortification."

Mr. Bennet sighed. "Yes, I suppose I understand you. Let me think on it, my dear. I am sure between the two of us, we can come up with a sufficient way to manage. Who knows, we may even enjoy ourselves before it is done."

Chapter Twelve

D espite Elizabeth's best intentions, nothing was resolved nearly as soon as she would have liked. She and Mr. Darcy continued to skirt around each other but never actually came face to face. Jane passed on news from Mr. Bingley that his friend had been required to spend nearly a week in town following the assembly, seeing to a family matter. He did not appear on her morning rambles, or when the sisters walked into Meryton.

Then Elizabeth, who never took ill, came down with a cold just prior to an event hosted by the Lucas family, where the Netherfield party was in attendance. Mrs. Bennet insisted that Kitty's cough was bad enough; did Elizabeth mean to hurt Jane's chances with Mr. Bingley by sneezing and sniffling into a handkerchief all evening? At least her father was able to attend and passed along Mr. Darcy's wishes for a fast recovery; Elizabeth had to make her peace with knowing that the gentlemen had reconnected amiably.

By the time a letter came for Jane, begging for her company at Netherfield, Elizabeth was ready to rudely invite herself along just to end her ever-growing frustration. She restrained, barely, and waved Jane off as the latter departed on horseback into darkening skies.

When a note was delivered the next morning, telling of Jane's illness from getting caught in the storm and hinting how much she would appreciate Elizabeth's presence, Elizabeth was caught between relief at the excuse and genuine concern for her sister. Jane *never* complained. That she should do so now was alarming.

Raised eyebrows and a nod was all it took to communicate between Elizabeth and her father, and in short order, Elizabeth set out for Netherfield on foot. It was a glorious morning for a ride, but Jane had taken the only mount not required on the farm, not to mention the only one trained to a side saddle. Elizabeth determined that she would ride Galahad back to Longbourn, once she had looked in on her sister. Three miles was not that far to walk, after all.

She made good time by cutting through the fields, and realized only as she mounted Netherfield's front steps that the bottom six inches of her dress and petticoats were covered in mud. She'd focused so much on Will, she'd forgotten she was not traipsing into Pemberley where she knew the back stairs and could change before she was presented. But there was nothing for it now and Jane remained her primary objective, so Elizabeth squared her shoulders and knocked on the door, prepared to meet her fate.

She was led swiftly to the breakfast room where the party was at the table, Jane noticeably absent. The gentlemen stood to bow; Elizabeth curtseyed.

"I beg forgiveness for the intrusion, but I received my sister's note and could not stay away," Elizabeth said, directing her words to Mr. and Miss Bingley. "How does she fare this morning?"

"My goodness, Miss Elizabeth, surely you did not walk the entire way here?" Miss Bingley drawled, her eyes picking out every spot of mud on Elizabeth's muslin.

"I did walk, Miss Bingley."

"Why on earth didn't you ride?"

The entire table turned to Mr. Darcy at his outburst. Elizabeth took the excuse to finally meet his eyes and bit back her smile, then answered evenly, "My sister took our only ladies' mount when she came yesterday, Mr. Darcy. I intend to retrieve Galahad from the stables and ride home once I have assessed Jane's condition."

"Galahad? As in, Sir Lancelot's son?"

Oh, he had noticed. Elizabeth had expected it, but she was pleased all the same. "A pale imitation of the original, I am sure, but I am fond of him all the same."

"The apothecary was here this morning to see Miss Bennet. He reported that she should not be in any danger, but ought not be moved throughout her convalescence," Mr. Bingley broke in. "As she is to stay here for some days, I wonder if you would wish to join her, Miss Elizabeth? I am sure it would increase her comfort greatly."

Miss Bingley appeared to be sucking on a lemon, and Elizabeth wondered if it was because it was the mistress's place to make the invitation or if Miss Bingley simply didn't want her present. Two seats over, Will gave a nearly imperceptible nod that told Elizabeth he approved, quite possibly even had something to do with the suggestion. Well, she had wanted a chance to reconnect with him when her mother wasn't present. And perhaps needling Miss Bingley would prove to be fun.

"Might I see Jane before I make a decision?" Elizabeth asked.

Miss Bingley opened her mouth, but before she could speak, Will pushed his chair back and stood. "I am finished with my breakfast and headed in that direction. I can show you to your sister."

Biting back yet another smile, Elizabeth curtseyed once more to her hosts and stepped aside to allow Will to pass, then followed him from the room. They passed three rooms beyond the breakfast room before she said quietly, "Did you mean to antagonize Miss Bingley? She will hate me forever, now."

Will stopped and looked down at her. She had forgotten how tall he was. "Are you teasing me, Miss Elizabeth? I believe I only allow friends to do that, and I am not sure how we stand just now."

Elizabeth felt her face drop, immediately contrite at not beginning the conversation better. Glancing up and down the hall, she stepped back into an alcove and forced herself to hold his gaze. "I am sorry, Will. I never meant to upset you. Did Papa explain—"

"Your worries about your mother and her expectations, yes. I will say, it is a new experience for me. I generally encounter young ladies hoping that they *will* trap me into matrimony, not that they will *not*."

"I hope you know me better than that," Elizabeth said, slightly indignant. "It was for your own peace of mind that I acted as I did." And for her own, if she was fully honest.

He inclined his head down the hallway, and they set off again, climbing the stairs to the upper level. "I know. It took me a few days to appreciate it, but I do understand. It would be rather like springing my aunt Lady Catherine on you without any warning." He paused. "Elizabeth, does it make you uncomfortable to stay here? From everything that you have said of Miss Bennet, I thought it would be a comfort to her to have you present, which is why I suggested the idea to Bingley. But I would not wish—"

Elizabeth stopped him with a hand on his arm. "I am not uncomfortable in the least," she said, "although I suspect that Miss Bingley will try my patience more than I like, over the next few days. And I suppose I shall have to pay attention lest I call you 'Will' in company and scandalize the entire neighborhood."

Will shook his head at her, face somber besides his laughing eyes. "You're right, that would never do. Here we are. Your sister's chamber, Miss Elizabeth. I shall leave you here and send a note to your father by your leave, requesting anything you and Miss Bennet may need for the next few days. Perhaps you would like to include a report on your sister?"

Elizabeth laughed. "You don't have to take care of everyone, Will—Mr. Darcy."

He raised an eyebrow, and for a second Elizabeth could see the resemblance to Richard. "Yes, I do," Will told her. "Do you mean to make it difficult on me?"

"Always," she said, then tapped on the door to Jane's room and slipped inside before he had a chance to reply.

*

Darcy rose even earlier than usual the next morning. He'd barely seen Elizabeth the day before, cloistered away as she had been with Miss

Bennet. When she did appear, her conversation was limited to polite banalities, and she left as soon after dinner as she could manage without being rude. He had known her over many years, however, and would be very surprised if she did not venture down for an early breakfast—so unlike Miss Bingley, who occasionally did not emerge from her room until midday.

So he was unsurprised when Elizabeth entered the room not long after himself, a sunny smile on her face to match the rays streaming through the windows. They exchanged polite greetings, she selected many of the same foods she had favored the last time they broke their fast together, and Darcy felt something inside him ease as she took the seat across from his, as she had so often in the past.

"I had thought to ride out this morning, Miss Elizabeth," he said on a whim as they finished their food. "Would you care to join me?"

She hesitated, but only for a moment. "It is lucky I requested my riding habit from home," she said. "Let me change, and I will meet you in the stables."

And so it was that within half an hour, they set out on one of Darcy's favorite paths, heading away from the house. No groom had offered to accompany them, and neither Darcy nor Elizabeth had requested one. It didn't occur to him until they were well gone that gossip might arise, and there was nothing to be done after the fact. Any additional action or comment would only call more attention to their situation.

"I like your Galahad," Darcy said aloud, pulling his attention back to the present moment.

"Thank you. My father purchased him when I was seventeen. I think he felt bad that he could not replace all of Pemberley for me, and a horse is the one thing I had asked him about more than once. Technically he is for all of us girls, but only Jane and I ride with any frequency."

Darcy could not keep his face from falling, though he hauled his usual mask back on quickly. "I am sorry your visits ended in the way they did, and were never reinstated. Georgiana and I always missed you when summer arrived and you and your father didn't."

Elizabeth gave him her impish smile. "Georgiana, I believe. But you? For all the trouble I gave you? I have recalled your patience with me many times, and sometimes I can scarce believe you tolerated me at all."

He grinned back. "You were no more bother than Richard, and often a great deal sweeter."

She looked away, but not before Darcy caught the bloom of color in her cheeks. "I wanted to write," Elizabeth said after a long pause. "When your father died, that is. I ought to have written, to Georgiana if nothing else. I just—" she broke off, sighing. "It felt like too much, all at once. Like everything was breaking and you and Pemberley and everyone else there belonged to a different world, one I had imagined. And I suppose—"

"Yes?" Darcy prompted, when it seemed that she did not mean to continue.

Elizabeth turned and looked at him directly. "I suppose I let George Wickham win. No, Will, hear me out. He said, in that last conversation, he said that he and I were the same. We weren't part of the Darcy family and never would be. We were the pets kept around for amusement. I didn't believe it when he said it, and I don't believe it now, but in the middle of everything I couldn't get it out of my head. I didn't want to intrude and give you one more obligation that had to be handled."

"I promise you, Lizzy, a letter from you would have been a great deal less stressful than dealing with my Aunt Catherine. If nothing else, I would have known your professed sorrow and condolences were genuine. There were so many hollow letters from people I barely knew, or those that my father actively disliked."

"Then I am sorry once again for my decision," she said. "Of course, it would have been a horrible breach of propriety to write you directly, but I am sure I could have contrived a way."

They had reached a clear space at the very back of the gardens, out of view of the house, and both horses stopped of their own accord. "Well, perhaps you would be willing to breach propriety in a different way," Darcy said.

Elizabeth raised an eyebrow. "More than riding

out unchaperoned, you mean?"

He grinned at her. "You owe me a dance. I was actually willing—nay, eager—to dance at a country assembly, and you ran away. Well, no one can see us here. So, Miss Elizabeth, may I have this dance?"

She stared at him for a moment, expressions chasing themselves across her face. "Mr. Darcy, I daresay you miss having me bother you. Does no one tease you anymore?" She held up a hand and shook her head. "Don't answer that. Why yes, gallant sir, I should be honored to dance with you."

Darcy swung down from the saddle and looped his reins around a tree branch before turning back and reaching up to catch Elizabeth. She fell forward as readily as she had five years prior, but stepped back promptly to tether her own mount. Then she turned and curtseyed; he bowed, and they stepped together.

"What are we dancing, Mr. Darcy?"

"With just the two of us here, and no music? What say you to a reel?"

Elizabeth laughed. "Very well, sir. You shall have your reel."

And then they were dancing. It took a while for them to agree upon a tempo, which then sped up as the dance continued, until they were spinning around each other at a pace Darcy rarely attempted, the greens of the gardens and the trees blending into the green sitting room of memory. Darcy raised an eyebrow at Elizabeth, daring her to continue the pace, and felt a *zing* of something as she grinned in response. He was too focused on his feet to put a word to the feeling.

They spun around each other, faster and faster and faster and—

Elizabeth yelped as she caught a foot on the hem of her long habit, pitching backwards, eyes wide.

Darcy reacted instinctively, locking his hands around her shoulders and holding her steady so she had a moment to find her equilibrium. "Goodness, Lizzy, I thought you were more graceful than that," he teased, slowly raising her back up to vertical.

"You try dancing with this dratted hem," she returned, chest heaving as she caught her breath. Slowly, she gathered up the offending skirt and took a step away from him—then froze.

Darcy stepped forward, arm reaching out to move Elizabeth behind him, even as his gaze followed hers. She stepped stubbornly to one side, peering around his shoulder.

"What is it?" Darcy asked in a low voice.

"I'm not sure," Elizabeth replied. "I saw a flash of something through the trees. Perhaps it was just a bird, but I was sure it was a person."

He stepped forward, intent on inspecting the area, only to be stopped by Elizabeth's grip on his forearm. "Don't," she said firmly. "It was likely nothing, although it is a reminder to both of us that we are not at Pemberley. I should not have gotten so carried away."

It was strange, seeing her look so serious and grown up. "Since when are you the voice of reason?"

A corner of Elizabeth's mouth quirked up. "The world is not kind to young ladies who step outside the common strictures, and I have three younger sisters." Her smile grew. "Besides, the whole point of this ill-conceived ruse was to keep pressure off of you, not force you to propose amid scandal. Come, let's ride back to the house. Surely some of our hosts will be rising soon?"

Darcy snorted. "Bingley, perhaps," he said, following Elizabeth to the horses and helping her into the saddle, then mounting his own horse. "The ladies and Hurst follow town hours. I doubt you'll see any of them before noon."

Elizabeth wrinkled her nose for just a moment, and he couldn't help but smile—she hadn't changed that much in essentials, it seemed.

They settled into a companionable silence for the return ride. Darcy thought back over their wild dance in the clearing and felt a smile spread across his face. What would his friends say if they'd seen him, the prudish gentleman who resisted any sort of interaction at balls? Could he ever hope to explain how different it was with Elizabeth, how his tongue never tied itself in knots when *she* was his partner?

It was only as they neared the house that Darcy recalled her comment at the end of their conversation, and the flow of thoughts in his mind halted abruptly. Once again, Elizabeth had made it very clear that she didn't want to trap him. It was a refreshingly unique sentiment. All he could think, however, was that she must be dead set against the possibility of marrying him —and why was it that the thought stung as much as it did?

*

"Good day, Miss Elizabeth. I see we have another early riser in our midst," Mr. Bingley said. "Have you eaten, or are you in need of directions to the breakfast room?"

Elizabeth felt her eyes dart to Mr. Darcy, who gave a nearly imperceptible roll of his eyes. They had separated upon arriving back at the house, and once she'd checked on a still-sleeping Jane, Elizabeth had followed the sound of voices, arriving at the front parlor just behind the gentlemen.

"I am not sure I would call this early," she replied. "I *have* eaten, and been out of doors as well, but did not wish to disturb Jane by moving around in our rooms."

Mr. Bingley shook his head and laughed. "You and Darcy. He is always going on about country hours, especially now that I mean to be a country gentleman. I admit I have yet to see the benefits, and clearly cannot hold a candle to the two of you, but I am here to give it my best effort."

"I find it a peaceful way to begin my day," Mr. Darcy remarked, watching Elizabeth claim a seat before settling into a chair with good light from the window. "I meant to say something yesterday, but was distracted by our additional guests. Breakfast is often an informal meal at Pemberley, and I hope you will not find it rude if I refrain from joining your sisters and Hurst at the table when they arise?"

"You are the landed gentleman of us all, Darcy. It is for us to follow your lead, not the other way round." Bingley flopped down between the two of them, somehow managing to look at ease rather than ill-mannered.

"Spoken like someone who has not spent nearly enough time around the foppish wastes of space that crop up in too many of the old families," Mr. Darcy replied. "Follow my lead if you will, Bingley, but do not do it blindly." How like his father he sounded in that moment!

"Have you any opinions to share on rising early?" Mr. Bingley asked Elizabeth.

It was impossible to not smile back at his genuine exuberance. "I will say that some of my favorite memories are from days that began with early mornings," she said. "Of course, most of them came from summer mornings rather than late autumn, but the sentiment remains the same."

Mr. Darcy gave a hint of a smile, but said only, "How does Miss Bennet fare this morning, Miss Elizabeth?"

Her smile dimmed. "She is still feverish, although I do not believe it is as bad today."

"Would she benefit from a more experienced opinion? I would be happy to send for my doctor in London."

Elizabeth blinked slowly, stifling the urge to roll her eyes at his fussing. But she managed perfect composure as she replied, "I thank you, Mr. Darcy, but that is hardly necessary. I would like to solicit my mother's opinion, if you are amenable to hosting yet another Bennet lady for a time, Mr. Bingley?"

As expected, Bingley was only too happy to accommodate the request, and it was settled between them that Elizabeth would send her mother a note. Mr. Darcy offered to convey it, once it was written, and Elizabeth moved to the desk set up with writing supplies. The gentlemen conversed quietly for several moments before Mr. Bingley jumped up.

"Drat! I am to meet with my steward, and quite lost track of the time." He hesitated, eyes darting between the two of them. A good host did not leave an unmarried lady and gentleman alone, and it would do no good to tell him they had broken that rule already today.

Elizabeth smiled, looking up from her missive.

"I am nearly done with my note, and once it is done I shall return to see if Jane has awoken. You needn't keep your steward waiting on my behalf."

Bingley hesitated, but she could see the relief in his eyes, and he hurried out with a quick farewell moments later, shooting one last glance at Darcy that she could not read.

"Bingley took me to task for my greeting yesterday, before you came in," Darcy remarked quietly when it was just the two of them once again. "Apparently it is rude and below me to question a lady as I did."

Elizabeth bit back a laugh, her estimation of Mr. Bingley rising. "Good. If he and Jane are to make a match of it, one of them needs to be able to have unpleasant conversations on occasion."

"Does she truly care for him, then?"

She stopped in the middle of folding her letter, shocked. "Can you not tell?"

"Not at all. Miss Bennet is very reserved, and quite different from yourself. I thought she may enjoy his company, but I never would have imagined her heart is engaged."

It would not do to say something rash, even if Elizabeth was instantly angry on Jane's behalf. "I will not betray my sister's confidence, but if you do anything to hurt her, I will do worse than put a frog in your bed. As for temperament, you ought to know better. How often do you wear a mask in public? Jane has been fawned over her entire life for her beauty. It makes her highly uncomfortable. But that is not something you would understand, is it, Mr. Darcy?"

He only gave her a look, but Elizabeth read the answer clearly. Yes, he could understand very well how Jane Bennet may decide to hide behind a mask of perfect calm.

She finished folding her note, and Mr. Darcy stood to take it from her, fingers grazing hers as the missive passed between them. "One other thing. I do not like lying to my friend and host, even by omission. Do you object to me telling him of our connection?"

All remaining anger faded away and Elizabeth sighed. "I fear I have done us both a grand disservice by not simply allowing the connection to be known from the beginning. No, I do not object to you informing Mr. Bingley of the whole truth. As for the rest of Meryton, perhaps we can allow them to assume that we became friends during my stay here? It is not that I care if people know, only that it will make us the main topic of conversation for a time, and I cannot relish that idea." She shot him a sideways look. "Although in that case, my mother will still do her best to matchmake. Promise that you will not hold it against her, or me? She means well, for all that there are times I think I will die of embarrassment at her methods."

Something passed over Mr. Darcy's face, and

she wondered what he was thinking in that moment. Aloud, however, he said only, "Of course not."

Chapter Thirteen

The day was not going according to Caroline's plans at all. She had risen late and spent extra time at her toilette to make sure she was looking her best for Mr. Darcy, only to come downstairs and find that he was not at breakfast but had ridden out—to deliver a note for Miss Elizabeth like an errand boy!

He'd returned, only to cloister himself away with Charles. That was not a bad development, for it surely served to strengthen their friendship as well as keeping Mr. Darcy well away from the impertinent Miss Elizabeth, but it did not allow Caroline a chance to show off her superb hostess skills. How could she convince Mr. Darcy she was the perfect woman to be the next mistress of Pemberley if he was not present to see how skillfully she handled the servants and arranged everything to suit him best?

Then came a dreadful half hour, when she was obliged to receive the remainder of the Bennet ladies. Miss Bennet was swiftly examined and declared much too ill to move, but not so ill as to worry any of them overmuch. Instead of leaving, the ladies proceeded to remain for at least twice as long as it had taken to see the reason for their call, and displayed all sorts of awful country manners. Why, the youngest girl had dared to ask Charles to hold a ball, and Charles had agreed to it! The only good thing Caroline could say of the encounter was that Miss Eliza had not appeared to look at Mr. Darcy even once. At least she had enough sense to realize how shameful her relations were, and to know that Mr. Darcy's opinion was the most important in the room to secure.

But he did not seem to hold the other Bennet ladies against her at all! Caroline contrived to be at his side when the unwanted party left, and she murmured to him, "At last! If only they would take Miss Elizabeth with them. Surely our servants are good enough to care for Miss Bennet in her convalescence."

"Care for, yes," Mr. Darcy replied, and Caroline began to preen before he continued. "However, no servant, skilled or not, can provide the same comfort as a most beloved sibling. Why, I would never dream of leaving Georgiana alone with naught but servants when she was ill, particularly not in a home where she knows so little of the inhabitants as Miss Bennet knows of us."

"Why yes, of course," Caroline was forced to

answer, for disagreeing so blatantly with Mr. Darcy was out of the question, particularly once he had mentioned Miss Darcy.

"Besides," Mr. Darcy continued, "while I understand that Mrs. Bennet and her younger daughters are not the sort of refined ladies one might find in Mayfair, I have not observed anything but proper behavior from the eldest two."

"Mr. Darcy!" Caroline exclaimed. "How can you say that, after the display we were treated to two days ago at breakfast? Surely you would not wish for Miss Darcy to appear in such a state?"

"Of course I would not wish it, but I would not condemn her if she did, especially if she came to be of service rather than to pay a call." He turned and looked directly down at her, and Caroline did her best not to shrink visibly from the force of his stare. "You are in the country now, Miss Bingley. Miss Elizabeth has lived on an estate her entire life. I daresay she understands the behavior that is expected of her."

He walked away and Caroline was left, for once in her life, completely speechless.

*

By the next day, Jane's fever appeared to have broken, and Elizabeth spent the morning in her sister's company. It was not until midafternoon, when Jane fell asleep, that she ventured out to join the rest of the party. She found them in the drawing room; the Hursts were both half-dozing on the sofa, Mr. Bingley was half-heartedly reading a letter, and Mr. Darcy was attempting to write one of his own, hindered by Miss Bingley's commentary.

The actions did not alter when Elizabeth entered, save for the long-suffering look that Mr. Darcy sent her when Miss Bingley was turned away. She smothered her smile and brought out the needlework she had with her, sitting near enough to the pair that she could listen in to what turned out to be a most asinine conversation.

"How delighted Miss Darcy will be to receive such a letter!" Miss Bingley exclaimed after a time, having failed to convince Mr. Darcy that she ought to mend his pen. "Pray tell your sister that I long to see her."

"I shall convey that when I write to Georgiana shortly, but at present she is not the intended recipient."

There was a pause, and Elizabeth waited to see if Miss Bingley would be so ill-mannered as to ask Mr. Darcy just who the recipient was.

"Oh!" she exclaimed. "How many letters you must have occasion to write in the course of the year! Letters of business too! How odious I should think them!"

Not a direct question. Miss Bingley deserved partial credit for that. Looking sideways beneath lowered lashes, Elizabeth met Mr. Darcy's gaze and gave him the tiniest flicker of a wink.

"It is fortunate they fall to my lot rather than yours, then, but this is not a letter of business. I write to my cousin, the Countess of Huntingdon."

Sophie. It had been some months since she and Elizabeth had last corresponded, due in large part to the birth of Sophia's second child that summer. Her friend was unfashionably involved in caring for her children and fully occupied with that pursuit.

"Will your cousin be interested to hear all about the banalities of life here in sleepy Hertfordshire?" Elizabeth asked before she could stop herself.

Miss Bingley appeared scandalized, as if she herself had not been prying just a moment before. "I am sure the countess has far more important things to occupy her time, and Mr. Darcy would not dream of burdening her with such trite reports."

Behind Miss Bingley's turned head, Mr. Darcy's lips pressed together into a thin line. "On the contrary, Miss Bingley. I have been relating the general inhabitants and activities of the neighborhood to Sophia, and I expect she will be glad to read the account. For all that she spends the full season in town, my cousin has always been fond of country life."

"Oh, of course! When one has access to such estates as Pemberley, it would be hard to *not* be fond of the country."

"Have you spent much time at Pemberley, Miss Bingley?" Elizabeth asked. "This is not the first time I have heard you mention it."

The other lady preened. "We spent part of the last two summers there."

"The Bingleys have family in Scarborough," Mr. Darcy added. "Pemberley is a convenient location to break their travels when they visit."

Miss Bingley's cheeks turned pink, and Elizabeth wondered if she had meant to hide that fact.

"It is lucky that you are able to travel north in the summers," Elizabeth said. "My aunt and uncle have remarked that they would prefer to leave London once the weather turns warm, but sadly my uncle's business will not allow for long absences."

"Oh," Miss Bingley said, drawing out the word to give it three times the usual number of syllables. "I did not realize you had relatives in town, Miss Elizabeth. Pray tell, where do they live?"

Elizabeth gave her a sunny smile. "Gracechurch Street, Miss Bingley. My uncle Gardiner prefers to be within walking distance of his warehouses so he can come home for lunch, and my aunt is prodigiously fond of their house. They joke about moving to a finer location, but I do not believe they will do so for some years."

"Gardiner," Mr. Darcy cut in, tone implying

he had been previously unaware of Elizabeth's connection. Highly surprising deception, for him. "You must mean Gardiner's Fine Fabrics."

"I do, Mr. Darcy. Perhaps the ladies in your life enjoy spending too much of your money on his wares?"

Mr. Darcy laughed, and from the corner of her eye Elizabeth noticed Miss Bingley start in surprise. "A very astute observation, if it were not for the fact that most ladies of the *ton* enjoy the same pastime. But yes, Georgiana occasionally buys from there, if she does not purchase from Lambton, and Lady Matlock and Sophia are both frequent customers."

"I suppose Miss Darcy will make more purchases in town, once she comes out," Miss Bingley said. "And I daresay that will be soon, too! She seemed so grown, so mature, when I last saw her. How I long to see her again! I never met with anybody who delighted me so much. Such a countenance, such manners, and so extremely accomplished for her age! Her performance on the piano-forte is exquisite." What accolades, for a young lady not even present! Elizabeth could only imagine what Miss Bingley hoped to accomplish with her words.

Before Mr. Darcy could reply, however, Mr. Bingley looked up. "I am in constant awe of the amount of patience young ladies must have to be so very accomplished—and I dare say all the ones I know are, for no one can speak of a young lady without also commenting on how accomplished she is."

"Charles! All young ladies accomplished? That is a preposterous notion."

"How so? They all seem to paint tables, cover screens, and net purses, play pianoforte or harpsichord or perhaps both, and can turn a tangle of thread and length of cloth into something marvelous, be it a fichu or lace trimming."

Elizabeth laughed. "My goodness, Mr. Bingley, you have listed more accomplishments than I could have managed, had you asked. You may not be accomplished yourself, but you seem to know a great deal about the state."

He flashed her a quick grin. "Unlike my friend Darcy here, I love to dance, and accomplishments are an easy topic to cover on the dance floor."

"Those are very fine accomplishments for London ballrooms," Mr. Darcy said, giving Mr. Bingley a hint of a long-suffering look. "I beg you to consider something more substantial when choosing your future partner, however, especially if you mean to purchase an estate. Netting purses will not create a menu or address the concerns of tenant women. I am very far from agreeing with you in your estimation of ladies in general. I cannot boast of knowing more than half a dozen, in the whole range of my acquaintance, that are truly accomplished."

"You might know more, Darcy, if you bothered to speak with any!" Bingley returned jovially. "But you intrigue me, so I shall ask. What is your list? What accomplishments must a lady boast before you would consider her to grace the halls of Pemberley?"

"Why, I daresay a woman must have a thorough knowledge of music, singing, drawing, dancing, and the modern languages, to deserve the word," Miss Bingley exclaimed, "and besides all this, she must possess a certain something in her air and manner of walking, the tone of her voice, her address and expressions, or the word will be but half deserved."

Elizabeth wondered if anyone else caught the stifled laugh in Mr. Darcy's compressed lips. "Those are accomplishments, to be sure, but I would also add that a lady must read extensively, both to improve her mind and to provide interesting conversation. I could not bring a lady home to Pemberley if she would not appreciate its library. And as I have said, she must be capable of managing the home and assisting with the tenants." He paused. "What would you add, Miss Elizabeth? The rest of us have given our lists."

She couldn't help the impish smile she gave him. "I do not profess any great knowledge in the matter, and so I shall only repeat what I have been told, Mr. Darcy. All gentlewomen must ride, particularly those on larger estates."

His eyes caught on hers and for a brief

moment Elizabeth could see the two of them on horseback, flying over Pemberley's emerald grounds without a care in the world beyond who would win the current race. Perhaps Sophia or Richard rode with them; perhaps it was one of those mornings when it was only the pair of them, just like yesterday. The moment stretched out, and Elizabeth wondered if Will—for he was Will just now—saw the same thing she did.

"How unfortunate it is for you, then, that your family has only one riding mount," Miss Bingley remarked, examining the nails of one pale hand.

Elizabeth blinked, looking away from Mr. Darcy. "I believe the intent was having the ability to ride, Miss Bingley. Besides, while I love Longbourn dearly, it is not a large estate. I am perfectly happy walking when Galahad is not available."

"Well! I suppose it is just as well for you that is the case," Miss Bingley said. "Goodness, look at the time! I do believe I shall call for tea."

*

It was preposterous. Inconceivable. In every way impossible. And yet, Caroline could not delude herself out of the truth. When she spoke to Mr. Darcy, he replied directly, with curt answers that did not further the conversation. He scarcely looked up from his letter, doing the bare minimum required to be considered polite. She had always considered this to be part of his mien, a noble bearing to be admired in his steadfast stand-off-ishness. Caroline had often imagined the striking image the pair of them would make once they married, both tall and reserved and haughty.

And then somehow, Elizabeth Bennet came along and made her reconsider everything she'd previously known about Mr. Darcy's character. Why, the impish county chit had very nearly turned Mr. Darcy *verbose*. He had *laughed*. And that moment when everything had paused and they just looked at each other, as if they both knew a delicious secret—Caroline had very much wished she was holding a cup of tea that could have been oh-so-conveniently upset directly into Eliza Bennet's lap.

Impossible that Mr. Darcy could like Eliza better than Caroline. Impossible that he could seem so much more at ease with her. They had only met a month ago, after all, and spent essentially no time together! Impossible.

And yet, the feeling of uncertainty that had begun with the Bennet ladies' visit was proving impossible to shake.

*

"By God, Darcy. If you hadn't told me about your prior connection with Miss Elizabeth, I daresay I would have been worried for your health!"

Bingley leaned back in his chair and surveyed

the friend that sat on the other side of the fire. It was the following evening and they were in Netherfield's office—Bingley's office at the moment, not that he could bring himself to think of it that way. Offices like this belonged to people like Darcy, who knew far more than Charles Bingley did.

Darcy was, just now, raising his eyebrow in that way that always made Bingley feel like he was back at Eton.

"Worried for my health? I'm sure I don't know what you are talking about."

"Come now! I've never heard you speak as much as you did over the last few days, and you only laugh like that when your cousin the colonel is around to prod you."

Darcy gave him a *look*. The man had a great number of them, usually small variations on a theme, and Bingley was proud of himself for having learned to read the face that many people found expressionless. This one said that Darcy didn't appreciate the teasing, but he was amused nonetheless; he thought that he should be annoyed more than he truly felt it.

"The comparison isn't surprising. Miss Elizabeth learned a great deal about teasing, and teasing me in particular, from Richard."

"Well, the end result surprised everyone. I thought Caroline was going to faint a time or two. I don't believe those in our party have ever seen you say more than a few sentences to a lady, unless she was a relation of yours." Bingley paused, wondering the best way to bring up what he actually wanted to discuss. "I am glad you don't dislike the Miss Bennets. Although did you have to offer them use of your carriage? I meant to win Miss Bennet's goodwill with the offer of mine."

Darcy shot him another look, this one all amusement. "Miss Elizabeth asked me directly, and as the gentleman who boasts a long-standing acquaintance *and* a friendship with their father, I thought it more proper to offer them mine. I doubt Miss Bennet thinks poorly of you for it."

"Yes, but—" Bingley bit his lip, then spit it out, "do you think she thinks *well* of me?"

There was a long pause, and Bingley felt himself tense in preparation of the response.

"As you so recently pointed out, I do not know Miss Bennet any better than you do, and you have spent more time with her since we arrived in Hertfordshire," Darcy said.

Bingley felt himself blink, surprised by the answer that was very different from what he had expected. Struck by a sudden suspicion, Bingley asked, "Has Miss Elizabeth told you anything of her sister's feelings?"

That earned him a stern look. "If Miss Elizabeth *had* said anything, I would never betray her confidence, and you ought not to ask it of me." He paused. "I will remind you that

Miss Elizabeth's reason for not claiming a prior acquaintance was to avoid pressure from her mother. That tells me that Mrs. Bennet is eager to see her daughters wed, and will likely push them at eligible gentlemen whether they think well of them or not."

Bingley opened his mouth, not sure what he meant to say but ready to protest.

"*However*," Darcy continued with yet another stern look, "Miss Elizabeth's actions tell me that she has a very different outlook on the matter, and it is clear to see how close she and Miss Bennet are. It is likely they would share many similar beliefs. If you wish to know more than that, Bingley, you will have to ask Miss Bennet herself."

Chapter Fourteen

To say that Mrs. Bennet was displeased when her eldest daughters arrived home before an entire sennight had passed was an understatement. "You ought to have stayed a week complete, Jane, for how is Mr. Bingley to fall for you when you have been shut away in your room? Although I will say it was kind of him to loan you his carriage, and what a fine carriage it was!"

Elizabeth exchanged a quick glance with her father while Jane bit her lip. "It wasn't Mr. Bingley's carriage, Mama. I am sure he would have offered, but Mr. Darcy did so first."

Mrs. Bennet rocked back on her heels. "Mr. Darcy!" she exclaimed. "And how in the world did that come to be?"

Jane looked to Elizabeth, who in turn braced herself. "I mentioned that I was hoping to return home soon," she said. "Perhaps he simply wished for us to be gone. I am sure we upset the balance of their prior grouping."

In reality, the conversation had been far more direct, but it wouldn't do to tell her mother that. Unattached young ladies did not beg favors from gentlemen they had supposedly just met.

"Well," Mrs. Bennet said after a long pause, still staring at Elizabeth. "Perhaps that is so, but it was kind of him all the same."

"I am sure Mr. Darcy did not have anything so selfish in mind," Jane added. "I spoke to him little, but he seemed to enjoy your conversation, Lizzy."

"Only because no one else in the party would speak to him of books!" Elizabeth exclaimed before her mother could say anything else. It was strange, after years of guarding Mr. Darcy and everything associated with him so zealously from her family, to admit even to general friendship. Elizabeth hadn't anticipated how hard it would be. Perhaps the visceral reaction that had caused her to hide at the assembly had more depth to it that she had originally allowed.

"Well, Lizzy, Jane, I am glad that you are home now," Mr. Bennet said, speaking up for the first time since his initial greeting. "We are to receive a visitor of our own tomorrow, and it will be better to introduce you girls all at once. I believe he is quite curious about you."

"Mr. Bennet, of whom can you speak?" Mrs. Bennet asked, Mr. Darcy momentarily forgotten.

"Why, my here-to-unknown cousin, Mr. Collins, who is heir to this place," Mr. Bennet announced. "I have had a most interesting letter from him, declaring his intent to heal the breach left by his father, and of course to meet the cousins that he has heard are the belles of Hertfordshire. Perhaps if I am lucky, he will enjoy speaking of books as well."

*

Mr. William Collins did not, it turned out, care to speak of books. He appeared to put stock in only two books, the Bible and Fordyce's Sermons for Young Ladies, and Mr. Bennet had to wonder if the latter was mentioned only due to the demographic in which he found himself. Even these volumes, however, paled drastically in comparison to how clearly he revered his noble patroness, Lady Catherine de Bourgh.

Having already heard of Lady Catherine—from her brother and brother-in-law, no less—Bennet found the parson's clear adoration all the more pitiable. To hear Mr. Collins tell it, the lady was benevolent and grand and most helpful with her liberal dispensing of advice. Five years ago, the Fitzwilliams and Darcys had painted a picture of her as a bossy, strident nag. It did not take much intelligence to determine which account was more likely to be correct.

In short, the man was both a delightful entertainment and a colossal disappointment, amusing but certainly not the sensible gentleman that one wished for when envisioning their heir. For the first time in several years, Bennet felt the stirring of unease that old Mr. Darcy had been capable of inspiring, wondering what would happen to his wife and daughters when this fool took charge of their home.

Interested in observing the guest, Mr. Bennet installed himself in a corner of the drawing room the next morning, where the family was wont to gather after breakfast. He took up his newspaper, much as he usually would in the peace of his study, but resigned himself to listening to the chatter instead of indulging in the day's news. Luckily, he did not have to wait long for the conversation to turn away from trivialities.

"I did not mention it yesterday, Mrs. Bennet, but I have another reason for journeying hence, and for my delight over the veracity of the reports regarding my fair cousins. You see, I find it the duty of a clergyman to set the example of matrimonial harmony in his parish, and Lady Catherine agrees most heartily. Furthermore, it has pained me, since the death of my esteemed father, to know that a breach exists between our families when future circumstances will benefit me greatly while disadvantaging my cousins. While such is the way of the world, it is no fault of my cousins that they have no brother, and this conundrum has long concerned me."

Did the man know that Mrs. Bennet would take his comment as an insult, that he had implied the fault for the lack of a Bennet heir lay with her? It seemed he did not.

Luckily for Mr. Collins, he blathered on before Mrs. Bennet had time to work up any significant amount of indignation, and his topic was one that was sure to endear him to the lady. "After long consideration, I have come to the conclusion that it is only right—one might say natural, even—that I select my bride from amongst my fair cousins, and I intend to put much thought to the matter during my stay."

Mrs. Bennet gasped, hands flying up to her chest. Clearly, she was delighted. Mr. Bennet, still half hidden behind his newspaper, could not take the news with nearly as much enthusiasm, and from the quick look that Elizabeth sent his way, she was clearly of the same mind. That tendril of unease reasserted itself, growing and twisting in Bennet's stomach.

But Mr. Collins was not looking at Bennet, or Elizabeth. He looked, or one might say *leered*, at Jane instead. Despite himself, Bennet could not help but wonder how his wife would react. Could she conscience tying her eldest, most beautiful and therefore most prized daughter to such a toadying man in order to keep her home?

"Mr. Collins," she said quietly, leaning forward as one would with a secret, "your news cannot but delight me; as a mother it would give me the most pleasure to see one of my girls so well situated, and in her own home as well! However,

I must tell you that the eldest Miss Bennet, while not officially in a courtship, may very well soon become engaged. I am sure you understand."

He may have understood, but Mr. Collins' face said he did not like the news at all. Obviously, the idea of possessing Jane had been one he relished, and one he did not like to give up. Mr. Bennet felt himself tense as Mrs. Bennet's mouth opened once again. How much stock would she put in the comments from yesterday, about the attention paid to Lizzy by Mr. Darcy?

"However, my next eldest—"

"Mrs. Bennet, a word?"

Before he realized what he was doing, Mr. Bennet stood, folding his paper and putting it aside. His wife looked surprised, but followed him readily enough from the room, happy with his excuse that a household matter required her opinion.

Bennet did not speak more until they reached his study, then turned to face his wife and waved her into the chair she had always favored. "My dear, I could not help but overhear your conversation with my cousin," he said once she was settled.

"Are you not excited? Such a thing for our girls, and I shall not have to leave my home! Oh, Mr. Bennet!"

He swallowed his smile; it was not for what she would have expected, anyhow. "That would certainly be good, which is why I stopped you before you could speak further. There is something I must tell you about Elizabeth, and I need you to listen to me fully."

Bennet waited for her nod, then added in a stern look when she would have burst into speech once more.

"Do you remember, my dear, the summers that Elizabeth and I spent in Derbyshire? We discontinued the trips when my friend passed away, as you know. What you do not know is that he left Elizabeth a significant sum to be used as her dowry. No," he said firmly, holding up a hand, "it is not something that can be used for purposes other than that, and it cannot be spread amongst the girls or transferred to anyone other than Elizabeth. The terms of the will were very clear. However, you ought to keep this in mind when recommending any of our daughters to Mr. Collins. With her dowry, Elizabeth could attract a gentleman of higher standing and better means than Mr. Collins."

Mrs. Bennet opened and closed her mouth several times before finally exclaiming, "But why was I not told? Such information is useless if not known. How are gentlemen to understand what Elizabeth can offer if the information is not spread? I must—"

"Sit down," Bennet said firmly as she made to rise. "Not a word will be said about Elizabeth's dowry, am I clear? I will not have my daughter as the source of gossip, or see you pushing her at penniless officers because you like their uniform color. Elizabeth and I have spoken on this matter at length. If she is ever serious about a young man, and believes he may be serious about her, she will let me know, and I will handle it from there."

"But Mr. Bennet, a man may not become serious about her if he thinks all that she can offer is fifty pounds!"

"If my goal were to see Elizabeth wed quickly, I may agree with that point, but it is not. I wish to see her wed *well*." Bennet paused, taking in the confusion on his wife's face. "Fanny, I know you worry about what happens when I am gone. I know you wish for our girls to be settled. We are not opposed in what we wish, only the particulars of it. You have heard the saying, I am sure, 'Marry in haste and repent at leisure.' Would you consign a single one of your daughters to misery, for the sake of seeing her wed?"

"It is misery to be turned out of one's home with nowhere to go and nothing to rely on but the sympathy of one's relatives! You will not be here to feel that, but the girls and I will," Mrs. Bennet exclaimed. "My brother and sister cannot take all of us in. At least one of our girls must be married well, and soon!"

It was a sound point, and he did not like it. His wife was considerably easier to handle when he could push her worries—her dratted *nerves*—

away and dismiss them as silly. She made it easy most of the time, but just now she sounded more like old Mr. Darcy than Bennet cared to admit.

"Enough, Mrs. Bennet," he snapped. "I am not in my grave yet, and I will thank you to let me manage my own family as I see fit. Recommend Mary to Collins, if you must. She may actually have him. If you push Elizabeth on him and she refuses, I will support her decision. And if I hear a single mention of her dowry, you will lose your pin money for the first quarter of next year. Do not test me on this."

His wife *hmphed*, but she knew better than to argue with that tone. "As you say, Mr. Bennet." She rose and swept from the room, in that moment not so different from the girl he had married all those years ago.

Bennet opened his newspaper to read in earnest. He had done his duty to Elizabeth, and if Mary reacted as he expected, to his whole family. The specter of George Darcy would have to be happy with that, for Bennet intended to remain in his book room for the rest of the day. The sooner he could put that conversation and the accompanying ill feeling from his mind, the better.

*

Bingley insisted on riding out as soon as the time reached polite visiting hours, insistent on ensuring that Miss Bennet's health continued to improve.

"Must you, Charles? She has only just left us, and was clearly well enough then. There is really no need," Miss Bingley said immediately.

"Perhaps, Bingley, we could go by horseback. There is a low area I have been meaning to show you, it will require proper management else it get too wet and not be able to produce," Darcy spoke up before his friend could retort. It was beneath him to insert himself in the argument, perhaps, but he already had a bit of a headache and Miss Bingley's shrill tones were sure to make it worse. And Bingley did truly need to see the area.

"Capital idea, Darcy! Let us go at once." Bingley sprung from his chair and departed, leaving his sister to glare after him.

"Mr. Darcy, I cannot approve of his behavior with Miss Bennet," the lady said, turning to him. "Surely you must agree; if he continues in this manner he will be raising all sorts of expectations. You have advised him from poor matches in the past; he listens to you when he will not hear what I say. You will help him again, won't you?"

What would Elizabeth say? He'd never mastered her way of making a point without coming across as rude. "I will offer my opinion if Bingley asks for it." No need to mention he had already done just that. "Now excuse me, I ought to ready myself before your brother leaves without me."

He exited, not overly pleased with his effort, but it would have to do. Miss Bingley's comment made him think, however. He *had* cautioned Bingley away from ladies in the past. Had Elizabeth not been involved, had she not made the comment about her sister's feelings and taken him to task for judging something based on appearances alone, what would he have done? Beyond that, had he done the same in the past? His rationale had been sound, and Bingley never seemed to remember the lady in question for long, but what of the ladies? It was a strange realization, noticing that he had never given thought to their feelings. How had they felt when Bingley's attentions suddenly stopped? It was a wonder that no angry brother had called out his friend for caprice.

Darcy was still ruminating on his past assumptions when they rode through Meryton. Only when Bingley reined in his horse did he shake off his thoughts and look around, wondering why they were stopping a mile short of their intended destination. The reasoning was easily found—all five Bennet sisters stood a short distance away, apparently accompanied by a strange gentleman and facing three officers. The youngest two girls were front and center; Miss Mary stood to the side by the gentleman not in regimentals, and Elizabeth was at the far back, tucked partially behind Miss Bennet.

The gentlemen made their way towards the

group, weaving around other passers-by. As they approached, Elizabeth's head came up and her eyes caught Darcy's.

Alarm shot through him: her face was pale, jaw set. What on earth would have her looking like that now, in a large group at a public square —and looking to *him*, after her insistence on not calling attention to their acquaintance?

One of the officers noticed her attention and swung around as well, following her gaze.

Wickham.

The world narrowed and Darcy could hear nothing beyond the pounding of blood in his ears. He kicked out of his stirrups and dismounted the way Richard had always preferred, landing with both feet on the ground and already in motion. There was something to be said for a well-trained horse; his mount wouldn't move unless thoroughly spooked.

His next conscious thought found him beside Elizabeth, his arm moving of its own volition. He halted himself just in time to hold it out for her to take rather than tucking her against him as he'd done the last time they faced Wickham together. Her fingers closed in a tight grip on his forearm; he would have to be content with that for the moment.

The moment dragged on. The world consisted of nothing beyond Elizabeth at his side and Wickham before him, all three pinned in silence beyond the thundering of his heart beat in his ears. Were they all remembering the last time they had been grouped in such a way? Darcy fought to push back the flashes of memory. And then—

"Good day, Mr. Darcy."

Darcy blinked and turned towards the voice that came from so far away and yet right beside him. Jane Bennet was smiling at him, her face serene, perfect. She held Elizabeth's other arm now; did she know who they faced? Or was she simply perceptive enough to realize that something was wrong and offer support to her sister?

"Miss Bennet," he managed. "It is good to see you looking so well; part of our reason for coming this way was to ensure the journey home had not caused a setback in your health."

Unsurprisingly, Bingley had joined the group before Darcy was done with his sentence, and immediately added in his own concerns and happiness at Miss Bennet's clear recovery. She turned to him, blushing, and Darcy returned his own attention to Wickham.

Elizabeth's fingers tightened further on his arm; she didn't want a confrontation.

"I see you have found a new occupation, Wickham," Darcy said, pulling on every ounce of self-control he had mastered over the years to speak calmly. "Richard will be interested to hear of it—had you heard he is a colonel now? I must write to him directly with the news."

Wickham's poker face was nearly as good as Darcy's, for only the barest flicker of fear showed before he smiled genially. Darcy understood the fear well. The three men had encountered each other only once after Wickham's departure from Pemberley. Richard's icy fury hadn't been focused on Darcy, but he'd been afraid of it all the same. He had wondered for a moment if he would have to keep Richard from pulling his sword on Wickham in the middle of London. They hadn't bothered to share life updates at the time.

"Not the life I had envisioned for myself, but one does what one can," Wickham responded, a twitch of a muscle turning his smile into a sneer for just an instant.

Darcy forced a laugh. "After all the times you insisted on playing soldier as a boy? This seems very fitting for you. Far better than a church living—you never could stand to be in the church for long. Imagine spending a whole career there."

"Is it so strange to think that a man might change with time and age?" Wickham asked.

"To change that much, in essentials? I would find that very strange indeed."

"La, do you know each other?" One of the youngest Bennet sisters—the one in the yellow bonnet instead of the pink—giggled as she asked the question, her gaze darting between them with glee. They had the attention of the whole group now, Darcy noticed.

"At one time, Miss Lydia, we knew each other very well," Wickham replied with infuriating smoothness, his smile charming. "I daresay you would have called us good friends."

It had been a *very* long time since that was true, but Darcy bit back his retort.

"But what a strange coincidence! To think that you should find each other here, so far from home, where you are strangers to everyone but each other!"

Wickham's eyebrows shot up as he processed the meaning of Lydia's statement, and Darcy felt Elizabeth's grip on his arm grow tighter.

"It seems you have made friends with the locals in a short amount of time, Darcy," Wickham said. "Perhaps we have both changed; you never were one for socializing with strangers."

"I'm afraid that is my fault," Miss Bennet said. "I was silly enough to fall ill while visiting Netherfield, and Lizzy came to nurse me. There were several days where I did little but sleep, and she therefore spent quite a significant amount of time in the company of our hosts."

Bingley laughed. "It was a relief to hand off speaking of books to someone else, even if both Darcy and Miss Elizabeth both took me to task for the scarcity of selection in the library."

"I can hardly blame you for the choices of the past inhabitants, Mr. Bingley," Elizabeth said, speaking for the first time. "Should your library remain so bare over the next twelvemonth, however, I may not be so kind in my judgment!"

"Books!" Lydia exclaimed. "Lizzy, you are so boring. If I had a new estate, I would never worry about books. There are much more enjoyable ways to pass the time if one is bored! Why, I should host a ball every month of the year."

"You had better be planning to marry a very rich man, then," Miss Mary said from the edge of the group.

Lydia rolled her eyes, mouth opening to retort, but Bingley said quickly, "I hope you will not think less of me for hosting only one ball this year, Miss Lydia, but I do have an invitation for all of you. Part of my reason for going to Longbourn today was to deliver this, for a ball to be held at Netherfield on the 26th of November. Will you see it gets to your mother, as the lady of the household?" he asked Miss Bennet, holding out an envelope.

Her cheeks turned pink as her gloved fingers closed around the paper. "On her behalf, Mr. Bingley, I thank you. I am sure she will be as delighted with the invitation as we are."

Beneath the youngest ladies' squeals and exclamations of excitement, Bingley took half a step forward and said, "I do hope, Miss Bennet, if your parents see fit to accept the invitation, that you might be willing to reserve your first set for me?"

Miss Bennet blushed deeper red and nodded. Darcy locked his jaw shut before he could blurt out a similar question to Elizabeth.

"It seems that I chose a well-situated regiment," Wickham said. "What soldier doesn't wish for balls and beautiful ladies open to befriending newcomers?" His eyes met Darcy's, then swept over Bingley and Miss Bennet before coming to rest on Elizabeth's tight grasp on Darcy's arm.

"Oh, Meryton is much more enjoyable now!" Miss Kitty said. "It was ever so boring before the arrival of the officers."

Wickham smiled, but he didn't turn towards the younger girls. Instead, his eyes fastened onto Elizabeth's. "Do you agree with your sisters, Miss Elizabeth? Is it enjoyable meeting strangers?"

Darcy's control on his expression slipped at last, and he took a step forward, only to be halted by a hard grip to his arm once again.

"I find that Meryton is certainly more eventful than it was before this fall, Lieutenant Wickham," she replied evenly. "As for my delight with the regiment, I shall require a bit more time to make up my mind." She turned to look up at Darcy. "Did you wish for an introduction to the bookseller? My father has requested that I pick up a volume for him, if you would like to accompany me."

"Yes, I would like that very much," he replied immediately. To have her away from Wickham would be nothing short of delightful.

"I look forward to hearing your decision," Wickham said, eyes still fixed on Elizabeth's face. "It will be very," he paused, "revealing, I am sure."

Her back straightened even further, and Darcy was reminded that Elizabeth had spent considerable time with Sophia as well as with himself as she said, "I am sure it shall be, Lieutenant. But I do not intend to hurry my decision. It would be quite a pity if a decision made in haste were to have lifelong effects, don't you think?"

She stepped forward, leading him away from the group after a quick exchange of glances with Miss Bennet. Only after they had collected his horse and made their way out of earshot did he say, "Are you well? Elizabeth?"

She let out a long breath, grip on his arm relaxing just a bit. "I know he is here now. He won't catch me by surprise again. I am glad that I was able to find my voice; it would not do for him to think me afraid."

He looked down at her, once again fighting the urge to tuck her close against him, or better yet toss her into the saddle and hold her tightly as they put as much distance as possible between themselves and George Wickham. What would she think to know his thoughts? Was he no better than Wickham himself, who had tried to take her just that?

No, Darcy thought viciously. No, he was

not like Wickham. That scoundrel had wanted Elizabeth for his own gain, for convenience. Darcy wanted to protect her, to comfort her, to put a smile back on her face as she had done so often for him over the years. He wanted to be able to keep men like Wickham from ever again causing her harm. Over the years, he had occasionally thought that Georgiana and Elizabeth occupied similar places in his life, but he would not delude himself now—he'd never felt like this about his sister. Georgiana was his to protect, to guide, to help raise to adulthood as their parents would have wished, and then to set free. Elizabeth was *his*, and so help anyone who tried to come between them.

Striding down the dusty road, Darcy was struck dumb by the realization that he loved Elizabeth Bennet as he had never loved anyone else—and as things currently stood, there was absolutely no way he could burden her with that knowledge.

Chapter Fifteen

ollins watched with shock and a bit of consternation as Cousin Elizabeth walked away without so much as a by-your-leave, the threesome of officers giving a more fitting farewell before they followed suit. It seemed that Mrs. Bennet had known what she was about when she directed him to Cousin Mary. He didn't relish the idea, for who wanted a wallflower when there were two others before her both in age and beauty? And yet Collins was not deluded enough to think himself competition for the kind of gentleman who now accompanied Cousin Elizabeth the rest of the way into Meryton.

"La, it is just like Lizzy to prefer boring Mr. Darcy!" one of the younger ones—was it Cousin Lydia?—exclaimed when the officers were gone.

A look flickered between Cousin Jane and the other gentleman, then the gentleman said, "Darcy will be grateful for the introduction to your bookseller, even if you find reading a boring pastime, Miss Lydia."

"Did you say Mr. Darcy?" Collins burst out. A random suitor was one thing, but Mr. Darcy! This was not to be borne.

Cousin Jane jumped a little. "Oh! Mr. Bingley, do allow me to introduce our cousin, Mr. Collins. He is a parson visiting from Kent. Mr. Collins, this is Mr. Bingley."

Bingley gave a pleasant enough greeting, then smiled. "Yes, my friend is Mr. Darcy. I apologize on his behalf; he can be rather single-minded when there is a task at hand. Particularly when it pertains to books."

Books, schmooks. For the first time, he agreed with Cousin Lydia: who cared for books? There were more important matters at hand. "But surely he is not Mr. Darcy of Pemberley? The nephew of Lady Catherine de Bourgh?"

Bingley and Cousin Jane exchanged another look; they must think him rude, not understanding his own connection to the great lady. He plowed on, explaining his great luck to have gained such a benefactress, and how honored he was by the distinction. Only then did he continue, "But Mr. Darcy is betrothed to his cousin! Anne de Bourgh is a true jewel, most befitting of her cousin's notice. Cousin Elizabeth must be warned so her hopes are not raised, not to mention that she ought to be chaperoned in the company of any gentleman not related to herself. Perhaps—"

"I understand perfectly, Mr. Collins," Bingley said. "Miss Bennet, I am not sure what your intended destination was today, but if you would care to walk with me, I am sure we can catch up to your sister and my friend."

Cousin Jane blushed becomingly; Collins blinked several times to turn his focus back to the matter at hand. "Of course, Mr. Bingley. I had nowhere specific in mind. Mr. Collins, may I entrust the oversight of my sisters with you? I am sure Mary would be happy to show you around Meryton so you may familiarize yourself."

Before Collins could come up with a rebuttal, they too were gone. Really, he ought to have gone after Cousin Elizabeth himself, to ensure that the warning was delivered properly and to give Mr. Darcy news he would surely be wanting from his aunt, but what was he to do now?

Cousin Mary looked up at him with a tentative smile. "It is not grand, but I am sure you will find something in Meryton to your liking. Is there any place in particular you would like to see? I am sure Lady Catherine would approve of your insights on our town, especially as you may have great influence over this area one day."

Her words took a moment to sink in, but once they did, Collins felt the smile growing on his face. "Why yes, I am certain you are correct. I had not thought of it that way."

Her smile was much less tentative this time.

"Come. I will show you the general layout of the town, and then perhaps you would like to accompany me to my favorite shop."

*

"We needn't hurry, Mr. Bingley. I doubt we can catch them, and I know their intended destination."

Bingley jumped a little, for all that Miss Bennet's voice was soft, serene. Recovering himself, he smiled and slowed his stride. "I am not intending to catch up to them. It's hard enough to keep up with Darcy when we start at the same time, and given where they are now, your sister must be able to set a similar pace. I only wished to put a bit of distance between ourselves and the rest of the party."

Miss Bennet smiled, and Bingley nearly forgot their topic of conversation. "Lizzy has always been a great walker. Lydia is the only one who can keep up with her when Lizzy decides she wants to move. It sounds like she is a good match for your friend."

The phrase gave Bingley an entry to the topic he had wished to discuss. "Do you—are you aware—"

"Of their acquaintance?" At Bingley's nod, she added quietly, "You mean, their *prior* acquaintance?"

"Yes, that." He too kept his voice down, conscious of the others around them on the streets. "From what Miss Lydia said, I could not be sure that you would. Darcy told me the basic overview while you were at Netherfield. I am glad he did—I was beginning to worry the man was sick! I have never seen him so relaxed and genial around a lady, perhaps not even excepting his sister."

Another smile, another flutter in his heart. "I do not pretend to know all the details, as I never visited Pemberley with Lizzy and Papa, but I know that she considered him a good friend for years, and it seems that he considered her the same. Any time the Lucas boys vexed her, Lizzy's response was always along the lines of—" Miss Bennet's cheeks colored, and she hesitated a moment before continuing—"'Will would never do that.'"

Bingley snorted, then stopped. "Wait. She calls him Will?"

Miss Bennet looked apprehensive. "As a child, yes. I haven't heard her refer to him in that way, well, since you arrived in Hertfordshire."

"No, you mistake me. The only other person I've ever heard use that name is Miss Darcy, and even she doesn't use it often. Darcy doesn't care for nicknames and he doesn't answer to them."

Miss Bennet's shoulders raised in a shrug. "All I can say is that Lizzy was quite young when they met, and she hasn't seen him for the past five years. I suppose it is natural that some of the childhood habits and interactions would carry over." But she didn't sound certain. "Is it true—I don't mean to pry—is Mr. Darcy truly engaged to his cousin?"

How sweet, to be worried for her sister, and interesting to know that she thought that might be a concern for Miss Elizabeth! "I do not know the particulars, but from what Darcy has said, it is a match only his aunt desires. He very rarely speaks of Miss de Bourgh, and I have heard his other cousins tease him about finding a wife. If he were engaged, I cannot imagine they would do such a thing, and they would know."

Relief brought a different kind of sweetness to her face. Cognizant of the increased traffic around them and far more interested in the lady beside him than he was in her sister, Bingley slowed even further. "I doubt our quarry shall be leaving the bookshop anytime soon, Miss Bennet, and I would not wish to see you overexert yourself so soon after being ill. What say you to stopping at the confectioners?"

*

Elizabeth stood at the door to her father's study, feeling weary. She had so wished to keep everything simple, to protect her friendship with Will, that she had immediately managed to make the situation far more complicated than it ought to have been. Even so, they could have muddled through well enough.

Wickham changed the equation. He'd always

been a wild card, unconcerned about anyone other than himself and always looking for a lark. He wasn't very different from Lydia in that way. At one time, she may have been able to convince him it was a game to fool everyone in Meryton, a fun ruse. He was clever enough to pull it off. But Wickham who felt himself ill-used, who still wished for the support old Mr. Darcy had rescinded and blamed Elizabeth for its loss —that was a dangerous foe indeed. Cleverness could easily be turned to mischief, and the glint in Wickham's eyes as he commented on how *revealing* her opinion of the regiment could be made Elizabeth think his revenge may be paid for with her reputation. If nothing else, she was guaranteed several uncomfortable interactions.

"Lizzy, is that you?" Mr. Bennet called.

She braced herself before pushing the door open and stepping into the room.

"Lizzy?" Her father set down his book and stood. "What has happened?" Heavens, she must look a fright to get that sort of response from him.

Elizabeth took a deep breath and forced herself to think rationally. Nothing was certain, and she wasn't fifteen anymore. Freezing in fear would not help the situation.

"We encountered someone in town this morning," she said. "A new lieutenant, just arrived to join the militia here. And yes, this time it is who you think."

*

It was with a great deal of apprehension that Elizabeth joined her sisters the following evening at a card party put on by their aunt and uncle Philips. Mrs. Philips, much like her sister Mrs. Bennet, loved to entertain and thought no man more handsome than one in a uniform. And while Mr. Bennet had promised to ensure that no officers were allowed at Longbourn, no such restrictions existed at the Philips residence in Meryton.

She had almost decided not to go, but it was far easier to gossip about someone not present, and Elizabeth knew herself well enough—if she was forced to imagine everything that *might* be happening while she waited at home for a report, she really would make herself sick. No, far better to go and face whatever her fate was to be.

They were welcomed in with a great deal of excitement. Clearly Kitty and Lydia had already made themselves popular with the regiment, and Elizabeth watched with amusement as Mary and Mr. Collins made matching expressions of disdain as the younger girls returned the effusive greetings. They disappeared into the throng already laughing, leaving the other four to enter at a far more sedate pace.

It took very little time to note that Mr. Wickham—Lieutenant Wickham, rather, for the red uniform was hard to ignore—was the favorite amongst the ladies of the group. Multiple pairs of female eyes followed him as he made his way through the group, and Elizabeth took in the jealousy on several faces when he made his stop by the group contaning her youngest sisters. Before long they were both hanging on his every word, and Elizabeth had to wonder if she would have been just like them, had she not had the benefit of knowing what lay under his charming façade. It was just one more uncomfortable thought in an evening full of them, but she did not like it all the same.

As time passed, however, she began to relax ever so slightly. Mr. Wickham did not appear to be intent on calling her out; he avoided her as much as she did him. Perhaps the absence of Mr. Darcy was what did the trick. She had never forgotten the strange sensation of being stuck between the gentlemen in a struggle she did not fully understand and wanted no part of.

It came as a shock, then, when he sat down between Elizabeth and Lydia at the table they had joined for a game. For once, Elizabeth would have been happy to let her youngest sister monopolize the conversation, but it was not to be.

"I ought to thank you for making my choice of seat so easy," Mr. Wickham said with a smile to Lydia. "It is not often a gentleman can claim a place between two beauties with such ease. Should I expect one of your local gentlemen to come attempt to scare me off?"

Lydia scoffed. "Our local gentlemen are nothing to the officers of the regiment! All of the interesting ones have married or left, anyhow. I can't blame them for going somewhere more exciting, but I do wish I could do the same."

"And the other newcomers, that I met yesterday? Are they not to your liking?"

"Mr. Bingley is to host a ball and that is delightful! But he only looks at Jane, and it is so tiresome hearing how beautiful she is. She may be beautiful, but I think that *I* shall be the first of us to marry, because I know how to have fun."

"Lydia!" Elizabeth admonished.

"You know it's true, Lizzy. You have been compared to her the most, I would expect you to agree. But then, you're just as boring as she is. I suppose you think stuffy Mr. Darcy is good company."

It was the exact topic Elizabeth had hoped to avoid, but there was nothing for it now. "I enjoy speaking with people who have new and different ideas," she said. "Not every conversation needs to be about bonnets and lace."

Lydia glared at her. "You think you're so perfect, Lizzy, but you're not any better than the rest of us. You and Jane can stay proper and boring forever for all I care. Just ask Charlotte Lucas what happens to girls like that."

It was a low blow, and Elizabeth saw her sister

realize it even as the words left her mouth. But Lydia was not the type to back down, especially not in front of a gentleman she wanted to impress. She cast about for something to say, something to bring the conversation back into safe territory.

Mr. Wickham seized the opportunity first. "It can be hard, can it not, to live with someone who always seems to do the correct thing. It is a struggle I lived with for most of my life. Even when you know they are not really perfect, and perhaps even have greater sins than you, the constant comparison from others is grating. No one should ever claim to be perfect."

Elizabeth opened her mouth to decry any such notion—heavens, she'd never once thought herself to be perfect—but Wickham and Lydia were no longer paying any sort of attention to her. Lydia's eyes glowed with the adoration of a teenage girl who had been made to feel important, and Elizabeth knew that anything she said now would just be further twisted against her. So she sat quietly, all interest in lottery tickets long gone, and wondered if it was only Lydia that Mr. Wickham intended to turn against her, or if this was just the beginning of his plan.

*

"Sophia! I did not expect to see you here!"

The Countess of Huntingdon, otherwise

known as his little sister, looked up from the letter in her hand and smiled, standing to greet him. "Hello, Richard. It is good to see you back from the continent in one piece, and earlier than planned, too! Do tell me you are done with battle for some time?"

He made a face and nodded her back into her chair. "I am free from Boney for the next few months, but there is another battle to be waged. I just had a letter from Darcy—you will never guess who he has encountered."

"Elizabeth Bennet," Sophia said promptly. "I correspond with both of them, and letters travel much faster when one does not have to be tracked down at a war office or military encampment."

Richard snorted and gave her a nod, ceding the point. "Do you know who else is there? I imagine it is a new occurrence, for I have just received this. No? George Wickham."

Sophia sprung up from her chair again, staring at him. "No."

"Yes. Apparently he has enlisted in the militia and is stationed in Meryton, only a mile from Longbourn."

She began to pace, chewing on her lip. "Is it by design? Or simply horrible luck for Lizzy?"

"That is one of the things I mean to find out, for I do not trust our cousin to handle this any better now than Uncle George did five years ago. You will have heard that he is visiting Bingley?

There is to be a ball next week, with the militia in attendance. Darcy mentioned it with even more than his usual annoyance. Apparently Elizabeth means to attend, even though they both worry that Wickham is up to some trick. I will send Bingley a note expressing my desire to surprise my cousin, and use that for my excuse."

Sophia laughed. "You can hardly show up uninvited to someone else's house *and* ball."

"Ah, but I can and I will, with not a whit of shame. Tell me, are you jealous?"

"Of course I am jealous! I have not seen Elizabeth in half a decade, *and* you shall get to meet all of her sisters at last."

"And perhaps pummel Wickham, not that you would care to do such a thing."

"Oh, I would like to do that very much. I am, however, wise enough to realize that sort of retribution is better left to you." She pursed her lips. "Do they fear that Wickham means to harm Lizzy physically, or by attacking her reputation? I could see either, from him."

Richard had wondered that as well. "I think it more likely that he will attack her reputation, especially since Darcy and Elizabeth have kept their prior acquaintance hidden. Had you heard that bit of utter baloney?"

His sister sighed. "Lizzy's last letter mentioned it. I understand her reaction in the moment, but it does make the situation more tenuous. Wickham was always good at twisting the truth of a situation around to make it suit his side of the story."

"I agree. My guess is he will try to ruin both of them in one fell swoop, and while Darcy can leave at any time, Elizabeth and her sisters don't have that luxury."

"Which means he won't leave her." She tilted her head. "She could always come here, you know. If a tactical retreat is the best option, I would be delighted to host her for the little season, or however long is required. You know Papa wouldn't mind."

Richard made a face. "Let us hope it doesn't come to that. But if scandal is imminent, that is far from the worst idea I have ever heard."

Chapter Sixteen

The next few days passed quietly, marked only by a brief visit from the Bingley sisters, then faded into what seemed to be endless rain. Lydia and Kitty spent much of their time bemoaning that they were kept from the officers, and the officers from Longbourn. Elizabeth, however, found herself far more interested in the middle Bennet sister.

To Elizabeth's perpetual shock, Mrs. Bennet seemed to have discerned that Mary was the one of her daughters best suited to be a parson's wife, not to mention perhaps the only daughter that might accept Mr. Collins. And Mary, without altering too drastically from her usually reserved self, clearly relished in the attention.

"I would disagree with you, Mr. Collins, on the idea that a proper lady must be easily led," Elizabeth overheard her sister say as she passed by the pair one day. "For what would become of such a woman, if she encountered a man who harbored ill-intent? Why, she would allow herself to be led into sin by that logic. No, I think it far better that a lady is resolute and unbending in her morals, especially if she is to be a mother and a leader in a community. You would not want your own children reared by someone lacking conviction, would you?"

Elizabeth promptly picked up a book and buried her nose in it. Mary's point was valid and Elizabeth could not find anything with which to disagree, but the tone! The looks that both Mary and Mr. Collins subtly sent Lydia, who sat across the room from them picking apart a bonnet and happily unaware that she was the subject of moral scrutiny! It was too much. She clenched her teeth together and refused to laugh. Lydia had remained stand-offish since the conversation with Mr. Wickham at the card party. Seeming to laugh at her would do no good at all, and neither did Elizabeth wish to draw Mr. Collins' attention.

It was only that night, preparing for bed, that Elizabeth realized Mr. Collins had shifted his opinion and agreed with Mary. It was not entirely unexpected, given his obvious deference to the female Lady Catherine de Bourgh, but it was a good sign all the same. Perhaps Mary would end up happy as Mrs. Collins, even if Mr. Collins was the last man on earth that Elizabeth could see herself marrying. She may never understand their relationship. But it was good to see Mary receiving attention from someone who could appreciate her for who she was.

*

"My dear Mr. Bennet, I do not know how this came to pass, but you have been entirely correct regarding Mr. Collins and Mary. Why, he has convinced her to dance at the ball, and indicated to me that he means to approach her for a private audience before he must return to Kent. Oh, Mr. Bennet!"

Bennet looked up from his newspaper and allowed himself a small smile at his wife's exuberance. "And Mary, my dear? Does she appear to enjoy his attentions?"

Mrs. Bennet seemed momentarily confused. "Why yes, she does, although she has not done any of the things I recommended to secure him. And that is the strange part, for Mr. Collins seems quite happy with her despite the lack."

Now he really had to fight back his smile. "Mr. Collins and I are rather different creatures, wouldn't you say? I suppose it stands to reason that we would look for different types of women to be our wives."

She frowned. "Yes, I suppose you are correct. I still cannot fathom—but as long as he makes her an offer and she accepts, I shall have no complaints. You do mean to give your blessing, do you not?"

"As long as Mary wishes to accept him, I will not withhold my permission." He hesitated, then pushed ahead. This had needed to be said since Elizabeth appeared at his door with fear in her eyes, and his wife was in a conciliatory mood just now. "Mrs. Bennet, as I have been correct on this matter, I request you hear me out on one other thing."

"Yes?"

"The officers, my dear. I know very well that Kitty and Lydia are young and mean no harm, but they are also naïve and not all officers are gentlemen. I will not forbid the girls from interacting with them, but neither will I have them invited to my house. Do not test me on that, Mrs. Bennet, for I shall throw them out if they turn up here."

She opened her mouth, excitement over Mary forgotten. He held up a hand.

"It is for our girls that I am doing this. I do not like to part with Mary, but I will do so because I know that she goes to a good, comfortable home and will one day live in this estate again. Jane, too, might quit our family sphere to live at Netherfield. An officer, if he is even a gentleman, is almost always a younger son. He has no estate and often little or no money. Can you see Lydia following the drum, cooking and cleaning for a husband with no servants to help her? Why, it would be cruel to waste one of our girls in such a way."

Mrs. Bennet stood frozen, clearly considering his words. Bennet remained silent;

contemplation was not a natural state for his wife, and he meant to give her plenty of time. At last, she drew a long breath and let it out again. "I do not like it, Mr. Bennet. Oh, I recall very well what it is to be young and delighted by a gentleman in regimentals! But I do agree, an officer would never do for Lydia or Kitty, not when Jane's marriage might throw them in the way of much finer gentlemen. That would be just the thing. Yes, I believe I shall tell Lydia she is to hold out for a lord at the very least. Lady Lydia, I can hear it now!"

He didn't bother to correct her—if any of their daughters ever achieved such a title, they would be called by their husband's title, not their first name. But Mrs. Bennet was happy as she bustled out, and she had agreed.

"Are you happy yet?" Bennet asked the empty air after the door had thumped shut behind his wife.

George Darcy didn't respond, which was likely for the best. If ghosts began to talk on the same day that Mrs. Bennet was reasonable, Bennet wasn't sure what he would be forced to think.

*

"Lizzy?"

Elizabeth looked up and smiled at Jane. "Come in, Jane."

Jane closed the door behind her softly and crossed the room to sit next to Elizabeth on her window seat. It was a wonderful location, and Elizabeth's favorite place in the house to read, but just now it was too dark to do so. Instead, Elizabeth had been staring out onto the grounds, mind drifting.

For a moment Jane sat silently, both of them watching barely-discernible tree branches toss in the rain. Then Jane said, "Lizzy, are you well?"

Elizabeth sat up straighter, shocked. "What do you mean?"

Jane gave her the look of an older sister who knows better. "You have been, ah, discombobulated since Mr. Darcy arrived in Hertfordshire, which is not that much of a surprise. I cannot begin to imagine your shock, and I know very well that keeping your acquaintance with him from Mama has caused you stress. But Lizzy, I am not blind. What happened that day we encountered the gentlemen in Meryton? With the newcomer that Mr. Darcy already knew? It does not seem a stretch to think you knew him previously as well."

Frowning at her sister, Elizabeth forced herself to remain relaxed, or at least to appear relaxed. "That was nearly a week ago, Jane."

"Yes, and you have not seemed yourself since then. I know it is hard for you to be trapped inside without your daily walks, especially with Mr. Collins here. At first I did not want to bring it up, because it was clearly not a pleasant encounter for you, and I thought that you would find me if it was something you wanted to discuss. But Lizzy, I have been worried and I can't stop thinking about it. Darcy seemed intent on getting you away, and you clung to him. I know there are no gentlemen here you have ever esteemed, but before that day, I could not even imagine you acting as you did. It is always you putting yourself in front of the rest of us."

Elizabeth turned her gaze back to the stormy night outside. What to tell Jane? Anything less than the truth would be disingenuous, and yet how could she even begin?

"His name is George Wickham," she managed at last, swallowing hard around the lump that threatened to close up her throat. Lord, but she never wished to think of this again, let alone speak of it. "He grew up at Pemberley; his father was old Mr. Darcy's steward."

"Were you friends with him as well, once?"

"No, I cannot say we ever were. He thought I was too young and—well, looking back at it now, I was a competitor for Mr. Darcy's affection. Old Mr. Darcy, that is. Will never liked him any more than I did, at least not while I knew them. I have heard they were good friends when they were small."

"Surely Mr. Darcy's affection lay first and foremost with his own children!"

Elizabeth felt the corner of her mouth pull up. "Will and Georgiana have always been reserved

—you've seen what he is like. Their father loved them, but he enjoyed the company of more energetic people. George was always good at making him smile or laugh."

"And you always took it as a challenge to charm everyone you met," Jane said, smiling.

You're just like me.

Was she really? On some level, was she like George Wickham, charming people who ought to have been giving their attention and affection to someone who deserved it more? Would she be better off retreating now, before she could cause any more harm?

No. No, no, no, no, no. She couldn't think like that. It led to places that Elizabeth did not care to remember and was determined not to visit again. Oh, if only Will was here!

But he was not, and Jane was still looking at her, concerned once again. Elizabeth took a deep breath and steeled herself.

"When I was fifteen, that last summer I visited Pemberley, George tried to elope with me. I think it entirely possible he would have attempted to kidnap me, when I wouldn't agree to go with him. Will found us in the midst of—everything, and got me away. It wasn't the only immoral thing George had done, but it was the first time old Mr. Darcy believed it. I was not a servant, and I was—it was apparent that harm had been intended. Will used to despair—but that is neither here nor there. Mr. Darcy ordered him to leave Pemberley. Knowing George as I do—did—I am almost certain he blames me for his change in fortune."

She turned back to her sister at last to find Jane white-faced. "Oh, Lizzy," she whispered, reaching out a gentle hand. "I knew as soon as I saw your face that day that something was horribly wrong, but even with how Mr. Darcy reacted, I wouldn't have guessed anything like that."

Elizabeth shrugged. "You had no reason to suspect. I certainly never spoke of it, and neither did Papa."

Jane looked up sharply at that. "Papa knows what happened?"

"Yes, and he knows Mr. Wickham is here. We discussed it, after that encounter."

Jane bit her lip again, only this time it appeared to be thoughtful, not hesitant. "I suppose that is why I overheard Mama telling Lydia that she mustn't put too much stock in the officers, for none of them besides Colonel Forster could afford to keep her in style, and he is already married. It is such a marked difference from her prior excitement I can only imagine Papa's influence is involved."

"Mama said that?"

"Yes. Although she also said it was still perfectly acceptable to flirt with them, if Lydia felt she needed the practice, so she has not changed in essentials."

Elizabeth huffed. "No, I suppose that would be

214

too much to ask. Still, it is good that she has given them any sort of boundary. I just hope it is enough. Mr. Wickham has already convinced Lydia to be mad at me, at the card party. If she thought she was being kept from having fun because of me, it would just make matters worse."

"Oh Lizzy, no wonder you have not seemed like yourself. What does Papa mean to do? Does he think you are in any danger?"

"From how Mr. Wickham behaved at the party, I am worried he means to turn the entire town against me before anyone is the wiser. But there is little we can do. Any sort of pre-emptive story telling would hurt my reputation more than his, especially since I was so idiotic about my friendship with Mr. Darcy. Don't look at me like that, Jane, it's nothing but the truth. And there is the chance that he will do nothing. He did mention that he had changed, in our first encounter. Perhaps he regrets how he acted." She didn't think it likely, but it was a possibility.

Elizabeth expected Jane to agree whole-heartedly with this idea, for her sister preferred to think the best of everyone. To her surprise, Jane said only, "I shall pay attention and let you know if I hear anything of note." She paused, then continued. "I do not wish to worry you more, but something else happened that day. After you left with Mr. Darcy, Mr. Collins mentioned that he is engaged to his cousin, a

Miss Anne de Bourgh. Of course, I understand much better now why he took you away so swiftly, but at the time our cousin's concern did seem reasonable if Mr. Darcy is promised to another."

The mounting tension faded, and Elizabeth allowed herself a laugh. "If he is, it is a marked change from their prior relationship, and Sophie never mentioned it."

"Your friend in town. I had not realized, or perhaps forgotten, that she is connected to Mr. Darcy."

"She is his cousin, and cousin to Anne de Bourgh as much as he is. I will say, "I appreciate that there is at least one person involved in all of this that I can call the same name that I used when we were children!"

"Such are the joys of growing up. And speaking of which, do you mean to dance with Mr. Darcy at the ball, seeing how you are no longer children?"

"Yes, just as I will dance with a great many friends and acquaintances I grew up with," Elizabeth replied tartly. He had requested the supper set before leaving her company the same day they saw Mr. Wickham, but Jane didn't need to know that just yet. "Be careful, Jane, or I shall begin to call you Mama."

"Don't be rude, Lizzy. Besides, Mama never would have asked. She would have insisted you dance." She paused, then smiled. "All the same, I am glad you are to dance with him."

It was the evening before the ball, and Caroline was trying to hide her annoyance. Mr. Darcy had yet to request a single set, or even to comment on the work she had done in the past week. Charles, at least, had complimented her on the work that had been done in so short a time—considerate of him, not that he had given her a choice in the matter. Did men really have no idea what it took to put on an event?

Watching her brother from the corner of her eye, Caroline determined that at least in his case, the answer was *no*. For all his love of socializing, Charles wouldn't have the first idea how to host a ball without her help.

Unfortunately, while her brother was clearly happy about the event tomorrow, Mr. Darcy was more of a mind with Caroline. There was no other word for it: he was currently brooding in the corner, glaring at the book in his hand with an intensity Caroline doubted that the volume deserved. While she could hardly blame him— she didn't want to socialize with the locals, either —it was making it hard for her to show off how well she had done at planning the last-minute ball and win his approval.

"I do wish you hadn't invited the officers, Bingley," Mr. Darcy said out of nowhere. So he was *thinking* about the ball, at least!

Charles had been staring into space, but

he looked up at his friend's voice. "I could hardly exclude them, Darcy. It would have been inordinately rude, not to mention the fact that there are so few gentlemen here without them. I know you do not care for dancing, but that is the point of a ball, and it is made far easier when there is a similar number of each sex."

Mr. Darcy huffed, and Caroline had just drawn breath to add her own thoughts when she was stopped by a commotion in the hallway.

"Charles, what on earth?" Louisa said, exchanging a look with Caroline, who rolled her eyes. Country servants left so much to be desired.

But her brother was grinning. "Apologies for keeping secrets, but I would wager that one of our guests for the ball has arrived. I was asked to keep this a surprise, and I did owe the gentleman a favor. I don't believe you will have any objections to *this* officer, Darcy."

Mr. Darcy stood at the comment, eyes fixed on the door with an intensity that made Caroline wonder just who he expected to step through it.

The gentleman who appeared was not one she had met before, or at least not one she remembered. Charles clearly knew him well, given the greeting they exchanged. "Bingley, I appreciate your participation in my surprise, and for hosting me," the gentleman said once the basics had been covered.

"Of course, of course. As many times as Darcy has hosted me, it is a pleasure to be able to return the favor to his family. But I don't believe you have met *my* family, unless you know Hurst? No?" Charles turned to the rest of the group. "May I introduce my elder sister and her husband, Mr. and Mrs. Hurst. And Miss Bingley, my younger sister. This is the Honorable Colonel Fitzwilliam, Darcy's cousin."

So they were to host the son of an earl. Caroline felt a thrill at the realization even as she determined that since he was a colonel rather than a viscount, it was only the younger son. Still, that was an achievement she had not been able to boast of before! Thank goodness she had decided to put her best work into the ball for Mr. Darcy rather than doing the bare minimum, as she had been so very tempted to do when Charles first told her of his plan. Why, she would melt through the floor if the son of an earl were treated to anything less than her best efforts, especially since he was related to Mr. Darcy.

But how that gentleman felt about his cousin's presence was far from certain. He had not moved from his spot, and after making an amiable greeting, the colonel pivoted to face Mr. Darcy, the expression on his face something Caroline couldn't quite name.

"What are you doing here, Richard?"

The colonel did not shrink from the stern tone as Caroline would have done. "Why, I could not resist surprising you after what you said in your last letter, especially since I find myself at leisure for the next few weeks. Bingley here was good enough to take pity on me when I wrote with the request."

"I dislike your meddling."

The colonel raised his shoulders in a shrug, the gesture reminiscent of someone Caroline could not recall, clearly still unconcerned at the hostility. "Perhaps I'm not only here for you. I have just returned from France, after all. Do you mean to turn away a weary soldier looking to escape the ruckus of town?"

From her angle, Caroline could see Mr. Darcy's expression clearly as his face flushed. Something like resignation passed over his face, and he sighed. "Apologies, Richard. You are correct, of course. And I *am* glad to see you. I just—" he stopped, shaking his head.

"Yes, I'm aware," the colonel said. He turned away decisively, eyes landing on Caroline. "Do I understand correctly that you are responsible for pulling together the ball? I must reserve a set before they are all gone, if you would be so kind as to grant me one."

It was not Mr. Darcy, Caroline thought as she graciously agreed to his request, but it was the son of an Earl. Perhaps the evening would not be a complete disaster.

Chapter Seventeen

S he doesn't know, does she?"

"No, and you aren't going to tell her."

Richard laughed, leaning back against the wall. "Oh, I don't plan on it. I just hope I'm close enough to see her face."

Darcy glanced over at where Caroline Bingley stood, reciting a list of final—and completely unnecessary—instructions to the housekeeper. Mrs. Nicholls undoubtedly knew the plan for the evening better than Miss Bingley did.

"Elizabeth didn't tell anyone for a reason, you know."

"Yes, and I still think it was one of her worse tactical moves. From what you've said, she probably agrees with me. Perhaps she will be glad to be done with the pretense."

Sighing, Darcy admitted to himself that his cousin was most likely correct. Still, he couldn't help but feel uneasy, as if revealing their deeper acquaintance would rob him of something precious, something vital. Is that how Elizabeth had felt when she made her snap decision the night of the assembly? If so, he understood far better now.

"Do you think Wickham will attend?" he asked aloud.

The expression on the colonel's face turned somewhere between vicious and gleeful. "I would be delighted to see our old friend. Seeing how he has always been the spineless type, however, I'm not sure I believe he will appear."

"Mr. Darcy, Colonel, will you be joining us at the door?" Miss Bingley asked, turning away from Mrs. Nicholls at last.

"We would never dream of taking attention away from you in such a manner," the colonel exclaimed, making the comment sound like a grand concession. Darcy repressed the urge to shake his head. He could have said the exact same thing and managed to offend everyone within earshot. Richard came off as the considerate son of an earl, and still weaseled his way out of a duty he didn't wish to perform.

From Miss Bingley's expression, Darcy was certain she had intended for him at least to join them at the entry, but Richard's phrasing had not left room for disagreement. Still, their hostess reached out a hand, though she stopped short of touching the colonel's arm.

"Colonel Fitzwilliam, I feel I must warn you, the sophistication in this neighborhood is not what you are accustomed to. Some of the locals are sweet, really, and I will grant you that the eldest Miss Bennet is truly a pretty girl, but I beg you not to hold high hopes for polished society."

Richard smiled the same way he did when indulging their aunt, Lady Catherine de Bourgh, in one of her tirades. "Ah, but I am nothing more than a weary soldier happy to be back on English soil. Besides, when one attends a country ball, Miss Bingley, one expects local gentry. As long as no one tries to shoot me or spills too much punch on me, I am sure I will enjoy my evening." He looked sideways at Darcy. "You must introduce me to this Miss Bennet. I have heard her mentioned before, and am quite anxious to see her for myself, assuming that Bingley does not protest too much."

Bingley's face lit up, Miss Bingley scowled before checking herself, and Richard calmly turned on his heel and led them away down the corridor.

One problem managed. Now they just had to see if Wickham would show up—and what mischief he intended to cause if he did.

*

Of course they were late. Usually when something like this happened, it could be attributed directly to Lydia or Mrs. Bennet, but this evening had brought a delay of entirely new origins. Mr. Collins, attempting to elegantly enter the carriage instead of hanging onto the handle like any normal gentleman of short stature and questionable physicality, had slipped and landed directly in the puddle left from the last several days of rain. He would not hear of them leaving without him, and Mrs. Bennet, keen on keeping her likely son-in-law and future head of household happy, agreed.

And so they waited in the carriage for him to change his outfit, touch up his hair, and perhaps have a deep conversation with his reflection in the mirror about the annoyance of puddles, if the time for his toilet was anything to go by. Poor Jane, promised to Mr. Bingley for the first, and not knowing if she would arrive in time to dance it!

At last their cousin heaved himself into the carriage and they all shuffled aside to make room for him, and then they were off. Jane held tight to Elizabeth's hand, face displaying none of the tension that her clenched fingers showed.

Through sheer luck, they made it into the ballroom just as the musicians were picking up their instruments to begin the dancing. Elizabeth had not promised her first dance to anyone, and knowing that Mr. Darcy had the supper set, she did not anticipate being asked. So her eyes were fixed on Jane and Mr. Bingley, both wearing equally relieved and happy faces, as the Bennet party entered. Then Mr. Collins tripped yet again, bowing to Mary—thank heavens she had avoided that chore!—and her attention was pulled away by him awkwardly righting himself.

"I do not see our friend," her father said in her ear, and Elizabeth felt herself relax as tension she had been forcing herself to ignore faded away. He could be hidden, of course, but perhaps she would be lucky this evening?

"But who is—*hmph*." Mr. Bennet snorted, although it was more of an amused sound than an annoyed one. "Perhaps that is why."

Slightly alarmed, Elizabeth caught the line of her father's gaze and turned in that direction. A tall man in regimentals was approaching them, and her heart leapt into her throat as she registered *soldier* and *Pemberley* before she met the gentleman's laughing eyes and realized just who stood before her.

"Might I request your hand for this dance, Miss Elizabeth?" Colonel Fitzwilliam asked, his voice strange in how familiar it was. "Hello, Mr. Bennet."

She placed her hand in his automatically, prior fear fading into a burst of excitement, "but you must confirm what I am to call you. It is Colonel Fitzwilliam now, is it not? One of Sophie's last letters said as much."

"Hello, young man," Mr. Bennet said. "I shall have to take Mr. Darcy to task for not warning us of your pending arrival."

"I am a colonel now, yes," Richard told Elizabeth, then gave Mr. Bennet a wolfish grin. "I didn't tell Darcy I was coming. He is rather put out with me; it has been great fun."

Mr. Bennet laughed, then his expression sobered. "Are you aware—" he paused.

"Yes, that is why I am here. So far he has not made an appearance."

"Good," Mr. Bennet said with a nod. "Now off with you both, before the dance is over. You must find me in the card room later."

The colonel agreed, then swept Elizabeth into the throng of dancers. "Did you really arrive without telling Mr. Darcy?" she asked.

"I did. You can imagine how much it frustrated him."

"Rich—Colonel!"

"If it makes it any better, I did tell Bingley. I didn't simply arrive and ask for a room. I believe he enjoyed Darcy's response as well."

Elizabeth bit her lip to hold back her laugh. Richard's grin grew larger, and Elizabeth couldn't help but think of the days when he was her partner in crime for their own tricks, causing mischief and teasing the quieter Darcy siblings into levity. The conversation turned to what they had done over the past five years, but the tone of the banter remained the same. As the set went on, Elizabeth recalled just why Richard had come to Hertfordshire, but she forced that thought away. George Wickham would *not* ruin her evening. Richard, Will, and her father were all present, and Richard had said that Wickham was not present. She knew him well enough to know that he had been thorough in that determination, so Elizabeth wrapped that knowledge around herself like a cloak and let herself dance as she hadn't since that last summer at Pemberley.

Before she knew it, the music was fading on their second dance, and the neat patterns fell apart as couples dispersed to find their next partners. Mr. Darcy came towards them, Miss Bingley on his arm and an exasperated expression on his face. She must have prevailed in pushing him to claim a set. Without meaning to, Elizabeth looked up and met Richard's eyes, biting back her grin.

Miss Bingley's nostrils flared, eyes darting between Elizabeth and the colonel, but she said nothing.

Mr. Bingley appeared from a different direction, Jane beside him. "I see you didn't waste any time finding a dance partner, Fitz," he said.

Colonel Fitzwilliam smiled. "With a lady like Miss Elizabeth before me, how could I resist? Do you mean to introduce me to *your* partner?" His eyes danced, and Elizabeth knew very well he had guessed Jane's identity.

Mr. Darcy huffed. Elizabeth resisted the urge to kick his foot.

"Colonel, this is Miss Bennet of Longbourn, Miss Elizabeth's elder sister. Miss Bennet, Colonel Fitzwilliam." Bingley turned slightly so he was facing Jane. "The colonel is Mr. Darcy's cousin and joined us just yesterday."

Jane curtsied; Richard bowed. "It is a pleasure to meet you, Colonel."

"And you as well, Miss Bennet. I have heard very much about you, and I can see now that none of it was exaggerated in the least."

Jane flushed.

"Is your next set open, Miss Bennet?" the colonel asked. Jane replied that it was, and they departed together into the reforming group on the floor. Elizabeth watched as Richard's dark head dipped towards her sister's golden one, saying something quietly. She caught Jane's surprised expression as she turned, which then flared into a smile. It seemed Richard had seen fit to say just who had provided his prior knowledge.

Mr. Bingley left the group as well to seek out a previously determined partner, Mr. Darcy gave Elizabeth another long-suffering look before turning to offer his arm to an approaching Mrs. Hurst, and Miss Bingley stalked off without saying a word.

Jane and Charlotte were both dancing, so Elizabeth stood alone on the side of the dance floor. As the first song of the set came to a close, she began to meander her way along the side of the floor in the general direction of the refreshments. People flashed by; Mr. Collins had apparently convinced Kitty to dance with him, and her pained expression was in direct contrast to Lydia's high spirits as she partnered one of the officers—Captain Denny, was it? Elizabeth didn't know. Her youngest sister caught her eye and wrinkled her nose before she was off and laughing again. Lydia, it seemed, was determined to hold a grudge even in the midst of the festivities.

And then, as the music faded, another gentleman in a red uniform stepped into her view.

"Miss Elizabeth, might I convince you to join me for the rest of the set?"

She locked her feet in place and looked up at Mr. Wickham. He was smiling; would anyone besides her notice the horrible glint in his eyes? She'd been tracking the Colonel and Mr. Darcy well enough to know that they were on the opposite end of the dance floor and even if they were not, what could they do?

What was she going to do?

"No," Elizabeth said quietly, coming to a decision. She would not let him bully her, not when he looked like that. Not when her nightmares from five years past had made a reappearance the night before. Mr. Darcy would not get his supper dance, but he would understand.

"You wound me, Miss Elizabeth," Wickham said, his voice far louder than hers. "Clearly it is not the uniform you object to, given your first partner. Is it that I am not the son of an earl?"

He'd timed it perfectly; his words rang out into the silence between sets and around them conversations died out as people turned to listen curiously.

"I do not feel like dancing right now, Lieutenant Wickham," she said, still quiet.

"You never did like to dance with me," he continued in that same voice. "Even as a girl, you clearly had your sights set higher than the son of a steward. Is that why you have no time for your old friend?"

"We have never been friends, Mr. Wickham," Elizabeth said, raising her voice as well. She would not be cowed. She wouldn't. "If you will excuse me, I mean to sit down. Unless you are planning on forcing me to dance?"

"So very proper." Wickham smiled at her, but there was nothing friendly in his expression. "You've convinced all these people you're an upstanding young lady. I wonder what they would say if they knew you and Mr. Darcy rode out privately, while you and your sister stayed at Netherfield? Or that you have known him far longer than the time he has been in Meryton. Tell me, did he convince his friend to come to this neighborhood on your suggestion? Did Miss Bennet decide that she needed a wealthy suitor, and Mr. Bingley fit the bill?"

Elizabeth had been mortified as he spoke about herself and Mr. Darcy, but Jane—to drag sweet, innocent Jane into this mess—her flushed face was no longer from embarrassment, but anger.

"Unlike you, Mr. Wickham, neither my sister nor I have ever attempted to entrap anyone. Mr. Darcy and I did not make a production of our prior acquaintance because neither of us cared for the additional attention. You know very well that my father is aware of the connection—do you think he would have condoned anything improper?"

Oh, would the musicians not begin the next song?

"I think Mr. Bennet would be delighted if he had a reason to visit Pemberley again. Perhaps he is in on your plan."

"Pemberley? Your father has been to Pemberley?"

Yes, *that* was clearly the important part of this conversation. "He has, Miss Bingley, as have I," Elizabeth said without looking away from Mr. Wickham. "I find it interesting, sir, that you accuse me of trying to entrap Mr. Darcy when it is you who is bringing to light these supposed transgressions, not I. One wonders what you mean by it."

"So then—you knew—you have known Mr. Darcy since before we arrived in Hertfordshire?" Miss Bingley stepped closer, voice shrill. Amusement flickered over Mr. Wickham's face. Had he chosen to bring this up by Miss Bingley, knowing she would fan the flames?

"I did," she answered as calmly as she could manage.

"But you said nothing. Why would you not claim a prior acquaintance? What did you mean to hide?"

Elizabeth turned to Miss Bingley at last. "Hide? I wished to hide nothing, Miss Bingley. As I reminded Mr. Wickham, my father is aware of our acquaintance; he and Mr. Darcy have met frequently during your stay in Meryton. My sister knows, and your brother was made aware as well; you might ask either of them. We simply did not *publicize* our friendship because we wished to avoid a scene very much like this one."

"So it's true?" a voice said in the crowd, and Elizabeth glanced sideways to see a wide-eyed Maria Lucas. "You and—and Mr. Darcy—you really have been keeping your relationship secret? Are you not ashamed?"

Elizabeth couldn't help but think the phrasing was odd, even as she fought to keep her composure.

"I'm not sure what I am supposed to be ashamed of," she managed.

"You do think you're always in the right," Miss Long said before Elizabeth could continue. "It's all very well to judge us, but what could perfect Miss Elizabeth ever do wrong? Of course you wouldn't feel shame for your actions! To ride out alone with a gentleman, indeed!"

"Fanny Gardiner always did think very highly

of herself," one of the older ladies said from the back of the crowd—for it was a crowd now, gathering around on all sides. Mrs. Goulding, perhaps? The world was beginning to spin around Elizabeth. "No shame at all when she decided she would be the next Mrs. Bennet. It's no surprise her girls would turn out the same. Just look, the only two eligible gentlemen to arrive in years, and you see who is primed to snap them up."

"Mr. Darcy and I are friends," Elizabeth said. This was ridiculous. She had to be dreaming; surely her long-term neighbors knew her better than this. "There is no snatching of any sort! That was the entire point of not publicizing our friendship."

For once, Miss Bingley appeared to be aligned with the locals. "I find it highly unlikely that a simple friendship would be covered up so well as this one seems to have been," she said. "The secret would hardly be worth keeping."

"What on earth is going on here?"

Richard's battlefield voice cut through the whispers and clammer like a knife. He stalked forward into the silence that followed, dancers and hangers-on alike scattering out of his way. Mr. Darcy followed in his wake, face like thunder. Wickham's face paled; clearly, he had not anticipated the colonel's presence any more than Elizabeth had.

"Take your jealous vitriol somewhere else,"

Richard told him in a conversational tone. "You are no longer welcome here."

"Who do you think you are?" someone in the crowd asked.

"I am a colonel in the regulars, the son of an earl, and have been a better fighter than George Wickham since we were both twelve years old—and he knows it," Richard said flatly. "I have also been acquainted with Miss Elizabeth for over a decade, as Mr. Bennet was friends with both my father and my uncle Darcy. My sister, the Countess of Huntingdon, counts her as a dear friend. I am extremely put out that she has been importuned in such a way. Is this a ballroom or a fish market?"

"Mr. Darcy—" Miss Bingley started, only to be stopped by a hand on her arm as Mr. Bingley held her firmly in place. For a moment, she was the recipient of glares from all three gentlemen.

Freed from the weight of Colonel Fitzwilliam's stare, Mr. Wickham took his chance to exit, hurrying through the crowd in the direction of the door. Mr. Bennet stepped into his place, face grave.

Her father surveyed the crowd quietly, and Elizabeth was reminded of being a small child facing her father's disappointment, waiting with ever-growing anxiety for him to proclaim her fate. If the shifting of those around them was any indication, she was not the only one.

"Come, Lizzy," he said after a long pause. "I

have no need for a community that will pick apart one of their own over the slander of a stranger."

One of his hands closed around her elbow, and Elizabeth let herself be steered out of the room, eyes locked straight ahead. She would not break, not here.

George Wickham *had* been clever, just as she'd feared he would be, and she knew exactly how he had done it. How easy had it been to charm the young ladies of the town, make them feel important under his attention, and then suggest how unfair it was that the Bennet girls seemed to enjoy perks not allotted to the rest of the ladies? He had given her a preview that evening with Lydia at the card party. Had he planned on Caroline Bingley's jealousy making a bigger scene, or was that simply her rotten luck? Elizabeth wasn't sure she would ever have an answer to that.

Sitting in the carriage opposite her father as it rolled back through the dark landscape, she felt the crushing isolation of being cast out by those who should have supported her as friends and neighbors, and knew that Mr. Wickham had planned his revenge well. But she was not naïve enough to think that was all he had intended.

They'll never truly care about you. If I loved Georgiana or Sophia, it wouldn't matter, even if they loved me back. We would never be allowed to wed. You can't dream of Fitz or Richard. You know that, right?

Whatever lies he may have told, Elizabeth knew that Wickham believed what he had told her on that awful day. So he had set her up to be compromised, linking her name with a man he believed would never offer for her, even if honor demanded it. She would either be cast out or ruined, her sisters along with her. Really, it was a masterful piece of work.

Elizabeth had no such doubts in Mr. Darcy's honor. He was the type to make whatever sort of noble sacrifice the situation required. The question was, would she let him?

Chapter Eighteen

Eight years. That's what Mr. Darcy had said tightly in the aftermath of the scene the evening before. Eight years of summering at Pemberley and shared childhood memories. Eight years of friendship with Mr. Darcy's favorite relatives, one of them the most admired and sought-after countesses of the *ton*. Eight years that Eliza Bennet had somehow convinced Mr. Darcy to conceal, for reasons completely beyond anything Caroline Bingley could imagine.

In a way, it was a relief to finally realize the hold that Eliza had over Mr. Darcy. There was nothing new or alluring about her; in fact, she was decidedly *not* new. And Mr. Darcy was a man of habit, Caroline had long ago noticed that. He was not someone forever seeking out new places and friends and experiences, not like her capricious brother. Eliza's appeal was therefore in her familiarity, perhaps with a bit of nostalgia, not because she was anything special.

She *certainly* wasn't anything special.

And if there was nothing special about Eliza Bennet—*obviously*—then that meant Caroline now had insight into Mr. Darcy she hadn't had before. All those times he had defended the Bennets or seemed not to notice behavior Caroline found intolerable, each instance he had seemed comfortable with Eliza in a way he never did with Caroline herself, it was simply a matter of time. Her presence and behavior were familiar to him, and it was clear that Mr. Darcy valued familiarity.

Caroline could be *very* familiar. It would not do to come on too strong, of course. She had known him for nearly two years now and he still held himself aloof, but much of that time had not been while they were staying at the same estate, in regular company. A long game must still be planned and played, but Caroline must reconsider the rules she had previously set. She must determine how best she could become *familiar*.

She would start today, when everyone would be pleasantly tired after the ball and inclined to lounge about the house chatting. The ball really had been a success after they had cleared up the unpleasant scene; perhaps she could elicit a compliment from the colonel in front of Mr. Darcy. If nothing else, bettering their acquaintance was sure to pay off. Caroline could see all of it so clearly, she had to keep herself from giving a childish twirl in front of her mirror in excitement and anticipation.

But when Caroline finished her toilette and made her way downstairs to find the rest of the Netherfield party, similarly late in rising, both Mr. Darcy and his cousin were gone.

*

Mr. Bennet leaned back in his chair and closed his eyes, sighing. Despite the late night the day before, Mr. Darcy and Colonel Fitzwilliam had appeared on his doorstep before most of the household was out of bed. Luckily, that meant that Mrs. Bennet and Mr. Collins had remained unaware of their visit. Mr. Bennet had no desire to experience more of the hysterics his wife had displayed upon her return to Longbourn.

The success of their planning was less certain. By the time they concluded the discussion, only two things had been decided: first, that Elizabeth would accept Sophia's invitation to join her in London, and second, that Mr. Darcy and the colonel would remain here to monitor the situation and see if Wickham could be dealt with for good.

"Is that what you would have done?" Mr. Bennet asked the empty room.

Like usual, no one answered. Instead, Mr. Bennet thought once more of the look on his daughter's face when the colonel had first suggested Elizabeth leave the area for a time. She hadn't wanted to go, that was clear to all of them in the room. It was not in Elizabeth's nature to run from anything. Then Mr. Darcy had leaned forward in his seat and asked her, "And if Mr. Wickham decides he isn't satisfied with harming your reputation? If he comes after you directly? Are you prepared for that eventuality, and to limit all of your activities so that he has no opportunity to do you harm? Do you *wish* to stay here, when your neighbors were so lacking in their support?" The slow draining of Elizabeth's defiant resistance to the idea would stay with Mr. Bennet for longer than he cared to consider.

And so his daughter had retired to her room to pack, while the visitors quietly took their leave and promised to return the following day. Mr. Bennet had been glad to see them go, relieved to regain the usual silence of his study. Now, however, he almost wished they were still there. It was much easier to resist the urge to speak to ghosts when one had living visitors.

A sudden shriek outside the room roused Mr. Bennet from his reverie, and he frowned at the door. It was early, surely his wife was not—

The door opened without a knock and Mrs. Bennet bustled in, her cheeks flushed and eyes alight. "Mr. Bennet, Mr. Bennet, it is the best of news! Such a thing for us, for our girls!"

Mr. Bennet raised an eyebrow. At least she was not babbling about Elizabeth as she had the night before. "I can celebrate better if I know what this news is, my dear."

"Oh! Mr. Bennet! Mr. Collins has proposed, and our Mary has accepted him. Only think, she shall be mistress of Longbourn after her mother, as must be right! We shall not need to fear the hedgerows after all. Oh! I shall go distracted!"

Mr. Bennet looked past his wife to find Mr. Collins—who rightfully should have made the first appearance—standing in the doorway. Mary stood hesitantly behind him, looking mildly annoyed but not in distress. Likely she also thought her mother should have remained in the sitting room, but it appeared that Mrs. Bennet's statement was correct. Mary had accepted Mr. Collins' proposal, not been coerced into it.

"Now, Mrs. Bennet, a time like this calls for celebration. Why don't you leave me to my part of this business, and go see Hill about cakes or the like?"

Her fluttering paused for a moment, and his wife pulled herself up straight. Then she was in motion again, hurrying back out of the room past the waiting young people. "Why yes, you are absolutely correct, Mr. Bennet. Cakes would be just the thing. Hill? Hill!"

The shouts faded off down the corridor, and Mr. Bennet nodded at Mary to close the door behind herself. "Well then, I suppose I know what this is about," he said once it was just the three of them. "Mary, you have accepted Mr. Collins' hand?"

"She has, and I am—"

Mr. Bennet silenced his cousin with a look he had rare occasion to produce, then turned his eyes back to his daughter. "It is a father's prerogative to ensure his daughter is happy with her choice," he said sternly, noting from the corner of his eye that Collins squirmed just a little. "Perhaps one day you will have cause to understand."

Mr. Collins drew breath, but Mary said quickly, "Yes, Papa, he has proposed and I have accepted his hand. I believe I shall be quite satisfied as a parson's wife, and of course later at Longbourn, although I do hope that is a long time in the future."

Touched at her clear sincerity, Mr. Bennet smiled fondly at his middle daughter. He would miss her, he realized, for all that they interacted little in day-to-day life. "May it be from your lips to God's ears, Mary. Now," turning back to Collins, he raised one eyebrow, "let us speak details, sir."

A great deal of drivel followed, but Mr. Bennet made himself listen. There were nuggets of information hidden within the multitude of extraneous words concealing them. Perhaps it was so in Mr. Collins' preaching as well? He made mention of his initial decision in a different direction—was that Jane, or Elizabeth? —but declared himself most pleased with Mary as the partner of his future life. They would live simply but comfortably, with a cook, a maid, and a man of all work, not to mention a great deal of interference from Lady Catherine de Bourgh. Collins meant to stay another few days, but then must return in time to deliver Sunday's sermon in Hunsford. He would be back once the banns were read, and just like that, Mary would be gone.

"Mary, you are agreeable to this? You do not wish to wait until after Christmas, or have time to plan a larger celebration?"

His daughter shook her head emphatically. "I would like to spend the holidays at my new home. As for an extravagant wedding, it is not seemly of a parson's wife to flaunt material possessions on the day she is joined with her husband in holy matrimony. And Mama would not agree with my choices, regardless."

The last statement, Mr. Bennet thought, was by far more true, not to mention surprisingly direct for Mary. Perhaps a bit of distance from her mother and sisters would be good for her, in time.

"Very well, you have my blessing. Mr. Collins, I expect we shall speak further on the marriage settlement before you depart for Kent. But for now, we ought to join the rest of the family and celebrate. Come, on with you now."

Collins led the way to the sitting room, with Mr. Bennet bringing up the rear. The younger gentleman hurried straight in—Mr. Bennet had noticed his partiality for Cook's cakes—but Mary paused and looked back, her expression somewhere between satisfaction and contentment. She may not love her soon-to-be groom, but Mr. Bennet was glad to see that Mary really did seem happy with the choice that she had made.

It was strange, he thought as he followed his daughter into the room. For once, George Darcy might actually approve.

*

Elizabeth watched Meryton disappear through the window with dispassionate eyes. Sophia had sent a Huntingdon carriage, a maid to accompany Elizabeth, and a letter promising a warm welcome at Matlock House, where she was currently staying with her parents. The carriage had arrived late the evening before, and Sophie had commented in her letter that 'it was likely for the best that she not encounter that Bingley woman at the moment' or she may have accompanied the equipage.

Elizabeth was grateful for the solitude. The silent maid on the rear-facing bench kept her eyes on her sewing, no doubt well-trained in pretending to not exist. While she generally would have preferred passing the journey in conversation, right now Elizabeth appreciated having the time to set her feelings in some sort of order.

There were two concerns, different but not unrelated, that had been ricocheting around her mind since the evening of the ball. First was the reaction of lifelong friends and neighbors, who had been willing to turn against her with less than a fortnight's work from Wickham. Elizabeth knew well that she was not Jane, good and sweet and universally beloved despite her envy-provoking beauty. Still, prior to the Netherfield ball, she would have said that she was liked and respected. Had that ever been true? Or had Wickham only targeted those who were most likely to harbor some sort of resentment or jealousy? It had been Maria Lucas—close friends with Lydia and always hungry for attention— who spoke up, not her sister Charlotte. There were rumors that Mrs. Goulding had once vied for Mr. Bennet's hand, and never forgiven Fanny Gardiner for winning it. Similarly, Caroline Bingley resented anyone she felt was a competitor for Mr. Darcy.

Elizabeth wanted very badly to tell herself that the majority of Meryton would have sided with her, believed her. Once again, though, she was not Jane. And there was no way around the fact that only Colonel Fitzwilliam and her father had spoken up in her defense.

The second concern was harder to name. She had felt it before over the years, a vague, nebulous idea that this was not her place in the world. Was it due to her time at Pemberley, or had she enjoyed Pemberley so much because this feeling already existed? Jane had certainly never shown signs of longing to leave Hertfordshire behind the way Elizabeth did on occasion. Did the denizens of Meryton feel it as well? Elizabeth loved her family and her home. She had never once considered herself better than any of the people who lived there. But that did not mean it was where she truly belonged.

She was disappointed in her neighbors. She was annoyed with herself for not seeing what Wickham intended in time to mitigate it. And she still had not decided what to do if Mr. Darcy was intent on being noble.

It was going to be a long ride.

*

As the carriage bore Elizabeth further away, Darcy and Richard rode into Meryton. It was a dismally uneventful trip, with Colonel Forster being held up in a prior commitment and unable to see them, but at least they did set up a meeting for the following day. If Darcy thought he detected a snicker or a sneer on several of the officer's faces when they looked at him, well, perhaps that was only his imagination. Either way, it would be dealt with before long. After the events of the ball, he had thoroughly come around to Richard's way of thinking that the Wickham problem ought to have been nipped in the bud a long time ago.

They returned to find the Bingley siblings in the sitting room, with wildly contrasting emotions. Miss Bingley was in such a temper that not even their entry stopped her from glaring across the room at her beaming brother.

"I must beg congratulations from you," Bingley exclaimed, turning towards them with an even larger grin. "I have only just returned from Longbourn and have the best of news. Miss Bennet has accepted my hand."

Richard strode forward with immediate congratulations. Darcy, as ever, followed behind with less exuberance. But not, he realized, less feeling. Miss Bennet was a far cry from the kind of woman he would choose for himself, but she fit his friend well. It was certainly not an equal match in terms of fortune—unless matters had changed significantly, only Elizabeth had any sort of dowry to speak of—but Miss Bennet was kind, of undeniably gentle birth, and beautiful. *And* Elizabeth seemed sure that her sister's feelings were sufficiently engaged. Bingley could have made a far worse match amongst the ladies of the *ton*.

It was a kind gesture for timing, as well. Darcy intended to make sure that Elizabeth's reputation did not suffer for long, but there were many suitors who may have held back while they waited to see how the Bennet family fared. He thought better of Bingley for proposing now. It showed that he meant to fully support his betrothed no matter the circumstance, and it didn't hurt that it would give Meryton something else to gossip about.

Richard and Bingley were still talking, and Darcy had just stepped forward to add his own congratulations when Miss Bingley appeared at his side, speaking low and fast. "Mr. Darcy, you must help me. This is a catastrophe, surely you agree. We must remove Charles from this forsaken county and smooth this over, no one ever need know. If we are gone today—"

She stopped, the rest of the room having gone silent. All three gentlemen had pivoted to stare at her. From the corner of his eye, Darcy noted that Richard's face was perfectly blank. His uncle Matlock wore that look when dealing with his cronies from the House of Lords. Bingley, on the other hand, was flushed red and growing more so by the second.

Darcy gave a quick shake of his head to Bingley, then looked down at the frantic woman in front of him. She was breathing hard, as if she had just been running, and for not the first time Darcy wondered just how deep Caroline Bingley's ambitions ran.

"And how, Miss Bingley, do you propose that I help?" He didn't pause for a reply. "Let us assume for a moment that I am in agreement and think this is an undesirable match. I suppose it depends on if the marriage contract has been signed; we shall assume it has not. I could speak to Mr. Bennet. Just this morning Miss Elizabeth left for an extended stay with my cousin Lady

Huntingdon in London; it would not be hard to suggest that Miss Bennet join her. Sophia tells me they are to stay at Matlock House, and Mr. Bennet has been friends with my uncle for years—I am sure Matlock would be willing to host a second of his daughters. Between Lady Matlock and Sophia, they would happily introduce Miss Bennet to those in town for the little season. Given her beauty and support from the countesses, she would garner a great deal of interest."

Miss Bingley's expression had shifted over the course of the conversation from hopeful to horrified. Now she spit, "Interest—in what? A lady nearly on the shelf, with no dowry, a host of unrefined sisters on the brink of scandal, and an awful mother who must be housed when their father dies?"

The hand behind his back curled into a fist, but Darcy kept his face calm. "You must not have heard. Miss Mary is to be the next mistress of Longbourn." Bennet had given him the news when Darcy accompanied the Huntingdon carriage to Longbourn that morning. "I am sure she will keep her mother with her. Should Miss Bennet marry—which seems likely, given that she *is* currently engaged and your brother is now honor-bound to see his commitment through— that leaves only three sisters. The younger two might remain at home or be sent to school, and I know of at least three estates where Miss

Elizabeth would always be welcome." It was not worth naming them. She would know. "And Miss Bingley, a gentleman does not ask a lady's age, but I know Miss Bennet to be around three and twenty now."

"You are two years her elder, Caroline. Does that mean you are on the shelf?" Bingley cut in, speaking up for the first time. Darcy was happy to see his friend had regained some of his usual countenance, and did not seem offended that Darcy had presented the situation with Jane Bennet being the more desirable partner. Knowing Bingley, he probably agreed.

Miss Bingley looked between the pair of them, gape-mouthed. "You mean to throw away everything Mother and Father strove for," she whispered to her brother. "You'll ruin any chance I have of making a good match. And you—" turning to Darcy "—Eliza Bennet has bewitched you. I don't know what black arts she has used, but—"

She cut off abruptly as Richard stepped forward and looked down at her directly. "My cousin is too much of a gentleman to say this directly, so I will say it for him. Elizabeth Bennet is a dear friend. She was my sister's closest friend in adolescence, and is beloved by my father. The Bennet family may not boast an impressive estate or riches, but they are not without connections. Your brother is never going to marry a duchess. He would gain more respectability by marrying a gentlewoman like Miss Bennet and leveraging her family connections than he would by reaching above his station and coming up short. Matlock, Huntingdon, and Darcy here command a great deal of respect amongst the *ton*. Your brother and Miss Bennet would be welcomed into all of those homes and circles, not to mention the friends they make on their own merits. As it stands right now, Miss Bingley, you would not. I would think carefully about your next words, before you sever any chance of those connections irrevocably."

Miss Bingley stood silently for a long moment, then turned and hurried from the room at a rate just short of a run. Richard and Darcy watched her go; Bingley dropped into an arm chair and put his head in his hands.

Darcy sat as well, stretching his long legs out in front of him. "I could have made that point, Richard." He did not like that his cousin had been Elizabeth's most vocal supporter the past few days, even if he did appreciate it.

The colonel snorted. "In two days, perhaps. My way was more efficient, and I feel better for having done *something* to defend Lizzy today, after that farce with the militia."

Darcy considered that, conceding the point silently. He would never relish speaking harshly to a lady, but Miss Bingley could not be allowed to continue as she had any longer. And thinking of things left unresolved— "Bingley?"

"Hmm?"

"Congratulations."

Chapter Nineteen

A t Richard's suggestion, he and Darcy stopped at Longbourn the following morning to collect Mr. Bennet before making their visit to Colonel Forster. "We've got a ranking officer and a rich gentleman, may as well add a righteously angry father to the roster," his cousin had said in the off-hand tone that he often used to fool people who were happy to believe him the coddled son of an earl. Darcy knew better; Richard had been stewing on the Wickham situation for over a week now, and his temper was simmering just below the surface.

The short ride into Meryton was tense silence punctuated by a few reminders from Richard of their strategy. Darcy wondered if Bennet was as angry as he himself was. The older gentleman had always been far harder to read than his cousin.

It didn't take long to reach their destination and tether their horses under the watch of a bored-looking soldier, then make their way to the colonel's office on the edge of the camp. There was a soldier there as well, and he waved them into the room without asking questions. They were expected.

They found Colonel Forster in a well-sized if simple room. He waved them into chairs across from his desk, Richard plucking one from the side of the room. Apparently Bennet's presence hadn't been anticipated.

"What can I do for you gentlemen today?" Forster asked once they were seated and basic greetings had been exchanged, his face a little too bemused to come off as genuine. By all accounts, he had been in the card room at the ball and seen none of the confrontation, but Darcy was sure he had heard plenty of tales, and not only from Wickham.

Richard leaned back in his chair and crossed his legs. "As one colonel to another, I assumed you would be interested in discussing the fact that an officer under your command has been slandering at least one member of this community. Hardly a good way to foster goodwill in your hosting location."

Forster didn't look surprised, confirming Darcy's assumption that Wickham had already fed him a parcel of lies. Indeed, he had the audacity to appear affronted. "That is a serious claim. I do not take kindly to my men being accused. No doubt you understand that sentiment."

Richard gave a single nod, face inscrutable. "I do. Which is why I am only telling you this because I am absolutely sure it is the truth."

"Interesting. I have had another man swear the same already, but in the opposite direction. I would be a poor commander indeed if I expected loyalty from my men but showed none to them in return." His smirk returned. "And this would not be the first time a gentleman has ruined a lady and tried to shift the blame for it to another."

A sharp glance in Darcy's direction kept him in his chair; Richard had been extremely clear that they were to leave the initial foray with Forster to him, no matter how angry they were. It would be interesting to see how long that command held if Forster continued in his current manner, and who would break first, Darcy or Bennet.

"Yes, I thought you might say something like that. Let us be clear, shall we? George Wickham insinuated that Miss Elizabeth Bennet has been compromised in some way by my cousin Darcy here, yes?" Forster nodded once, looking slightly unsure for the first time. "And how has Wickham explained his knowledge of the matter and his decision to bring this up in a very public location, in a way designed to drag one of the foremost ladies in this community through the mud?"

Forster's eyes darted to Mr. Bennet before replying, "I have heard that Miss Elizabeth and Mr. Darcy knew each other prior to his arrival in Hertfordshire. When he did arrive, they resumed their, ah, arrangement. Lieutenant Wickham knew both of them during their previous acquaintance. He was friends with Mr. Darcy at the time and fancied Miss Elizabeth, but she chose to ignore his affections in favor of Darcy's money and connections, since she has no dowry and Longbourn is entailed away. As for his current interest, I believe he still feels affection for Miss Elizabeth and is pained to see that she has been forced into a situation that will never evolve into a proper courtship and marriage. When she refused to dance with him at the ball, he was hurt and reacted accordingly."

"Interesting. And you have known Wickham for how long, exactly?"

Forster bristled; Richard raised an eyebrow, his face set like granite. The silence stretched on until Forster said with a resentful air, "A fortnight."

"Ah. Well in that case, of course the matter is clear. It makes sense that you would know more about a man in two weeks than Darcy and I possibly could in over two decades of close acquaintance. And as for Elizabeth Bennet, someone you have never met, you are obviously a better judge of character than her own father and those of us who have known her since her childhood. My sister, the Countess of Huntingdon, cannot know Miss Elizabeth as well as you despite years of close friendship, and my father Matlock would surely turn her out of Matlock House, where she is currently staying, if he weighed your estimation against his own years of acquaintance with the lady in question."

Forster's face had been slowly turning red, and now he sat forward and said, "I cannot help but notice that you have not denied a single one of the claims made by Lieutenant Wickham."

"All in time, my good man. I have one more question for you to consider, first. If Wickham really does care for Miss Elizabeth, and wished to see her treated well, why would he have spread rumors about her prior to the incident at the ball? It was clear to me from the crowd's response that this was not the first time he had spoken poorly of her."

"Why, he is hurt and feels betrayed. It is not uncommon for soldiers to share concerns with each other." But Forster did not look as smug as he had at the beginning of their interview.

"Of course, the men share their happiness and heartaches. And yet, in his two weeks in this regiment, Wickham has spread this story to you and to a large number of the local inhabitants. He did not come to Mr. Bennet to discuss his concerns, nor did he approach Darcy directly. In short, he told no one who could actually make a difference and all of those people who were sure to spread the story. Do you employ common gossips in this regiment, Colonel?"

Richard didn't wait for a response. Instead,

he continued, "Now, let us address those pesky claims. Darcy, have you and Miss Elizabeth ever been, shall we say, romantically involved?"

"What? No!"

"But you do claim a prior acquaintance with the lady."

"Yes. She visited Pemberley for multiple summers as a child. I met her when she was seven and I was fifteen. Do you often plan trysts with children, Colonel?"

"Easy, Darcy," Richard said in a pleasant tone. "Now, let us assume for the sake of this conversation that you were interested in Miss Elizabeth, and she in you. Would you have any reservations to courting and marrying her?"

Richard had let him know this question was likely, but Darcy still thought of how Elizabeth had felt tucked against him as he replied seriously, "Not at all. If we cannot silence the gossip that Wickham has started, it is as good as done. I refuse to allow a lady I hold in such high esteem be ruined by that scoundrel when I can offer her my name and connections as a shield." He looked sideways at Bennet. "Assuming your agreement and her own, of course."

Bennet bowed his head in acknowledgement. "Let us not make any hasty decisions, but I cannot imagine a situation where I would not give you my blessing. You know the truth of Lizzy's dowry, I assume?"

"Yes, let's clear that up as well," Richard cut in.

"What is the amount, Bennet?"

"I would have to verify with my brother Gardiner, as he manages the investment, but I know it is upwards of three thousand pounds now. It may not be as much as some ladies, but I would hardly call it nothing."

"I believe that has addressed all of Wickham's claims save for one," Richard said, looking back at Colonel Forster. "I can tell you, in all the times I saw them together, I never once saw a shred of affection in Wickham's interactions with Miss Elizabeth. I would have not even called them friends, for they rarely interacted. However, perhaps something was there, because when she was fifteen, he attempted to force an elopement on her. She was vehemently opposed."

"You were there to witness this?"

"I was not. Both of these gentlemen were, however."

Forster turned suspicious eyes to Darcy, then Bennet. Whatever he saw in the latter's expression made him blanch; Darcy didn't dare turn his head to see for himself.

"I do have the letter Darcy sent me, just after the incident," Richard said, pulling a missive out of his inner coat pocket. "Note the postmark, if you would. I wouldn't want you to think us guilty of fabrication." He handed it over and Forster accepted gingerly, expression turning more and more resigned as he read.

At last, Forster refolded the letter and

returned it to Richard. "Do you gentlemen have anything else to tell me?" he asked, voice flat.

They'd discussed this as well. "Wickham has a habit of running up debts he has no intention or means of paying," Darcy said. "Perhaps he has grown out of this. I would like to believe he has. But it may behoove you to see what he currently owes the local merchants, and his fellow officers in debts of honor. It would reflect very badly on the militia if its members are unable to settle up."

Richard snorted. "Darcy, this is why you are the gentleman and I am the colonel. It speaks well of you for wanting to believe men like him can change. I do not care to leave matters to chance." He reached into his coat again and pulled out a stack of papers. "Wickham's debts, Colonel Forster. I have been buying them up when I am home from the continent."

This had *not* been discussed, and Darcy looked sharply at his cousin. Richard only shrugged. "I told you I wanted to deal with him years ago," he said, clearly unrepentant.

"But this—this is upwards of two thousand pounds!"

"It is, and I do not believe I have been able to collect all his vowels. With debts of honor, it would not surprise me if he owed closer to double that amount."

Colonel Forster stared at the papers in his hand as if they might bite him. After a moment, he let out a long breath, then looked up at

Richard with a level gaze. For the first time in their acquaintance, Darcy could picture the other gentleman commanding troops. "You have prepared for this. How would you like to handle it?"

Richard smiled. "I thought you were a reasonable man, colonel. I have other long-term plans, but for now the simplest option is most likely the best. Wickham has been avoiding his creditors for years. No doubt they would agree with me that a stay in Marshalsea is fitting."

Another pause, and then Forster nodded. "I will make inquiries into his local debts. When do you mean to collect him?" They spoke details for several minutes, then Forster said, "Very well. Is there anything else I can do for you today?" This time, he appeared completely genuine.

Richard gave a smile that was anything but friendly. "I believe an apology is in order."

Forster flushed. "Apologies, Mr. Darcy, and to your daughter, Mr. Bennet. I will not attempt to excuse my behavior."

Darcy bowed his head in acknowledgement. Colonel Forster had proved much easier to convince than he'd anticipated, although he knew a large part of that was due to Richard. Bennet, however, did not seem inclined to accept.

"You will leave this place in several months, Colonel," he said. "You and your men go onto a new place, with a fresh start. My daughter was born here, and she may never be treated the same, by people she has known all her life. I am intelligent enough to realize that a majority of the blame lies with George Wickham, but you willingly played a part as well. Find me when you have a daughter of your own. We will talk about forgiveness then."

*

Mr. Collins hurried back towards Longbourn, ignoring the chilly November wind. He'd walked into Meryton at his Mary's suggestion, to grace the local shops with his benevolence one more time before he left for Kent. Granted, it was a rather meager benevolence right now, but Mary had said the shopkeepers would understand and remember when he took over as master of Longbourn. Just one more sign that he had picked the correct Bennet sister for his future partner in life!

But it was not Mary he thought about as he walked. No, his thoughts were full of Miss Elizabeth, and they were far less pleasing than his ruminations on his soon-to-be wife. Collins knew very well that gentlemen did not eavesdrop, but he had not been able to stop himself when he heard the name 'Darcy' followed by a question about courting and marrying his cousin. And Mr. Darcy's answer! He could not believe the man, who Lady Catherine spoke of so fondly, would cast aside his engagement to Miss de Bourgh for a penniless girl with none of her consequence. There had been something about Miss Elizabeth's dowry, but in his astonishment Mr. Collins had not heard everything. He could only imagine cousin Bennet had been reminding Mr. Darcy about her lack of funds, and even this had not swayed the gentleman.

He'd realized his trespass at that time and continued on, but he'd heard enough. This must, simply *must*, be reported to his patroness so she could stop Mr. Darcy from falling prey to Miss Elizabeth's clutches before his future—and Miss de Bourgh's—were ruined for good.

*

Charles Bingley stood in the middle of his entryway, completely perplexed. He was a man accustomed to a rapid shift of events, and he generally managed to face them with unfailing optimism. Today, however, was proving beyond even his equanimity.

Layered below everything else was his ongoing euphoria over Jane's acceptance of his proposal and his excitement at their future life together. That was simple and straightforward. Thinking about Jane made Bingley happy. Being with Jane made him even happier. If only the rest of his feelings were that easy to categorize.

Darcy and the colonel had returned from their morning excursion with grim faces.

Ony after breaking through the typical Darcy reserve—uncharacteristic from the colonel, but then Bingley had never known him in a serious situation—did they reveal the plans to address the ongoing rumors in Meryton about Miss Elizabeth, now including Colonel Forster's assistance in addressing Lieutenant Wickham. Bingley liked Miss Elizabeth, and he knew Jane had hoped to have her stay with them at Netherfield after the wedding (*the wedding!*). She would be heartbroken if her sister couldn't return to Meryton, and Jane's sadness, or supposed sadness, made Bingley sad as well.

There was also a touch of anger, even less common for Bingley. He was mad at Wickham, and mad at the people of Meryton for believing his salacious lies. Darcy was one of the most upstanding gentlemen Bingley had ever met, and Miss Elizabeth had seemed well-loved prior to this instance. For the local residents to turn on her felt like a betrayal by the community Bingley had grown fond of in the last two months.

And then there was Caroline. Bingley wasn't annoyed with his sister. He wasn't upset by her, or embarrassed by her. He wasn't even angry, although he supposed it would be understandable if he was. No, he was simply perplexed.

He'd returned to Netherfield after visiting Jane to find a note waiting for him. Caroline had stayed in her rooms since Richard's set-down the day prior, and quite honestly, Bingley had been pleased with the reprieve. He had no interest in being subjected to more of Caroline's vitriol. That only made the paper in his hand all that more confusing.

Charles –

We're to London this afternoon, Louisa and Hurst and I. It was only decided this morning between us, and you and the other gentlemen are out. Mrs. Nichols is aware of the plans, and has assured me she has the next week's menu prepared for you, Mr. Darcy, and Colonel Fitzwilliam. She will likely cause you less headaches than I have.

Let us know when the wedding will be, should you wish for our attendance. I assume Mr. Darcy will stand up with you; please assure him that I will not make any undue demands on his attentions, person, or time.

Your sister,

Caroline.

It was written in Caroline's hand, and Bingley could hear her voice in phrases, but the whole was so overwhelmingly unexpected that he scarcely believed what he'd read. She'd called the housekeeper by name! It was the least one would expect of any mistress of a house, and somehow even that courtesy was shocking, coming from Caroline.

The door opened and Darcy strode in. "What is it?" he asked.

Bingley shook his head, holding out the note. Darcy took it hesitantly and scanned it, then handed it back, face inscrutable. "I feel worse for what I have to tell you now. I leave for town myself, tomorrow."

"I know you never meant to stay the entire winter. I assume the colonel will accompany you?"

"Yes, he only has so much time on leave, and his mother has commanded his presence for part of it."

That made Bingley smile. "I would not expect the colonel to bow to such an order, but I have met Lady Matlock."

Darcy seemed to hesitate, then said, "He has a delivery for Marshalsea as well. That is part of why I am to leave so abruptly—we thought it better to have the both of us accompany Wickham."

That was news. "Is it handled, then?"

"Wickham is handled," Darcy said, pulling a face. "His rumors will not be silenced so easily. But I will have some good news for Elizabeth, at least. Bingley, I do not like leaving you here all alone. If I—"

"Go to London," Bingley said, cutting him off. "I understand why you are going, and it gives me a perfect excuse to spend all my time at Longbourn. My future mother-in-law, whatever her faults, sets a superb table. I can't invite Jane here without a hostess, even if you were to stay."

Darcy agreed somewhat reluctantly and headed on his way, but Bingley remained where he was for a few moments longer. The edges of his confusion were fading away, customary positivity reasserting itself. It was certainly going to be an interesting few weeks, that was for sure.

And at the end of it, he got to marry Jane.

Chapter Twenty

Elizabeth's first few days in London had passed quickly. She had worried briefly that seeing Sophia in person would end awkwardly after their five years apart, but that fear had disintegrated almost as soon as her feet hit the cobbles in front of Matlock House and Sophie swept her inside with a warm welcome.

Lord Matlock was much as she remembered him, his dry wit reminding her just why he had gotten on so well with her father, and Lady Matlock—whose long-established visit to Brighton each summer had kept her from Pemberley—was pleasant if somewhat reserved. Elizabeth was also introduced to Sophie's two children and happily claimed a place as an honorary aunt, and in turn took Sophie with her to visit the Gardiners.

After two days of shopping on Bond Street and a visit to the theater, Elizabeth was only too happy to awake to a day not full of activities. She broke her fast with the family and had just settled herself into a small parlor, intending to read for a time, when a carriage pulled up and disgorged a lady in very expensive clothing several years out of fashion. Elizabeth smiled in amusement but thought little of the visitor. She would be to see Lady Matlock, not Elizabeth.

So she was utterly surprised several minutes later when the door flew open with a bang, revealing the lady and a clearly repentant footman trailing behind.

"You!" the woman exclaimed in strident tones.

Elizabeth rose on instinct, but said nothing. What *did* one say in response to a greeting like that?

"Are you Elizabeth Bennet?"

"I am."

"My name is Lady Catherine de Bourgh and I have traveled here with utmost haste after hearing a report of a most alarming nature. You cannot be ignorant of what I speak, and I assure you that I shall not be leaving this house until I have heard you deny all of it."

Having heard stories about Lady Catherine for years, Elizabeth could indeed guess at the subject she would find so alarming, but what on earth would have caused her such indignation that she felt the need to leave Kent to have it decried in person? How could she have heard anything?

"You are wrong, your ladyship. I do not know what report you are referencing. Perhaps you would like to join the other ladies in the main parlor and we can speak of it over tea?"

"I would not like that, and I am disappointed in you. I will not be lied to; do you hear me?"

No wonder Will and Richard and Sophie talked about their aunt Catherine with such uncharacteristic disrespect. "I will not lie to you, but if you wish me to address any report, you will have to tell me what it is. I have no idea of what you are referencing."

"Very well, if this is how you insist on continuing, I shall gladly oblige. I have always had a forthright manner, and I do not intend to change that now. I was told, just two days ago, that not only is your elder sister to be most advantageously married, but that it is a near certainty that you will soon follow her to the altar and be wed to my nephew, Mr. Darcy. I know this to be blatantly false, and indeed to not dare demean him by believing it, but I set out at once to hear it denied by your own lips. What say you to that, Miss Bennet?"

What would Sophia say? Nothing likely to help in this situation, because Sophie very well might decide that telling off her aunt was perfectly acceptable under the circumstances. "I would say, Lady Catherine, that you traveled quite some distance to address a report you declare impossible in the first place. One would wonder why you did so."

"Because I know who you are, Miss Bennet. I remember my brother writing about you and your father, always finding a way to hang around Pemberley. Your name was linked not only to Mr. Darcy's, but to George Wickham's as well. What a long game you have played! How long have you and that father of yours wanted Pemberley, since Longbourn is lost to future generations of your family? Well, you will not get away with it, not on my watch. Mr. Darcy is engaged to my daughter Anne. *She* will be Mrs. Darcy. *She* will be mistress at Pemberley and Rosings. Not an upstart with no dowry like you!"

For heaven sakes, it was like facing Mr. Wickham all over again.

"If Mr. Darcy is engaged to your daughter, then any supposed report to the contrary must be false. Or do you think so little of his honor?"

"Their engagement is of a particular kind, it was agreed to in their cradles and has long been held as the fervent wish of his mother as well as hers! But what do you mean, supposed report? You did not engineer it yourself?"

"I have never heard it."

"And will you swear that it is untrue?"

"I will not. You have come hence today for no rational reason I can see, and while your manner may be forthright, I have no cause to be equally so."

"I will pay you. What will it take for you to leave my brother's home and never bother a single member of my family again? Three thousand? Five? Ten?"

Something in Elizabeth snapped. She had spent the last week worried about Mr. Wickham, then her reputation, and now this horrible lady thought her a leech who would give up all her closest friends in exchange for a payment? It was not to be borne.

"I do not accept your disgusting offer, and I never shall. Do not think me ignorant of who *you* are either, Lady Catherine. I have heard Sophie and Richard and Will speak of you for years, and what I have heard today only confirms what they have told me. You care nothing about what Will wants, only what is most convenient for *you*. You look at him and see Pemberley and Darcy House and ten thousand pounds a year. You're right, I've spent time at Pemberley and I will love it for the rest of my life, but at least I am capable of seeing Will as a separate identity from his estate."

"Brava, Miss Elizabeth," a voice said from the doorway. Startled, Elizabeth looked up to see the earl, Mr. Darcy just behind him.

"Henry! You must assist me, this hoyden is intent on ruining us all! Darcy is to marry Anne, aren't you, Darcy? I insist that someone shall tell me what I came here to hear!"

"And I insist that you stop the raucous screeching. Good God, are you a lady or a fishwife? Mother would be ashamed of you, Catherine." Clearly, Richard had learned how to deliver a set-down from his father. Elizabeth would have been amused, had she not been overwhelmed with less enjoyable feelings.

Lady Catherine opened her mouth, face turning nearly purple. Lord Matlock raised his chin, eyes flinty. Whatever that expression represented, it was clearly one Lady Catherine knew better than to cross. With a glare, her mouth closed again.

"Much better. Perhaps you would care to join me in my study, so we might discuss your sudden appearance in my home." The words were not a request.

The pair departed, leaving only Mr. Darcy, his expression grim. He took a step towards her, and Elizabeth retreated before she realized what she was doing, as if she could outpace whatever news had put that look on his face. She hadn't expected to see him for days.

"What's wrong?" she asked. More details were slowly filtering through the shock of her conversation with Lady Catherine, including the fact that Mr. Darcy was in travel clothes. "Why did you come straight here, instead of Darcy House?"

One of his eyebrows rose. "You mean, what is wrong beside my aunt acting like—like—"

"Like a dockside fishmonger, I believe Richard used to say," Elizabeth said, and had the satisfaction of seeing Mr. Darcy's eyes flare wide. She and Sophia hadn't been supposed to learn that expression. "Yes, besides that."

He took a few more steps into the room, and

this time Elizabeth managed to hold her ground. "I thought you would wish for an update as soon as possible. Was I wrong?"

She linked her hands before her, refusing to fidget with her dress or turn her fingers over each other. "I don't believe anyone is ever in a hurry to receive bad news, Mr. Darcy."

A wry smile. "It's not all bad. Wickham also left Hertfordshire this morning, and will be spreading no more lies. Richard and I deposited him at Marshalsea, and with the debts that Richard has been buying up for the last few years, he won't be free to bother you anytime soon. Colonel Forster, once we convinced him of our story, was only too willing to assist."

"And yet?" Elizabeth asked. She'd braced herself for the worst, and dragging out the suspense was stretching her nerves tighter and tighter.

Mr. Darcy studied her evenly for a few long moments. "And yet, gossip cannot be removed so easily. I believe, as does your father, that it will fade in time. But at the moment, there is still a great deal of talk about you—about *us* —in Meryton. We do not think it would be a comfortable place for you at the moment, and there are your sisters to think of as well."

Elizabeth closed her eyes. It was the most logical outcome, based on what had occurred at the ball. A single whispered rumor was hard enough to quell, and the ones about her had been said loud and clear. Meryton would not let go of this entertainment easily. And yet she had still hoped, clinging to the belief that perhaps things were not so bad, that everything would blow over by the time she was to return home with the Gardiners for Christmas. Her neighbors would adjust their reasoning once they were away from the festivities and the punch bowl. They couldn't possibly be so cruel. For all that she wondered if Meryton was the best place for her, she had never fully considered what it would mean to have it closed to her for good.

Blinking rapidly, Elizabeth opened her eyes to find that Mr. Darcy had advanced so he stood an arm's length away. He was looking down at her with blatant concern in his eyes, and Elziabeth wanted nothing more than to take that final step and bury her face in his chest, like she had done the last time George Wickham threatened to ruin her life.

The realization hit her with the force of a blow, and Elizabeth swayed on her feet. She loved Mr. Darcy not only as the boy she had known but as the man standing in front of her now, loved him beyond any bond of friendship, however strong. Perhaps in a different life they could have found their way together, but now? Her dowry was nothing compared to the ladies in his circles and the only connections she could boast of were his own, but those were not insurmountable obstacles. Her reputation, though—she had as much faith in his honor as she ever had, but how could she even consider accepting when he had Georgiana to think of? A marriage based in scandal would hurt her as well as him. And that was assuming he felt anything for her other than the same tolerant friendship of their youth. A bold assumption, that. She had always been a child to him, another little sister to keep out of trouble.

That was her answer. As easy as it would be to let him take care of this—take care of *her*—she would not be a duty. Maybe before her realization they could have married and managed as friends, but not now. It would break her heart to love him when he only felt friendship in return.

"Elizabeth," he said, voice full of concern, and she dug her fingers together to keep from shuddering. "I know this is a great deal to take in, but you won't be abandoned or forced to live off charity. You aren't the only person being spoken of, after all, and I couldn't bear to see you injured when I have the power to stop it. Elizabeth, would you do me the honor—"

"Don't do it," she said, voice barely stronger than a whisper. She took a deep breath and tried again. "Don't do it. You're about to be noble and self-sacrificing and I don't want to hear it. I won't be a duty. I won't. Good day, Mr. Darcy."

And so saying, Elizabeth whirled and ran from the room, forcing down her mounting sobs until she had reached her own chambers and turned the lock behind her. Then, and only then, she threw herself down on the coverlet and sobbed as she hadn't done since she was fifteen.

She was breaking, everything was breaking around her, and she loved him. Oh, how had she never seen it before, never even suspected the truth of her own feelings? Even when Wickham had thrown the idea in her face, she'd brushed it off. Her overwhelming joy at seeing Will again in Meryton, her ill-conceived plan to hide the association from her mother, all of it made so much more sense through the lens of her realization. And none of it mattered now. All that Elizabeth could do about it, in the aftermath of Wickham's machinations, was put her head down and cry until she fell into an uneasy sleep.

*

Darcy was at breakfast the following morning at Darcy House, halfheartedly picking his way through food and glancing at the day's paper, when the door opened and Sophia strode in without announcement. "What on earth did you do to Elizabeth?" she asked by way of greeting, pulling a chair out and dropping into it before his ingrained manners could send him to his feet.

"What do you mean? Is she well?"

His cousin gave him a quelling look. "Do you think I would be here if she was well? She was locked in her room all of yesterday afternoon, requested a tray for dinner, and said next to nothing when I insisted on seeing her. Mother is convinced that Aunt Catherine caused her retreat, but neither Father nor I can see Lizzy being that cowed, not when Father said she was holding her own if not winning the argument from what he could hear. All he can say is he left *you* with her, and she's been in this state ever since."

Unbidden, Elizabeth's face from the day before flashed in Darcy's mind. She'd been pale, tense, clearly distraught. It had taken nearly all of his willpower to not follow when she'd fled from the room. But even then, he hadn't imagined the distress would last for so long.

"I brought news from Meryton. Wickham has been handled, but the rumors are still rampant, and Mr. Bennet doesn't believe it would be good for her or her sisters if Elizabeth is to return home soon."

Sophia gave an impatient shade of her head. "That is old news, and Elizabeth would have told me that. We've discussed it in depth. There's something else."

Darcy clenched his teeth. His entire being rebelled against telling her more. But Sophia would get the truth out of him before she left, and he didn't want Georgiana walking into the conversation, which would become more likely the longer he stalled. "I proposed," he said tersely. "Or rather, I attempted to propose, before she told me she didn't want to hear it and ran away."

And that hadn't stung, not at all. Apparently Elizabeth's aversion to marrying him still stood, even when she was facing ruin.

Sophia's face had gone perfectly blank. She sat in silence for a long while, then blinked rapidly. "That could do it," she said, as if to herself, then focused on him again. "How did you propose?"

"Does it matter? She clearly doesn't want to marry me."

His cousin rolled her eyes, exasperated. "It matters a very great deal, and you are an utter dolt when it comes to this sort of thing. How did you propose, Darcy?"

He huffed. "I said, I don't know, I said that she didn't have to worry about being cast out without somewhere to go, especially since my name was being spoken along with hers. I believe I said I couldn't bear to see her harmed when I had the power to do something about it. She didn't let me get a full question out before she cut me off and left."

Sophia let out a long breath, a great deal of tension leaving her body. "That would do it," she repeated.

"Do what?" Darcy asked acerbically. "Prove that Elizabeth Bennet is absolutely repulsed by the idea of marrying me?"

"Have you spoken of it before?" Sophia asked, looking at him sideways.

"That was the base of the entire farce in Hertfordshire! She didn't want to feel pressured into marrying me by her mother."

Sophia held up a hand, and Darcy swallowed back his next retort. "Has she ever said she doesn't want to marry you? Or did she say that she doesn't want to be forced into it? Or see *you* forced into it? What exactly did Elizabeth say yesterday, Darcy?"

He huffed again. "I don't remember, exactly. Something about me being noble and she didn't want to be a duty, so she wasn't going to listen. It wasn't a very coherent conversation."

"Darcy," Sophia said slowly, "I know you're already feeling pig-headed about this, but humor me for a moment. You're assuming that Elizabeth doesn't care for you. What would yesterday's conversation look like if you assume that she *does*? What would her perspective be?"

Darcy stared at her, not comprehending. "I would assume it ends with a positive answer, not fleeing the room."

"You really are a dolt. Very well, let me lay this out for you. Assume that someone you care for comes in during a conversation where a relative is accusing you of entrapping them. Embarrassing, but not insurmountable. But then, you are reminded that you are ruined and can't go home, and it seems that this will be of an enduring duration. Imagine receiving news that you are no longer welcome at Pemberley because of George Wickham. And then, in the next breath, you're told it is not a concern, because this person knows their duty. How would you feel? Would you feel relief? Would your pride even allow you to hear that suggestion?"

Silence reigned for what felt like an eternity as Darcy stared at Sophia, her words slowly percolating through the hurt still clouding his mind. "Are you saying," he said at last, "that Elizabeth cares for me?"

"I don't know," she said bluntly. "She won't tell me what is bothering her. But I think, from what you've told me and from everything that I know of her, that you ought to consider it as a possibility. It's the only reason I can come up with that makes this situation make sense."

*

Elizabeth –

I hear from Sophia that you have not been well, and I am more concerned than you can imagine, especially if I have added to your distress in any way. I would very much like to speak with you. This is perhaps in the opposite way of what one might consider usual, but that does not surprise me, not where you are concerned: you accused me, yesterday, of being self-sacrificing and noble. If I promise that I plan to be utterly selfish, will you hear me out?

I await your answer.

FD

Chapter Twenty-One

It was with a great deal of trepidation that Elizabeth stepped out of the house the next morning, following Mr. Darcy out to the gardens in back. She'd barely been able to look at him, so embarrassed was she over her behavior the day before, not to mention her newfound shyness. She was determined to not act in a way that would give her away, and yet felt that it was an endeavor doomed to failure. How was she supposed to hide something like that from Will?

Luckily, he said nothing as they started down the path, simply holding out his arm nonchalantly. She took it, grateful for the chance to bring her heart rate back down to a normal level before needing to speak. But even then— was her grip tighter than it usually would be? Or looser, as she overthought everything? Was she standing too close? Heavens, she could not bear the idea of becoming like Caroline Bingley, constantly hanging off Mr. Darcy like a limpet.

They made it nearly to the center of the

gardens in silence, and Elizabeth began to worry instead that perhaps Mr. Darcy did *not* mean to say anything, when he at last stopped and turned to face her.

"I've been trying to decide the best way to begin since I requested this meeting, and I am no closer now than I was then to feeling prepared. I can only hope you know me well enough to understand what I want to say, because lord knows spoken communication is not one of my strong suits."

Elizabeth forced herself to meet his eyes. It felt odd to not tease him about his reticence, but she could not even manage to open her mouth.

Mr. Darcy let out a long breath. "Am I correct in understanding that Aunt Catherine was not the crux of the problem yesterday?"

She hesitated, instinctively wanting to deny the statement. After a pause, however, nodded once in confirmation.

Mr. Darcy gave her a smile far too understanding for her taste. "Elizabeth, I won't insult your intelligence by pretending you don't comprehend the situation. Your father and I spoke after the incident with Wickham, and I am sure you know most of what was discussed. Given your comment yesterday, I can only conclude that you have a mistaken view of my motivations."

So they were going to speak of his proposal, even if they didn't call it what it was. Elizabeth crossed her arms across her middle, tucking the edges of her pelisse closer around her. It could be attributed to the November wind, couldn't it?

Mr. Darcy shifted so he stood between her and the wind, seeming to edge slightly closer. He looked undecided, then took a decisive step forward, words pouring forth like water spilling from a dam.

"Lizzy, how old am I? How many seasons have I gone through? I have met scores of ladies, and none of them ever held my interest for more than an evening or two, and do you know why? Not a single one of them measured up to you. I would find myself in a ballroom surrounded by titled heiresses and all I could think was what you might say about their hair, or their manners, or the drama of the evening. I just didn't realize my feelings were beyond those of friendship until I saw you again. I promised to be selfish and so I will. I want to marry you, Lizzy. I want the right of protecting you from all of the George Wickhams of the world. I want to spend every summer at Pemberley with you, and watch you try to keep a straight face when you have to punish our sons and daughters for sliding down the banister and breaking ugly vases. If there is anything I regret about this situation, it is that it takes away some of your ability to choose, to tell me no if that is what you wish. But do not think I am proposing out of a sense of obligation. Nothing could be further from the truth."

Elizabeth blinked, feeling her eyelashes brush against her cold cheeks. She felt *everything*: the chill wind, the tangle of her skirts around her legs, the slight warmth emanating from Mr. Darcy, the pounding of her heart. Her mouth opened, but no words, no sound at all, came out.

"If I have misjudged," Mr. Darcy said, and her eyes jumped back to his, "you need only tell me, and I will never speak of this again. I will do everything in my power to find you a place away from Meryton, away from any taint of Wickham, where you can be happy. It's up to you, Elizabeth. I would be honored—*delighted*—to have you as my wife, but I will leave right now if that is what you would prefer."

She still couldn't speak, but shook her head against the idea of him leaving, slowly at first and then with more vigor. It was her turn to take a half step forward, one of her hands reaching out quickly and then withdrawing, unsure of the rules in this new game.

The growing concern on Mr. Darcy's face cleared, and he closed the final distance between them, warm fingers closing over her own. "Elizabeth, will you marry me?"

And then she was beaming, voice working at last as her brain finally caught up with the situation. "Yes," she whispered. "Yes, I will marry you."

He closed the final step between them, standing nearly flush against her as he brought her hands to his lips, one after the other. "You might have saved us both a night of heartache, had you let me speak yesterday."

Elizabeth snorted. "And here I was thinking you had completely forgotten how to tease, without my coaching these past several years!" She sobered, then, and told him in halting terms of her realization the day before, and how convinced she had been that he spoke only from a place of obligation, not any true feelings.

Mr. Darcy listened, and soothed, and then said wryly, "How do you think I felt? Any time the topic of marriage arose in Hertfordshire, you were so adamant that we not be pressured to marry!" He turned so he stood beside her, tucking her far closer to his arm this time, and they began to wander through the gardens again despite the chilly wind.

"I still would not have you pressured into anything," she said, "but beyond that, I can only say I was blind to the depth of my feelings. I knew how much you used to hate the ladies who clung to you in hopes of a proposal, and I could not bear to have you see me like them. Especially not with Caroline Bingley providing such a blatant example!"

"I have never once thought of you in that way. In fact, I remember more than one time where I thought that you and Sophia and Georgiana were the only ladies in the entire world around whom I could fully relax. And I promise you I have absolutely no desire to marry either of them."

Elizabeth halted, turning to look up at him. They stood there, frozen in place, until the hint of a frown crossed Mr. Darcy's face and he asked, "Is anything the matter?"

She shook her head. "No. It is just, I can hardly believe this is real. I feel as if my world has been set on its ear in the past day, and I am a little bit afraid that if I close my eyes for too long, you will disappear." A particularly strong gust of wind hit just then, and Elizabeth could not stop her shudder. At once, Mr. Darcy pulled her tight against him. She fit snugly beneath his arm, and any thought of cold vanished in her delight at being held so close. Elizabeth felt her cheeks flame and knew she was blushing. How could she not, at such a wanton thought? And yet, how could it be wanton when it felt so familiar and *right*?

"Will," she whispered.

He smiled down at her, face close to hers. "I have missed you calling me that. Now come. You are cold, and I refuse to start our engagement with you catching a chill. I promise I will stay close by for however long you wish, so long as I can see you out of this wind."

*

In a turn of events that would have mystified Darcy, had Lady Matlock and Sophia not been the ones in charge, a full dinner party was held that evening to celebrate his engagement to Elizabeth. He still wasn't sure how they had managed to gather both Lord and Lady Matlock, Henry and his wife Isabel, Richard, Sophia and her just-returned husband Francis, Georgiana, and Mr. and Mrs. Gardiner, let alone plan and prepare multiple courses for a dozen people. Only as the ladies rose to remove to the drawing room did he think to wonder if Sophia had begun the preparations the evening before, after she had visited him at Darcy House.

It didn't matter. Not nearly as much as seeing Elizabeth laugh throughout dinner, or catching her eye as she looked back before quitting the room, her gaze very nearly pulling him from his seat and into the hallway after her.

"So that is how it is to be, eh?" Richard asked, accepting his glass of port and giving Darcy a smirk.

"Now Richie, don't be rude just because you want a lady of your own," Henry said from the opposite side of the table. "I'm sure if you are a very good boy and remember to wash behind your ears, someone will take pity on you and keep you company."

Richard sat up a little straighter, his eyes gleaming as he surveyed his older brother. Before he could return fire, however, the earl pointedly cleared his throat and both men, viscount and colonel alike, gave a slight wince at the sound.

"I am glad to have finally met Miss Elizabeth,"

Huntingdon said, clearly agreeing with the earl that a topic change was in order. "I have heard so much about her from Sophia it was strange realizing I'd never actually laid eyes on her before."

"Let me guess, you were expecting someone taller," Richard said.

Huntingdon shot Darcy an apologetic look, but laughed. "The thought did cross my mind."

"I didn't even notice until she stood next to Georgiana and they were the same height," Matlock said. "Although I suppose that says as much about Georgiana's height as it does about Elizabeth's."

Darcy shook his head. "I hadn't noticed at all. She was always the smallest of us," he nodded at Richard, knowing his cousin would understand he meant the two of them and Sophia, "but it never stopped her from joining in. I think it would have been stranger if she *had* grown taller."

Out of nowhere, Henry burst out laughing. In response to the multiple looks he received, he only shook his head. "I keep remembering Mama confronting Darcy—was it two years ago? —about finding a wife, and his comment that he hated talking to ladies he didn't know. She should have asked for a list of your childhood friends; you may have found Elizabeth again much sooner."

"She was hardly a secret," Darcy said. "She and

Sophia corresponded regularly, and I know you and Bennet stayed in touch," he added with a look to his uncle.

Matlock grinned. "Yes, but would you have accepted the suggestion if it came from any of us? I'm not sure anyone has ever told you this, Darcy, but you can be a bit stubborn on occasion."

The table burst out laughing, even Gardiner, whom Darcy barely knew. "Well, at least we know his wife will be up to the challenge," Richard said, continuing the laughter. "You won't be able to hide away from Elizabeth, or intimidate her with your silences."

The laughter continued, but Darcy's mind caught on the idea of what it would really be like to have Elizabeth for his wife. He had considered his love for the adult Elizabeth, and his memories of Lizzy as a child, but never combined the two. Now, however, he could picture it clearly: reading with her in the hidden nook, letting their children run in the gallery on rainy days, walking the grounds, sharing early-morning rides. Would she dare attempt leaping from her saddle into his again? And if so, could he control himself now? Perhaps that was a better thought for later, in the privacy of his own room. And as for thinking about *their* rooms at Pemberley—yes, that was absolutely better considered later.

Darcy had just decided to abandon the rest of his port and rejoin Elizabeth when Richard said suddenly, "Father, how on earth did you manage to keep Aunt Catherine away tonight?"

The earl looked amused. "That, son, is a secret I shall be keeping to myself."

"So you told old Duke what's-his-name you'd support the latest hairbrained scheme, if the duchess invited her for dinner?"

From the corner of his eye, Darcy watched as Gardiner nearly choked on his mouthful of port.

"I never support hairbrained schemes," Lord Matlock replied evenly, even as the corners of his eyes crinkled with the hint of restrained laughter. "It is a bad policy on principle. Now come, all of you. You're keeping a newly betrothed man from his fiancée."

Darcy eyed the last swallow of port in his glass, then held it up. "A moment," he said; around the table, the gentlemen paused. "To Mr. Gardiner," he said, turning towards the tradesman who had done a remarkable job of looking comfortable with his boisterous, titled company all evening. "Had you not brought Mr. Bennet and Elizabeth to Derbyshire, I would have met Elizabeth under very different circumstances, and likely been a worse man for lack of knowing her."

"Gardiner!" was echoed around the table, glasses thrown back and set down again.

"Now," Darcy said, placing his own glass down with the rest, "you are correct. It has been far too long away from the ladies already."

They all laughed, but not a single man got in his way as he hurried from the room. And if they thought him a fool, well, Darcy didn't mind. Elizabeth was worth being foolish over.

*

Bennet –

I hope you forgive my presumption, when you see the announcement in tomorrow's paper. Neither Darcy nor your daughter thought you would mind, and I thought it might do both of them some good to so obviously have the support of myself and my wife. You will have guessed by now, but I will say it all the same—so they are to make a match of it after all! I admit I did wonder, the last time we were all together at Pemberley, but Elizabeth was so young then I could not be sure. I believe George would have been quite pleased.

I mean to continue with my presumptions and to start with I shall say that it is long past time that I met your wife. Darcy has told me of the continued stain on Elizabeth's reputation, thanks to Wickham, and I have an idea of how it is to be addressed. I hear that you have an annual assembly not long before Christmas; we shall arrive that day and make our entrance once it is underway. Who "we" shall comprise is yet undetermined, but at very least will include myself, Darcy, and your daughter. I mean to greet you with great enthusiasm, so do be sure to attend. Elizabeth says you are to learn from her mistakes and not run away. I do believe she has inherited your humor, my friend, but she makes a valid point all the same. Between Wickham's removal, your daughter's engaged state, and a confirmation of our friendship, I think it likely that if Elizabeth is able to brazen her way through the evening with her head held high, the majority of society will decide further gossip is not worth the effort.

If my idea does not work, then we shall remain only a short time. In line with this, I have encouraged Darcy to procure a special license. That way they may marry wherever they like, should the local church not feel welcoming. I have heard talk of a double wedding with Darcy's friend and your eldest; this, I shall leave to the younger generation to arrange.

I shall end here, for Catherine has been standing outside my door these last ten minutes demanding I grant her entry. While it has been amusing, and a good lesson to her, my patience begins to grow thin. Why she ever thought Darcy could be made to marry Anne is beyond me, but it seems that I shall be the one who must dissuade her of this dream for good. Ah, well, her aim has always been worse than my reaction time.

Most sincerely,
Matlock

Mr. Bennet sat back in his chair, eyes returning to re-read bits of the letter even though he knew he had read it fully the first time. So Lizzy was to be married, and from the other hints that Matlock gave, she was pleased with the situation. Darcy had certainly seemed amenable when they discussed the possibility, and Bennet had wondered himself if his daughter saw her former friend and playmate through the lens of romance, but he had not cared to think on it for long. Lizzy in love meant Lizzy leaving, and he could not relish that idea. Not even knowing that she would return to Pemberley, and he could spend his summers there once again.

"Well," he remarked aloud, ignoring the suspicious lump in his throat, "The estate will recoup her dowry, and you can't tell me that she won't be cared for. Your lad will see that she never wants for anything. Are you happy now?"

No voice spoke in his head, but across the folds of time Bennet recalled George Darcy's smile as he had looked at Elizabeth. Yes, his old friend would be happy. And despite the bittersweet realization that Elizabeth was soon to leave home for good, Bennet admitted to himself that he was happy as well.

Chapter Twenty-Two

T hey had discussed in detail if returning to Meryton was a good idea, even with their engagement announced and George Wickham removed. The hurt caused by her neighbors turning against her still lingered, and Elizabeth had spent the better part of an afternoon pacing around the chilly garden, wondering if it was better to write off the town and its inhabitants altogether.

In the end, it was part of a letter from Charlotte Lucas that tipped the final scales.

...I ought to say I told you so, for I distinctly recall suggesting that perhaps your Mr. Darcy was hoping to be caught, not avoiding it. Perhaps I also should have realized that it would take a great deal of emotion for you to act the fool at his arrival—is the saying not that we are all fools in love? You shall have to tell me if it is true, as I have no experience in that area. Regardless, Eliza, I write with most sincere congratulations and best wishes for your

future as Mrs. Darcy.

It was a thrill to see the announcement in the Times. Mother made the most amusing noise when she first read it, and then of course Father had to repeat several times, "The Earl and Countess of Matlock are pleased to announce the engagement of their nephew, Mr. Darcy of Pemberley in Derbyshire, to Miss Elizabeth Bennet of Longbourn, Hertfordshire." You can imagine which words he stressed the most.

Had you been the first Bennet lady to become engaged, or even the second, your news may have garnered a great deal more interest, but it seems that in the wake of Mary and Jane's prior announcements, there is only so much to be said about any one of you. I believe the timing of it worked for the best as well—Mr. Wickham's substantial debts came to light not long after your departure, and as the public opinion of him has swayed accordingly, I believe the general feeling is that any transgressions (whether they are real or perceived) on your part are smoothed over by the end result.

Your mother in particular greatly enjoyed flaunting that her daughter's engagement (to a gentleman of ten thousand a year!) was announced by none other than an earl, while Mrs. Goulding, to whom this was recounted loudly, chose to believe a no-name charmer who did his best to bankrupt the town, and didn't that prove what following jealousy would get you? Granted, both Maria and

Lydia at the very least seem convinced that anyone as handsome as Mr. Wickham could not truly be a villain, but even they are losing interest in Mr. Wickham's continued absence...

Doubtless her father would have some clever quip about the foibles of human nature, but Elizabeth would not be so quick to forget nor forgive. She did wish to attend her sisters' weddings, however, and so if Meryton could pretend it had not turned against her so viciously, Elizabeth was willing to tolerate the majority in order to see those persons, like Charlotte, whom she still truly esteemed. And so it was decided: Elizabeth was willing to attempt the plan laid out by Lord Matlock. To Meryton they would go.

*

Although she had not been part of the late-entering party at the previous assembly, Elizabeth felt a sense of déjà vu as she stepped into the Meryton assembly hall on Will's arm. It was the same room, the same people, and—unfortunately—the same feeling of simultaneous joy and anxiety as when she had first laid eyes on Will that night.

There were differences, of course. Only her father, Jane, and Mr. Bennet knew to expect them, and despite Charlotte's assurances, Elizabeth knew that at least some of the attendees would be less than pleased that she had reappeared. But she herself had changed as well, and as Elizabeth climbed the last of the steps up to the assembly hall door, she sank into the confidence that came from Will's hand hovering at the small of her back and the knowledge that whatever occurred in the next hour, it could not be any worse than what she had already endured.

Richard had been called away for several days on military matters, but Sophia had insisted on joining the party. She had also put her foot down about Elizabeth's attire and consequently Elizabeth was dressed finer than she had ever been for an event in Hertfordshire. She'd argued that it would be better to attend as she had before, given that she had already been accused of thinking herself better than her neighbors. Sophia had taken the position that if Meryton was going to gossip about her anyhow, she might as well have a gown that stood up to the scrutiny. Elizabeth still felt she might have won, had Lady Matlock not backed her daughter.

"You are attending not as the Elizabeth Bennet your town has always known, but as the guest of an earl and the intimate acquaintance of his family. In light of that, of course you are previously acquainted with Darcy and feel comfortable interacting with him informally. Your attire will show you belong in his sphere, and make them question if *they* belong in *yours*."

And so Elizabeth entered in a gown of pale green silk, feeling somewhere between beautiful and ridiculously overdressed. Heavens, was *she* the Caroline Bingley of the evening?

There was no time to question her choices now. Standing behind the earl and Sophia, her hand on Will's arm, Elizabeth could just make out Sir William Lucas as he immediately made for the door at their entry, faltering slightly as he recognized Mr. Darcy. Others in the vicinity turned their way as well, and Elizabeth fought down the instinctual panic at once again being surrounded by staring eyes.

But this time, she did not stand alone. Just before it would have been seen as rude, Lord Matlock shifted his focus away from the approaching Sir William and strode further into the room. Elizabeth could hear the smile in his voice as he exclaimed, "Bennet!"

Her father came forward with an enthusiasm he typically reserved for new books. "Matlock! Welcome to Meryton. And Lady Huntingdon, a very belated congratulations on your marriage. Did Lady Matlock accompany you this evening? The viscount or the colonel?"

"Mr. Bennet, so good to see you again," Sophia said in her countess voice. "My mother and brothers were wanted at prior commitments, but I couldn't pass up the chance to visit after hearing Lizzy talk about her sisters for so many years."

"Perhaps this will be the year I convince you to join us in London, if only for a few days?" Matlock said. "You know you are welcome at Matlock House. We shall host a few dinners of our own to entertain you."

"Parties? You don't know me as well as you claim, if that is your inducement," Mr. Bennet replied.

That was Elizabeth's cue. She stepped forward, forcing herself to ignore the crowd, who had begun to murmur amongst themselves. "But Papa, you should see his library! Obviously it is nothing to Pemberley's, but for a townhouse even you could not find it lacking."

One of Mr. Bennet's eyebrows jumped up as he turned his attention towards her—apparently, he had not been briefed on her new attire. But he stepped forward smoothly and kissed Elizabeth's cheek. "Lizzy, glad to see you returned safely. And Darcy," he added, reaching past her to shake her fiancé's hand. "I believe your father would have been pleased," he said, in a tone not meant for the listening ears.

"I appreciate you saying so, sir," Will replied. "I can only say that I am very pleased, myself."

Sir William, who had been hovering on the edge of their group attempting to look inconspicuous, broke in now. "Bennet, I never expected to see you stealing my job. You must introduce me to our newcomers."

The usual wry look snapped back onto Mr.

Bennet's face, but he said readily enough, "I have no desire to be Master of Ceremonies. That is a title much better left to you. I am simply greeting a friend and his daughter, whom I have not seen in far too long." He waved the pair forward. "Lady Huntingdon, Matlock, if I may introduce Sir William Lucas, my closest neighbor and our Master of Ceremonies for events like these?" At Matlock's nod, given after a tiny pause, Mr. Bennet turned. "Sir William, this is the Earl of Matlock. He is an old friend, and Mr. Darcy here is his nephew. We used to spend our summers together in Derbyshire. And this is his daughter Lady Sophia, who has become the Countess of Huntingdon since I saw her last."

"A pleasure to meet you," Sophie said. "You must be Miss Lucas' father. Lizzy spoke of her quite often in our childhood."

Sir William flushed with pleasure and turned, no doubt looking for Charlotte. Feeling relieved despite the fact that she had never worried overmuch about her reception from that quarter, Elizabeth allowed her attention to move to the others in the larger group beyond her father.

One person down, the rest of the room to go.

*

Bennet noticed the moment that his daughter relaxed, and how Darcy seemed to take his cue from her. Elizabeth always had been the better of them at reading a crowd. They stepped further into the room together, and in a moment Mr. Bingley and Jane had come forward to greet them. None of them expected the night to pass without comment or snub, but thus far Matlock's plan appeared to be working. The first step in ensuring Elizabeth's reception and reputation in Meryton had succeeded.

And in order to achieve it, Bennet had just lost any hope of peace and quiet for the next month. He heard his wife coming before he saw her and braced himself for the pending storm. It was worth it, for his Lizzy. Perhaps it had been foolish of him to think he could hide the connection from Fanny forever, despite the years that he had kept the secret. Perhaps he ought to have told her in privacy at home. But no matter the past, the farce was over tonight.

"Mr. Bennet!" she exclaimed, then stopped, seemingly unsure of how to continue. He watched his wife's eyes dart over the scene around them, taking in the earl and Sophia speaking with Sir William and Charlotte, Elizabeth and Darcy, Elizabeth's new gown, and then back to his face.

To his utter shock, her next words were in a low tone. "Mr. Bennet, when you told me Lizzy had a dowry unlike our other girls—did Mr. Darcy find out?"

Bennet bit back a laugh. "Mr. Darcy knew before I did. His father was the one who left her the money."

"Oh." She seemed to process that for a moment, staring at Lizzy. Then her gaze jumped back to him. "The other man, they are saying he is an earl, and the lady a countess. But surely not? I would have known if you were friends with an *earl*."

The old uncomfortable twinge of guilt bit at him. "It is not a friendship I advertised to anyone. But yes, he is an earl, and he has asked specifically to meet you."

Mrs. Bennet perked up at once, hurt momentarily forgotten, and Bennet pushed aside his self-reproach. Instead, he walked his wife to where Matlock still stood with Sir William, Charlotte and Sophia having moved to join Jane and Elizabeth.

The introduction was swiftly made, and Bennet had nearly decided his wife had been replaced by an imposter when Matlock's relation to Colonel Fitzwilliam was mentioned.

"But why did you not bring him with you?" Mrs. Bennet exclaimed. "There is little I love better than a man in regimentals, and my younger girls are just the same. They are just there, dancing. Does your son care to dance, Lord Matlock?"

Bennet caught a glint of humor in the earl's eye. "Both my sons dance, Mrs. Bennet, although the viscount has expressed a preference for his wife."

"Oh! But of course that must be so. Are they

newly married? Why, Mr. Bennet has never cared much for dancing, but we did make a fine couple on the dance floor when we were young." She shot him a reproachful look.

The earl was definitely amused now. "In that case, Bennet, you won't mind if I steal your wife for a set? If you would care to dance the next with me, Mrs. Bennet?"

She flushed a vibrant red color Bennet could not remember seeing in years, if ever. He hadn't been aware Fanny *could* blush like that. None of the things that mortified others ever seemed to touch her. Almost shyly, she accepted and they joined the others making their way to the dance floor as the next set formed.

Bennet noted Darcy and Elizabeth among them, the latter of whom was greeted by multiple people as they moved through the crowd. There were some who watched his second-eldest with suspicion, but as Bennet observed, most of those eyes shifted to his wife. Lady Lucas managed to keep a straight face after a single look of surprise; Mrs. Goulding did not manage so well, appearing to suck on a lemon. Bennet didn't bother to suppress the rush of satisfaction he felt. Mrs. Goulding had been amongst those who lambasted Lizzy the loudest, and he had heard rumors that she and his wife had recently had words over the matter. Letting his eyes sweep the room, Bennet began to wander in the direction of Mr. Goulding.

They had discussed embarrassing wives before; perhaps a reminder of that and an introduction to Matlock would buy him an ally against future gossip.

A loud, familiar laugh sounded from the dance floor and Bennet smiled even as he rolled his eyes. Nothing, it seemed, could keep Fanny's spirits down for long. Maybe she would even forgive him for keeping this secret, for the thrill of reminding all of Meryton of her dance with the earl for the next decade or so. If he was very lucky, Matlock wouldn't mention the idea of hosting them in town, and it would all become a pleasant memory without any considerable effort on Bennet's part.

Well, he could hope. But in the meantime, there was still work to be done, for Lizzy and for all his other girls. Shaking his head, still rather bemused at how he had been roped into this plan, Mr. Bennet headed towards Mr. Goulding. Old Mr. Darcy, he couldn't help but think, would surely approve of the meddling.

*

It was long past the time that Darcy usually would have sworn off dancing and either found a quiet place from where he could observe, or departed the gathering altogether. He did not claim to have enjoyed the evening's festivities —there had been one dance with Elizabeth's youngest sister Lydia that was particularly trying—but it was the final dance of the night, Elizabeth's gloved hand was clasped in his for their second set of the evening, and Darcy had to admit that he was enjoying this particular moment very much indeed.

She seemed to be of the same mind. They had not been able to speak freely for most of the night, dancing with various partners or making their way around the room together to weed out remaining whispers and lay what rumors they could to rest. It had been utterly exhausting for Darcy, and he knew that for all the positive reception they had received, those who remained standoffish wore heavily on Elizabeth.

But they were here together now, no one had insisted they leave the assembly, and Elizabeth seemed as ready as he was to focus on happier things.

"Jane is amenable to a double wedding," she said, giving him a shy look. "She and Mr. Bingley thought to wed just after the first of the year. What would you think of joining them, assuming no further complications arise?"

Darcy smiled down at Elizabeth, wishing he could hold her closer than the dance allowed. That she felt comfortable remaining in Meryton, when the decision had been so uncertain at the start of the evening, filled Darcy with joy. He hated the idea of Elizabeth being in any sort of distress. "I wish to marry you, and soon. The details of exactly when and where do not matter so long as you are my wife."

She blushed, and he bit back his smile of satisfaction. This was new, being able to fluster Elizabeth, and Darcy intended to fully explore it. No doubt she would find some new way to tease *him* in retaliation, but even that would be enjoyable. He'd never minded her teasing nearly as much as he had pretended.

"Will you spend the holidays in town? I assume you will want to be with Georgiana."

"Actually, I thought I might ask Georgiana to join me in Hertfordshire," Darcy said. "Bingley doesn't mind, and she expressed an interest in meeting your family. I believe after so many years of hearing you talk about your sisters, she is quite curious to see them for herself."

"She and Sophia will have to compare notes," Elizabeth said, laughter in her eyes. His cousin seemed set on furthering a friendship with Miss Bennet; what she thought of the younger Bennet girls was far less certain. Darcy looked forward to hearing her opinions once they were in a more private setting.

Elizabeth continued, "I will not lie, I selfishly was hoping that you would remain in Hertfordshire if I chose to do so, and I have enjoyed renewing my friendship with Georgiana these past few weeks. It would be pleasant to see more of her."

"You know you'll see plenty of her in the future. Or have you forgotten you'll be coming home with me after the wedding?"

Her cheeks turned pink again and Darcy laughed. Several of the neighboring dancers shot him startled looks. Darcy ignored them. He would likely shock a large contingent of London's *ton* as well, not that he intended to become *social*. After years of feeling hunted across ballrooms, however, it was delightful to finally enjoy dancing, the way Bingley and Richard always seemed to do. He'd always enjoyed dancing with Elizabeth more than anyone else. They just hadn't been able to perform in public prior to this year.

"You know, I'm fairly certain my father would have insisted on hosting a come-out ball for you, either in London or Derbyshire, had he not passed when he did," Darcy said.

Laughing eyes met his. "Would you have danced with me? Or just stood on the sidelines and glared at everyone?"

"I wouldn't have glared at you. Or Richard and Sophia." He thought for a moment, wondering what that would have been like. "I would have danced with you. I would have claimed it was my duty, but I wouldn't have minded."

"Wouldn't have minded!" Elizabeth exclaimed. "Mr. Darcy, you do know how to make a lady feel special."

Oh, how he wanted to kiss her when she gave him that look! "And what if I tell you that I would *not* have liked seeing you dance with all the other dandies in attendance? I am almost positive I would have brooded until Richard noticed and proceeded to tease me mercilessly until I came to my senses and proposed."

"That very evening?" she asked, grinning up at him.

His smile was smaller, but no less genuine. "Perhaps not that evening. But I believe I would have realized my feelings far sooner, had we continued to be in company."

Elizabeth sobered, and he was beginning to worry he'd upset her in some way when she said, "I think it was good, the time we had apart. We both needed to grow up, to become individuals in our own right. For all that I teased and challenged you, I think I would have idolized you a little bit too much, had we not been separated for a time." She spun away from him in the dance, going through the pattern before coming back to grasp his hand once again. "It was always going to be you, though."

The certainty of her statement may have surprised many of those in the room, but Darcy knew exactly what she meant. "I'm glad you feel that way as well. I wasn't sure, given your actions the last time we were in these rooms."

She rolled her eyes and said, in a clear subject change, "You haven't told me where we are to go, when we leave here. What home shall we be going to, oh grand sir?"

"I thought you might prefer to be asked. We

could go to London and perhaps host a much-delayed coming out ball for you, even if we don't call it that. We could make for Derbyshire directly, as long as the weather cooperates and the roads are passable. Or we could take a wedding trip, if you have somewhere in mind. That could always be delayed for warmer weather, as well."

Elizabeth pursed her lips. "It might be enjoyable to spend some time in town for the season, whether we host anything or not. I never have seen Darcy House, did you remember that? But after that, the only place I wish to go is Derbyshire." She looked up at him, eyes luminous, and instead of flashes of the past, this time Darcy glimpsed his future even before the next words came out of her mouth. "It's been far too long since I've spent summer at Pemberley."

About The Author

Jennifer Kay

Jennifer Kay started writing stories in kindergarten. She rarely got past designing the cover, but the habit stayed with her, and before long the covers turned into short stories and the  stories into novels. In college, Jen discovered Pride and Prejudice and it's safe to say life has never been the same. She has a minor in English but primarily writes as an escape from her day job in engineering—and yes, all her coworkers call her crazy. Jen lives a long way from Pemberley with her husband, a dog named Darcy, and two cats. She can be reached at jenkayauthor@gmail.com.

Books By This Author

Snowflakes At Pemberley

The Kidnapping Of Elizabeth Bennet

A Better Understanding

Darcy's Angel

A Lady's Pride

Before A Fall

The Ski Lift (Novella)

What Happened In Lambton

(Novella)

Darcy's Tempest (Novella)

Printed in Great Britain
by Amazon

38288915R00182